Trail Blaze

by

Philip Soletsky

Trail Blaze by Philip Soletsky

Cover Artwork: Rachel Carpenter Artworks

ISBN-10: 153985714X

ISBN-13: 978-1539857143

To Joe Ruhl

Who understood Valerie's heart better than I did.

Also by this Author

Firefighter Mysteries

Embers
A Hard Rain
Dirty Little Secrets
Little Girl Lost
Trail Blaze

Standalone Thrillers

Avarice

But first, a word from our sponsor...

That's a joke – I don't have a sponsor. This is all me: writer, editor, typesetter, cover layout guy, marketing, and sales, and I'm happy with that. I like doing all the work myself and I love my books, and my fans are awesome, and there are so many more of you than I would have ever thought possible. I've sold over a thousand books, and hope to sell thousands more, and this is where you come in. If you enjoyed my earlier books and if you enjoy this one, please tell someone. It's as simple as that. Word of mouth is my best advertising. Also please consider leaving a review at Amazon. You don't have to write a huge missive. Here, I'll help you out. Just write "A+++++++. Wow!!!" Note that I used seven plus signs and three exclamation points – you may choose to use more. Also, much as I feel like I'm contributing to the downfall of humankind just by saying this, you can follow me on Facebook for updates about signings, author events, and announcements of when I'm having sales or when new books are coming out.

Now, without further ado, I bring you *Trail Blaze*.

One

I squatted, my dog, Tonk, between my knees, my hands resting on his flanks. I leaned forward and whispered in his ear, "Go to your mommy, Tonk. Go to your mommy." I lifted my hands and, instead of leaping into action, Tonk lazily turned his head and looked up at me.

I was trying to teach him a trick I had seen on a segment of *60 Minutes* wherein a dog had been trained to seek out one of a number of family members by name. That dog, I believe it was a Border Collie, had appeared almost comically alert, launching itself ecstatically from one family member to the next whenever a name was called. Tonk, an English Bulldog, was perhaps not built for such athletics, but I had thought he would quickly get the gist of the trick. Thus far I would have to call the results less than successful.

He glanced in my wife, Valerie's, direction where she stood at the far end of our backyard. After a moment's contemplation his tongue lolled from his mouth. Tonk looked at Valerie without intent, and possibly without recognition. His gaze said something along the lines of, 'Hey, lady, I think this guy is talking to you." Perhaps if I tried hiding a squirrel down her shirt.

"Come on, Jack, it's such a beautiful morning. I want to go for a hike," Valerie called.

She had a point; it was a beautiful morning. Almost a remarkable one given that it was the second week of December in New Hampshire. Right around Thanksgiving we had seen a few flurries and ski resorts were talking about an early opening, but here it was seventy-four degrees, and we were all running around in T-shirts. It was the latest Indian summer on record, if political correctness hadn't forced a name change, and if it was still called that when it fell in December.

Whatever you chose to call it, it was the perfect day for a hike, the sky blue, the sunlight warm on my back. I felt energized and alive, and it wasn't just the weather; I had a lot of other reasons to feel good as well. Valerie and I were slowly mending the rents in our marriage. The stitches in my face were out, and though the scar wasn't particularly pretty, I was OK with that. Most importantly, no ugly mysteries had been dumped in my lap, and no one around me had been killed or tried to kill me in months. This, I thought, is what Batman's life might become if he ever relented and hung up his cape and cowl. Peaceful.

I smiled to myself and gave Tonk an encouraging rub on his head. "In a second. He's almost got this." I made little shooing motions and whispered, "Your mommy, Tonk. Go to your mommy."

"Does the phrase, 'you can't teach an old dog new tricks' mean anything to you?" Valerie asked.

"Hush yourself." I took hold of Tonk's jowls and turned his head to me, staring deep into his doggy eyes, "Don't listen to her; you're not too old to learn tricks. You're just a puppy."

"He's twelve," she said.

That thought gave me pause, and I took a moment trying to verify it for myself, working from other events fixed in time and in my mind – when I got my PhD in physics, when Valerie and I had gotten married, when we had bought this house in New Hampshire, when I had joined the Dunboro volunteer fire department. Closing in on my fortieth birthday, I thought she just might be right. "Wow, Tonk, you are old," I rubbed his face, "so very old."

Never vain about his age, Tonk didn't seem to care.

I stood, trying a different tactic, using my louder, alpha-dog, not-to-be-ignored voice. "Go to your mommy, Tonk."

Valerie suddenly threw down the dog biscuit she had been holding, turned and stalked off.

Elderly or not, Tonk raced over and snagged the biscuit on the first bounce.

"Val?" I jogged after her.

I found her standing, her head down, at the corner of the house where the driveway curved into the garage.

"Val, what-" I began, and then saw the florist delivery van idling in the turnaround, the driver exiting through the rear cargo doors. He held an enormous bouquet of white roses. Such lovely flowers – pity they were not from me.

After solving a mystery of her own earlier in the year, a murder in nearby Milford no less, Valerie had gained some notoriety and spent a brief period in the public eye. She had accumulated some fans, and been convinced by a publicist named Kymbyrly to get a wildly asymmetric haircut, nearly a crew cut over her left ear, hanging down to her collarbone on the right, a sloped wedge of bangs that draped over her right eye. It looked something like a blonde wig that had slid to one side, and it annoyed the crap out of her. Now, months later, her hair was

3

growing in, though not nearly quickly enough for her taste, and all of her fans had found other idols to worship. All of them except for whoever kept sending her two dozen white roses every other week.

I had been convinced bouquet number one was from her boyfriend, the oily residue left over from an affair, which I suspected had been with an attorney named Craig Lerner. When I had confronted her, Valerie had denied it. Not the affair – that she admitted to – but she was sure that her boyfriend, her ex-boyfriend she had pointedly amended, had not sent them. Having had an affair of my own, I was in little position to point fingers under what I believe is formally known as Einstein's Postulate of Glass Houses and Stones. Still, I must confess to an undercurrent of distrust on my part, and this was yet another landmine in the war-torn field of our reconciliation.

Bouquet number two had made me more suspicious still and had given Valerie and me cause for another wonderful border skirmish. At number three I had called the florist who told me only that the orders had arrived in an envelope with cash, our address, and the request that the roses be delivered. There was no return address and the cash in the envelope was for more than the flowers and handling costs – quite a bit more – and the florist wanted to try and return the change. Did I have any idea who was sending them? If not, did I want them to stop the deliveries? Despite the overwhelming creepiness of the whole thing, at bouquet three I had said no.

This particularly delivery represented bouquet number ten, and I sure as hell didn't want to lay eyes on number eleven.

"Valerie Fallon?" the driver inquired.

Still staring at her shoes, Valerie took a deep breath and let it out as a prolonged sigh. She looked up and stepped forward, snatching the bundle from him angrily. I barely managed to snag the envelope from where it was taped to the green florist paper as she steamed past me towards the garage.

4

I examined the outside of the envelope. It was blank except for the printed name of the florist in the upper corner, just like the other nine times. The plain white card inside read only, "From me." Ten for ten there too. The florist had told me the note cards came in the envelope with the cash.

Valerie tore the lid off a garbage can standing next to the garage door and stuffed the roses deep inside with a cramming, punching motion, using far more brutality than was required. White petals, thin as satin and delicate as snowflakes, fluttered to the ground around the can. She concluded by slamming the lid down with a clang.

"Something wrong with the roses?" the driver asked as he held out a clipboard.

I grabbed it from him and carved some random squiggle on the appropriate signature line, practically tearing through the paper. "This is the last time," I growled at the driver with as much hostility as could possibly be packed into those five small words.

"Hey, talk about killing the messenger," he said, trying to inject some levity.

I gave him the clipboard along with a glare that could have cut steel battleship plating.

He accepted both and stepped away backwards, keeping his eyes on me. "OK, I'll let my boss know," he said quietly.

The driver got into his van and left. Valerie returned from the garage.

"Recognize the handwriting?" I asked, perhaps unwisely, holding the card up for her to see.

"For the tenth time, no." She gave her asymmetric haircut an irritated flip.

"Twenty dozen roses, Val," I said, perhaps with more accusation and exasperation than I had intended. Seriously, what kind of crazy person sends two hundred and forty roses without identifying themselves?

"I said, 'no,'" she snapped, a quick flash of lightning in the storm clouds of her grey-green eyes. Whatever emotional tripwire I had unwittingly stumbled over in the backyard had been exacerbated by the flowers. Valerie seemed to have been certain that every delivery of roses would be the last, and for the first four or six dozen appeared even flattered by the gesture. Ten bouquets later, it was starting to freak her out.

"I'm just saying," I replied in what I hoped was a soothing tone of voice.

She took the card from me, crumpling it into a tight ball as she made a return trip to the garbage can. There was another clang as she lifted the lid, chucked the ball inside, and slammed the can closed again. She stood like that, her head tipped down, one hand holding onto the handle of the lid as she visibly collected herself. Finally she looked up. "Let's go for a hike," she said.

"You sure you still want to go?"

"Yeah," she said, but she said it in a resigned sort of way, like a political prisoner tortured for hours before finally signing a confession.

I knew then that hike in this instance no longer meant what it meant to most people. We had been taking many such "hikes" together, which usually turned into long discussions about us, often with a fair amount of fighting and yelling involved, in the relative seclusion and privacy of the White Mountains. Maybe they were necessary steps in the healing of our marriage and were leading us to a better place. For the most part, however, they didn't feel like that, at least not to me.

Without another word, Valerie headed for my pickup truck.

Tonk, always game for a ride, trotted along behind her. She loaded him into the rear cab space, and then got into the passenger seat and closed the door. She would wait there until I joined her, perhaps sleeping in the truck overnight if I chose not to, an alternative I never seriously considered. No, really.

"OK, then," I said to no one and went inside.

I retrieved a backpack from the front hall closet and loaded it up with snacks and bottles of water, plus a sandwich bag of kibble for Tonk. I threw in a couple of sweatshirts. Sure, it was in the seventies now, but could easily dip below freezing near dark. I also stuffed in two flashlights. Lots of people get caught in the White Mountains because a hike takes longer than they think it will and the winter sun can drop behind the high peaks surprisingly early. They then find themselves in the dark, ill-equipped, and in need of rescue. Through my service in the fire department I had often been on the rescuing side of that equation, and I was determined not to change sides. I also put a Swiss Army knife in my pocket. Not that it was a particularly useful tool; the big knife blade was only three inches long. But I kept it sharp and it made me feel manly and rugged carrying it, ready to gut a black bear if called upon to do so.

I went back outside and climbed into the truck and we set out, I and my dog and the woman I loved and whatever emotional suicide vest she had strapped on, for a "hike" on a stunningly beautiful early winter's day. Our destination was a trail in the White Mountains so remote and overlooked that it seemed like our own secret place. We had never seen another soul hiking there in all our visits, and no, I'm not going to tell you where it is.

Despite her mood, I was hoping this would turn out to be just a normal day in a normal life.

But seriously, what the fuck do I know about normal?

7

Two

Our hiking spot is a couple of hours north of our home in Dunboro, New Hampshire which is tucked down near the state's southern border. Only Brookline snuggled in between keeps us from actually touching Massachusetts and getting cooties.

Driving up through the notch, along the Kancamagus Highway, past the pebbly grave of the Old Man of the Mountain, the scenery is beautiful. Something about the way that road weaves up close to peaks many thousands of feet high makes me, and by extension my problems, seem small and insignificant. Most of the trees had long since lost their fall foliage, but the evergreens were, truth in advertising, still green. The orderly channels and trails of the ski resorts we passed were coated with only a thin, crusty rind of ice with veins of dirt visible throughout. Their lots empty, they were out of luck, but still crossing their collective fingers for a white Christmas.

Valerie continued to simmer while we drove. If I've learned anything in more than ten years of marriage, and Valerie would probably be the first one to tell you that I haven't, it's that prying won't get Valerie to talk about anything until she is ready to. I ran the events in the backyard through in my mind trying to identify what I had said that triggered her current mood. "Go to your mommy, Tonk. Go to your mommy." I shook my head; I had nothing.

When we arrived we found the parking area almost completely overgrown. The weeds whispered against the undercarriage of the truck as we pulled in. I climbed out into knee-deep grass.

"Wow, I guess they forgot to pay the lawn service," I said. It took some time to stomp down the plants enough to close the truck door without slamming a bunch inside, but I finally managed it.

Tonk jumped out of the passenger seat and disappeared into the brush up to his eyebrows. Driven by some deeply ingrained instinct to mark territory, Tonk would feel compelled to tinkle on every blade of grass more than four inches high. He had his work cut out for him; the place was a weed-choked mess.

"I like it," Valerie said. "Secluded, like we're the last people on Earth."

That illusion was ruined by the sudden appearance of another car.

It nosed into the lot, stopping short when the driver saw us. The car was a Ford Focus; the color reminiscent of Cheese Doodles. The windows were tinted enough that I couldn't identify the driver, but I could tell from the shape that it was a man and that he was alone in the car.

He idled there, watching us, which felt suspicious to me until I put myself in his shoes. He had, as had we, expected to find an empty, private hiking spot. And yet here was someone else, and it surprised him, much as it had us.

After a moment, he drove in. Apparently not the friendly sort, he parked as far away from us as possible. That wasn't very far; it was a small lot. While I clipped a leash on Tonk, the man killed the engine and got out of his car. Lean, mid-twenties, dark hair. I didn't really notice much about him. What I did notice was Valerie's reaction. She stared at him in rapt fascination. Sure, he was wearing very short and tight running shorts, and he did a number of stretches for her entertainment, toe touches and whatnot, his backside on display like a howler monkey in heat, but seriously, Val, show a little decorum. I was thinking of telling her to take a picture; it would last longer. I realize that's a really old joke, and I was hoping to come up with something more original, but the guy snapped on a hunter orange backpack and jogged off up the trail before anything better occurred to me. When he was out of sight, I expected Valerie to fan herself with her hand, maybe making little Victorian panting noises or perhaps say "Hubba, hubba," but instead she shook her head and shrugged to herself.

I snagged the backpack out of the space behind the driver's seat and slung it over one shoulder, high school cool.

Without a word passing between us, we started up the trail.

It was a peaceful walk, the crunch of grit beneath my shoes, birds, stirred by the unseasonable warmth, out and about in full-throated song. Or rather it would have been a peaceful walk if not for the emotional tension which hovered like storm clouds, dark as bruises, on the horizon of my thoughts.

The path became more rocky and sloped uphill at a steep angle, developed some challenge to it. We spent a little time sucking wind and getting into the swing of it. The trail narrowed, with close woods on both sides, the deep scent of pine in the crisp air. About a half a mile farther ahead there was a spectacular wow moment where the woods fell away at a sudden rocky promontory. Someday a lawyer would hike up here and demand a safety railing, though the drop off was only thirty or forty feet. But for now the view, unobstructed by that railing which did not yet exist and above the tree line, would be breathtaking. I was looking forward to it even as I waited on pins and needles for Valerie to finish organizing her thoughts, continue the conversation we had paused earlier.

She didn't make we wait long.

"Do you remember the afternoon in Dr. Layton's office?" Valerie said to my back because I was walking ahead.

Dr. Layton was a fertility specialist we had consulted after months of unsuccessfully trying to have a baby. He had discovered the cause: benign cysts, non-life threatening, in her uterine walls.

I glanced over my shoulder and was astonished to see her crying, fat tears rolling silently down her cheeks. How could I not have heard her crying, not heard the tears in her voice? I stopped and took her hands, "Val?"

She pulled one hand loose, swiped at her tears, didn't give the hand back to me. "Do you remember?" she repeated the question with some irritation.

"I remember. That was when he told us, um," I was a little at a loss for words.

"He said I was infertile," she spat, finding the words for me.

Those words I had known; I had been searching for kinder ones, gentler ones, and in truth Dr. Layton hadn't said the cysts made her infertile exactly, only that getting pregnant and carrying a child to term were highly improbable. Regardless, it would be a moment I would find difficult to forget, if for no other reason than shortly thereafter we had given up trying, the sexual component of our marriage cut away, sectioned off like a lobotomy. No, not like that; a lobotomy is a big deal. Our physical relationship died a simple and uncomplicated demise

11

with no more difficulty or fanfare than trimming ones toenails. I wondered if someday I would find myself looking back and consider that the final straw that had doomed our marriage, despite whatever it was we were trying to do here today, the lack of a normal sexual element pushing us inexorably onwards towards the brink.

She pulled her other hand from mine, slid past me and took the lead, pushing at a goodly clip. Tonk struggled to keep up with his twelve-year-old body and stubby bulldog legs.

"I remember," I assured the back of her head.

She trudged grimly upwards, grinding gravel and twigs angrily under the treads of her boots, her breathing starting to labor. "I felt so sorry for you," she said.

That was such an unexpected pronouncement that I had to replay it over in my mind several times to convince myself I had heard her correctly. It took me several more to formulate a response. "For me? Why?"

Her response was immediate. "Because I was defective."

"Oh, Valerie, no."

"I am. I'm defective." She insisted. "You got ripped off. You thought you were marrying a whole woman, and instead you got me."

I was speechless. We had wanted children, sure, but there was adoption, and there might yet be some fertility treatments that we could try, and in either case it wasn't a death sentence. We still had each other, and we still had our love. And yet my brain, ever so helpful, reminded me of my first feeling, my gut instinctive reaction at Dr. Layton's pronouncement. I did love her less. Or I had at that moment. What I felt now, layered under the patina of time and shellacked with two thick coats of extramarital affairs, was more complicated.

She increased her pace, and I fell behind. I have an old ankle injury, pretty much healed up and for the most part I don't even think about it, but on steep inclines with unsure footing it still slows me down.

Her shoulders hitched, and this time I heard the tears in her voice when she said, "I'm never going to be mother to anything but a stupid dog. You deserve so much better."

'Go to your mommy,' I had said to Tonk. I shook my head. Now her reaction made sense. I can be such a clueless ass sometimes.

With a burst of speed, I began an awkward lurching sort of lope that probably looked ridiculous but was all my ankle allowed. I managed to put a hand on her shoulder just as she plowed through the bushes and out onto the promontory. I turned her towards me and hugged her close, spun us around on the rocky outcrop so that she was looking out over the drop and I was looking back at the trail. Tonk's leash became tangled around our knees. She was stiff in my arms, unyielding, all closed down.

"It's not like that."

"Oh, God, Jack," she said as she tried to force me away.

I held her against me, my own tears threatening, "It's not true. I don't feel that way at all."

"No, Jack, look!"

Her tone made me release her, and I turned to see what she had seen. I followed her finger which was pointing down the slope. At the bottom lay a hunter orange backpack, a motionless body nearby.

Three

"Is he dead?" she asked, looking down as she again swiped at her tears with the back of her hand.

"I don't know." I couldn't see any blood and his limbs were still attached, the joints all at natural, human angles.

I shucked the backpack and stepped out of the tangle of Tonk's leash. The path down was tricky but not particularly dangerous. The slope was loose rock and soil, but there were plenty of trees along the way to grab onto. I picked a route and started climbing. Valerie stayed at the top watching me.

"Dial 911." I told her as I cleared the lip. "Tell them we have a hiker that took a spill, mid-twenties, unknown injuries. Let them know there's a volunteer firefighter on the scene, and they'll get an update as soon as I have more information. Also tell them that responders are going to need climbing gear."

"What's the name of this trail?"

"Shit, I don't know. Maybe it doesn't have a name. Give them

14

the GPS coordinates off your phone."

When I was halfway down I stopped and leaned against a tree to catch my breath. My earlier estimate of this drop had been way off base. It was more than fifty, even closer to sixty feet. Maybe the lawyer and his railing would have been a good idea. The runner had likely burst through the bushes and launched over the edge before he even knew what hit him. But he had pulled into the overgrown parking area, so he must have been here before. How could he not have known about the cliff? Maybe he thought it was further along the trail.

I looked around the tree I was clinging to. I still couldn't see any injuries, and I thought the man was breathing. "Fire department!" I shouted. "If you can hear me, move your fingers."

I waited.

Nothing. Damn.

I resumed climbing. It was going to be a bitch getting him back up this slope to an ambulance. Maybe there was a route back to the lot that was easier than climbing up, but you'd have to know the terrain to find it. I hoped one of the responders was a local, someone who knew this area.

"Jack," Valerie's voice floated down. "I can't get a signal."

Better and better. "We'll call on the way to the hospital."

Where was the nearest hospital of any consequence anyway? Not to knock the north country, but a lot of their emergency rooms are little better than witch doctors shaking chicken bones at you. You would sometimes literally come across a one-man trauma center where the doctor was also the mayor, the dog catcher, and sometimes the town undertaker – as if that wasn't a conflict of interest. I knew there was a serious ER in Littleton about an hour away. It serviced several major ski resorts, and therefore had considerable experience with broken bones and internal injuries, not to dissuade anyone from the fine New Hampshire tourist sport of skiing. Littleton was where we would go.

Optimistic thoughts; I was getting way ahead of myself. This had essentially just become a solo rescue mission, and it would involve a one-man carry that might take hours and would exacerbate whatever injuries the man had. There was the possibility he was already dead, but we don't allow ourselves to think that way in the fire service. Treat every response as a possible rescue and not a body recovery until you know differently. They drum that into you in the academy.

I reached ground level. The man was face down, and definitely breathing. If he had landed that way, he might have cracked ribs, or internal injuries, maybe a head wound. He could have had his teeth and so much debris driven down his throat that he could be on the verge of choking on it. But he was breathing, so the smart thing to do would be to make no attempt to move him and have Valerie drive to get help. Naturally the car keys were in my pocket. I thought briefly about tossing them up to her, then realized that if I missed the throw or she the catch, we could spend the next ten hours searching for them in the brush. Her climbing down or me climbing up, the drive back to civilization – it could all take so long that he might die before help arrived.

I should roll him over, I thought. Just roll him over carefully and see how life-threatening his injuries were, the reasoning being that I should work with absolutely as much information as I could gather. But I worried about puncturing a lung with a bit of broken rib by rolling him. I worried about complicating neck and spinal injuries if he had them. If he had significant bleeding in his throat, rolling him over could drown him.

The problem with being the first on scene at a bad call is that you begin to doubt yourself and your actions. The moment you start questioning every decision you make is the moment you freeze up and do nothing, which helps no one. On the other side of the coin resides the Hippocratic Oath: first, do no harm, though firefighters don't take the Hippocratic Oath.

I called up, "Climb down, Val. I'm going to need your help. Be careful!"

I watched as she started down the slope, the pack slung over her back, then turned to my patient. I leaned over, pressed my shoulder against the back of his head and used one arm to stabilize it, then used my other arm to roll him. It's difficult to do that solo and keep everything in alignment, keep stress off the neck and spine, but I had seen the technique for it once in an emergency first aid class and thought I did a pretty good job of it. The patient didn't complain, though his being unconscious probably helped.

There was no blood coming out of his ears, nose, or mouth. Better yet no brains or spinal fluid. I ran my hands gently over his head looking for and not finding a lump or depression in his skull. I pressed his abdomen testing for rigidity, a fair sign of internal bleeding. He had a six pack of abs I could feel through his shirt that made it difficult to tell, but everything seemed to be in order there. Maybe he had a serious spinal fracture, which I had zero ability to diagnose. If so, it made carrying him out of there without crippling or killing him difficult for a team of trained experts with the proper rescue equipment, let alone solo and improvising like mad.

I stood and looked back up to check Valerie's progress. She was taking a moment's rest against the same tree that I had. Tonk wasn't with her so she had likely tied his leash against something at the top. She peeked around the tree at me, and suddenly her face contorted in fear. "Jack! Look out!"

I began to turn around having no idea what direction the danger might be coming from or what it might be, and something struck me hard in the back of the head. I was sent reeling before I managed to arrest my stumble by grabbing onto a tree.

When I straightened up I found the man was no longer lying on the ground, but up on his feet. He was coming at me, his arm already in motion, clutched in his hand a military-looking knife that would have scared my baby Swiss Army knife into running home crying with its tail between its legs. His fingers were woven through the handle which was designed like a set of brass knuckles.

I was trying to get my arm up, but knew well in advance that it wasn't going to get there in time to ward off the blow that was coming. A message to brace for impact sizzled along my nerve endings like the warning to the crew of a submarine about to get hit broadside by a torpedo. I heard Valerie screaming, a piercing horror-movie shriek, so loud I debated if they would hear it in Littleton. My last thought was wondering if they would send help if they did, or if they would consider it the screech of some escaped exotic bird. Then the butt of the knife hit me in my left temple and snapped my head back against the tree I had been holding onto, and I was gone.

Four

When I came to, I was lying face down with my hands behind my back. I tried to open my eyes and only the left one responded. Still, the shaft of light my one eye let in was too bright. It blasted into my brain and made the world swim sickeningly. I clamped my eye shut and swallowed hard until the nausea passed.

I could hear two voices somewhere to my right.

Valerie: "What are you doing? Stop it!"

A man's voice: "Stop struggling."

Valerie: "Why are you doing this?"

Man: "For us."

Valerie: "What us? What are you talking about?"

Man: "Stay still. This will all make sense in a minute."

I cracked my one eye open more slowly and rolled onto my side, which made my nausea spike again. I waited absolutely motionless until it subsided. The man had Valerie's arms behind her and was ratcheting on a pair of flex cuffs like the police use to detain prisoners at mass arrests. My probing fingers told me that it was likely a twin to the one around my own wrists. They were made of extruded nylon with a tensile strength of about a ton, unbreakable for all practical purposes. My ankles were bound together with a zip tie that had been ratcheted tight. I patted my pocket and found my knife and car keys gone. Both backpacks were sitting side by side a short distance away.

The white noise in my head was fading down to a dull roar, which was a pretty good indicator that I hadn't suffered a concussion. Unfortunately in the last several months I had become something of an expert at self-diagnosing those. I noticed there was blood down the front of my shirt. My nose had bled some, but it didn't feel broken, though it was clogged with clots and I had to breathe through my mouth. The right side of my face felt stiff, and my eye was gummed shut with dried blood from the wound on my forehead which was starting to throb like a mother.

The man noticed me watching and gave Valerie's cuffs a final yank to tighten them up which made her cry out in pain, and then he forced her onto the ground on her butt. He came over and crouched next to me. His monster knife was tucked into a black leather sheath attached to his belt.

"Good, you're awake. Hope I didn't hit you too hard, Jack."

This guy knew my name. What the hell? He reached over to touch me on my forehead where he had socked me and I flinched away. This seemed to disappoint him.

"Do I know you?" I asked.

"No," he said, getting up and walking back to Valerie, "we've never met. But Valerie knows me. Why don't you introduce us?" he asked her.

Valerie looked up at him. "I'm not sure, I, um."

"Oh, come on! I know you know me!" he insisted. "I saw you staring at me in the parking lot."

She kept looking, her face blank. She shook her head slowly, "I'm sorry, I don't."

"Jumping Jesus on a chariot!" he stalked away from her, then turned and stomped back. "I sent you all those flowers."

"You never signed the cards."

"I shouldn't have had to! You should have just known!" He frowned. "Look, the last time you saw me my hair was lighter, brown. I dyed it darker. Does that help?"

She focused on him for several seconds. "You're Craig's assistant," she ventured cautiously. "Kevin?"

Bad enough to be fooled and have my ass kicked so effortlessly, but to have it done by someone named Kevin?

He clapped his hands together in a kind of angry celebration, a fully 'roided jock on a post-game high. "Yes! Fuck yes! Kevin. You do know me!"

"Kevin," I asked, "What's going on here?"

"Right down to business; I like that," he said coming back my way. "I bet under different circumstances we'd be friends."

"And what circumstances are these?"

"You're married to the woman I love."

21

Oh, boy. Kevin was a loon, not to besmirch New Hampshire's fine upstanding loon population.

"Kevin," Valerie said gently, "Jack is my husband."

"That's only because you met him first. You will love me."

"I love him."

"After all he's done? After the way he's treated you? I heard what you told Craig."

What had she told Craig, I couldn't help but wonder.

She took some time composing her answer, her eyes focused at an uncertain middle distance. She said at last, "Craig was a mistake," with less conviction than I would have liked, then drew a breath, let it out, and turned her focus back to him. "This is insane, Kevin."

"It's not insane," he said tightly. I expected him to fly off the handle, but instead he walked towards her calmly, menacingly. He snatched something out of his backpack as he went by, but I couldn't see what from where I was lying. Whatever it was, I could tell that Valerie didn't like it from the look of fear and confusion on her face as he approached. When he reached her, he placed a foot against her shoulder and pushed her over, then flipped her onto her stomach and jammed a knee in her back to keep her in place. He grabbed her hair and wrenched her head back, and then he shifted his weight, his body blocking my line of sight. His handling of her, the coldness of it, this woman he claimed to love, was chilling.

"No! St-" Valerie shouted, her cries cut off mid-word.

"Valerie!" I yelled, and tried to reach her. Bound hand and foot, all I managed was flopping around like a fish dying on the beach.

Her feet free, she kicked like a demon, managing to glance her heels off his shoulders once or twice, but he didn't seem to care. After perhaps fifteen seconds of her grunting and him swearing under his breath, he said, "There, done." He stood up, grabbed her by the shoulders, and hauled her up by the scruff of her shirt. She pedaled her legs, trying to run away, but he held on. He spun her around and slammed her back against a tree hard enough to make her wince and causing a small shower of dry pine needles to rain down upon them. She slid to the ground and ended up sitting at the base of the tree looking up at him. "Stay put," he told her.

When he stepped away I could see there was a large red ball stuffed in her mouth. It had been forced behind her front teeth and stretched her lips tight around its bulk, a wide leather strap that latched somehow at the back of her neck kept it in place.

"Whew," Kevin said as he came towards me, swiping his hands against one another as if removing dust, a man who had just completed some arduous manual labor, like changing a tire on a very large truck. "She put up more of a fight than you did." He crouched back down. "Seriously though, tell me the truth, there are times you've wanted to shove a gag in her mouth. Am I right?"

He waited as if he expected me to really give him an answer to that. When I didn't, he again seemed disappointed, another thoughtless slight on my part.

"Anyway," he got up and went to his backpack again and started rooting around inside, "now we can talk without distraction, and Valerie, she can be quite a distraction as I'm sure you're aware. Did you know she stood backstage at *Nightline* while Kymbyrly fussed with her hair, joking with me wearing just her bra, like she wasn't half-naked?" Kevin was referring to a brief media circuit Valerie had made while in the public eye. His eyes took on a wistful look with the recollection, and he stopped pawing through his backpack. "Her bra was practically see-through."

23

He glanced in her direction, "You have killer breasts. Really, world class."

Valerie's cheeks burned with humiliation. She mouthed at the ball, like a horse working a nettlesome bit.

"Confidentially, Valerie can be quite a flirt," he said to me.

I knew that Valerie liked to flirt, and that she was good at it. I liked to flirt too, though did so with much less skill. I like to think as a couple devoted in our love, a little sexual banter with members of the opposite sex was harmless because we were confident that it wouldn't lead to anything. I had turned out to be wrong about that with Craig. I had also failed to consider instances where the object of the flirtation turned out to be a lunatic. Perhaps it was a policy we should revisit in the future.

Kevin remembered what he was doing and dug into the backpack again. I dreaded what he might be looking for. The gag and the flex ties had been in there; nothing good for our team had come out of it as yet.

What he retrieved was my pocket knife, which he tossed in my direction. It landed in the dirt a few feet away.

I looked at it.

"Go ahead," he urged. "Cut yourself loose. I've got big plans for our day."

I didn't like the sound of that, but wormed my way over and retrieved the knife. I folded out the blade. As I said previously, it wasn't much for length, but at least I kept it sharp. I watched Kevin suspiciously as I worked at the cuffs behind my back. It was tough going because they had been ratcheted tight, and I didn't want my wrists to end up slashed to bloody pieces in a rush to free myself. At last I felt one cuff strap break. Cutting my other hand loose took just a couple of seconds more. Lastly I severed the strap holding my ankles together and stood up. My hands and feet were all pins and needles from lack of circulation.

I compared the baby knife I held versus the big daddy knife on his belt and debated attacking there and then. The owner of such a knife probably knew how to use it, maybe had even taken some training. I was just a guy who had purchased a Swiss Army knife at Target. I'd used the screwdriver a couple of times, the corkscrew, and once used the blade to cut a seatbelt at a car accident. I was definitely not Rambo material.

I also reconsidered my original assessment of his physique. He wasn't built like a runner at all. His shoulders were broad, broader than mine, and his torso veed down to a narrow waist. His calves, exposed by his shorts, were huge and when he gestured his biceps and triceps popped like those of a power lifter.

Rather than getting my brains beaten out in some ill-conceived attack, I thought it better to see what he had to say first. He didn't ask for the knife back so I folded it up and put it in my pocket. I rubbed at my wrists trying to work blood back into my fingertips.

"Good," he said. "So here's the deal. You ready? Because it's going to blow your mind." He paused, perhaps listening to a snare drum roll that only he could hear, his face flushed with the excitement of his upcoming plans. "You and I are going to fight to the death. The winner takes Valerie."

Five

I was struck speechless. Someone should have made a note of
the date and time; it doesn't happen often. This, I thought, is
what I must look like without speech. My mouth agape, my one
eye open wide; the embodiment of the slack-jawed yokel.

He looked at me eagerly.

I probed gently at my bloodied eye, prying with thumb and
forefinger, trying to get it open without success. Water would
have helped, and I debated and rejected the idea of asking for
one of the bottles out of our backpack. Who knew what would
set him off?

He waited, an expression on his face like that of a Labrador
when it sees you reaching for a favorite tennis ball: focused,
hopeful, and coiled with barely-restrained, wild energy.

I abandoned working on the eye. "You're serious," I said at last,
the only two words my brain was capable of stringing together. I

was almost expecting this to be an episode of *Candid Camera*, or an elaborate scene from the TV show *Punk'd* wherein Ashton Kutcher played heinous impractical jokes on his friends. Shouldn't there be cameramen jumping out of the woods and rappelling down from the trees like ninjas right about now?

He dispelled this notion by nodding. "Two men fighting over the woman they love, the hero emerging triumphant. It's romantic, right Valerie?" he called over his shoulder to her.

She, of course, didn't answer.

Romantic was maybe one word for it. I thought crazy was a more suitable one, though I suspected where Kevin was concerned the word crazy was in serious danger of overuse.

He leaned towards me, which caused me involuntarily to shy back, and added sotto voce, "and make no mistake, I'm the hero here."

I shook my head, not in denial, but to see if I could rattle my jammed-up thoughts loose. I couldn't get my brain to engage, the gears of my mind refusing to mesh with the mad machine Kevin was spinning up. This never happens in real life, a part of me kept insisting.

Except when it does.

Some guy in, I believe it was, Cleveland had kept not one, not two, but three women hostage as sex slaves for ten years, even fathering children by some of them. Two guys in California had time-shared a single woman in much the same way for months before she had managed to escape. Women went missing all over the country every day, never to be heard from again. Was it such a stretch to imagine that some of them ended up locked in

27

makeshift dungeons? Without having told anyone of our plans to come out here today, would Valerie be the next one, my body lying undiscovered, the flesh striped from my bones by small animals, my bones bleaching quietly in the sun thereafter? We had been at home two hours ago playing stupid pet tricks in the back yard, and now I was here trying to figure out how to negotiate with someone who harbored a very different view of reality from the rest of us. It defied belief.

I waited in the dead silence that followed Kevin's pronouncement, straining to hear the sound of another human voice, hoping there might be other hikers nearby, or the rumble of a car in the distance. Even the hollow droning of a plane passing by overhead at forty thousand feet would have been a comfort. Instead the world around us was deathly still, holding its collective breath to see how this might play out. We were completely and totally alone out here.

I noticed then, much to my chagrin, that his knuckles were rough and calloused, while his palms looked soft. Sure, maybe there were plenty of perfectly innocent manual labors that could lead to such an unusual wear pattern, but the activity that my brain latched onto first, latched onto and wouldn't let go of, was boxing, sparing, working the speed and heavy bags with bare hands. I flashed on that scene from *Rocky* where Sylvester Stallone punches slides of beef. Oh, Valerie, why couldn't you have flirted with an asthmatic, malnourished, video gamer?

"Kevin, that's…" I paused there, the word crazy perched tenuously on the edge of my lips. I thought it would be wise to leave that unsaid. Valerie had called him crazy, and look what it had gotten her. I had to choose my words carefully. I held up my hands in a placating gesture, realized as I did so that my hands were framing my head, like painting a bulls-eye on my face, and let them drop again. The phrase 'Let's be reasonable' came to mind, like we were two businessmen discussing a somewhat thorny deal. I left that one unuttered too.

Kevin's face twisted up, his mouth in a grimace or half a smile, a sociopath's stew of sadness and mirth and I had no idea what else. "Jack, don't disappoint me." The tone of his voice was that of a dire warning, though what punishment he had in mind if I refused to fight him, what he could do to me that was worse than beating me to death while my wife looked on, I couldn't imagine. Yet somehow, I knew, I didn't want to find out. Not one tiny bit.

I had little interest in following Kevin down his rabbit hole, but at least at the present didn't see as I had any other choice than to play along. Stall, get some distance, find some help – my plan at that point was no more detailed than that.

"Are there any rules?" I asked.

He pondered that for a moment, I think surprised by the question.

While I waited for his answer, I took another crack at my stuck eye. If I was going to fight for my life, I wanted to do so with stereo vision. I managed, finally, to pry it open. Flakes of blood fell into the eye and it stung like hell. I rapidly blinked them away.

After some internal debate, Kevin raised a single finger. "One rule," he said. He went over to Valerie who tried to scrabble backwards away from him but seemed to have forgotten that she was up against a tree. He grabbed a fistful of her shirt and hauled her to her feet, and then proceeded to pat her down, or rather feel her up. Unless he expected to find whatever he was looking for tucked inside her cleavage or wedged deeply into her crotch, in which case his search was as professional and expert as anything the TSA was doing to airline passengers a million times a day, though he lingered on her breasts for a long time even by TSA standards. Valerie withstood his attentions stoically, but the very second he gave her an opening she kneed him in the groin.

It looked to me like it connected, and I experienced that momentary sympathetic gut clench that all guys do upon seeing a fellow male take one in the nads, but then I figured this was my chance and began closing the distance between us rapidly.

Somehow the blow didn't faze Kevin at all. He flowed around behind Valerie. That's the only way I can describe it, like some kind of martial arts move. One hand twisted a fistful of her hair, lifting her up on her toes, wrenching her head back. The other slid the knife from its sheath and leveled it against her exposed throat. The whole thing happened so quickly that I had covered only two or three steps of the distance between us before skidding to a halt.

Valerie panted shallowly through her nose, her eyes glassy with terror. She teetered on her tippy toes, afraid to let her weight down on the blade of the knife.

"Wow," Kevin said seductively, "I bet you are a lot of fun in bed." He pulled her against him, his hips cocked forward, pelvis pressing against her backside. He dipped his head to nuzzle her behind the ear. He then removed the knife from her throat and hooked her ankles with his foot, sweeping her legs out from under her. Her arms bound, she was unable to arrest her fall and hit the ground hard. She drew her knees up to her chest, mewling in pain through the gag.

He sheathed the knife, completely unconcerned for how injured she might have been. I was worried sick, but heartened that she seemed to come out of her fetal position fairly quickly.

"Now, where were we?" He looked down at Valerie and that

seemed to spark his memory. "Oh yeah." He rolled her onto her stomach and dug her cell phone out of the back pocket of her jeans. He dusted it off, even taking a moment to blow the grit from the screen, then threw it at the ground hard enough that it exploded into thousands of pieces on impact. He held a hand out to me. "I'm going to need your phone."

"I don't have one."

He made a face. "Come on. Everyone has a cell phone."

"I don't." I had once, until a group of terrorists had taken it from me and hurled it off the Ernest P. Heflan scenic overlook in Dunboro. Verizon and I were in something of a contract dispute as we debated who should pay to replace it. That seemed like a too complicated a story to go into at that moment. If he was really interested, he could buy the book.

He shrugged. "OK, have it your way, but here's the rule: it's just you and just me. You call for help, I see a helicopter in the sky or a ranger in the woods, and I'll kill her. And believe me, I'll make sure it hurts and you won't recognize the remains. Got it?"

His ability to so callously harm Valerie, whom he claimed to love, to further threaten her with mutilation and death if he didn't get his way, caused a sharp pain in my guts, like someone was twirling up my small intestines like spaghetti on the tines of a fork. Did I have any option other than to go along?

"I understand," I said. "You want to do this now?"

He changed his stance subtly, his gravity centered, his hands loose at his sides. "If you like."

"How about later?"

"That's up to you." He watched me warily.

"How about next New Year's Eve, Times Square, at midnight?"

He gave a humorless chuckle. "Valerie said you were funny." He looked down at Valerie still writhing on the ground and said, "You're right, he's funny." He casually stepped over her and stood between her and me, like a dog cutting me off from a bone that he clearly thought was his. "No, here's the deal. Come at me whenever you like, any time within the next twenty-four hours. If we haven't settled this by then, I'll take her and disappear, and you'll never see us again."

I glanced at my watch to make a note of the time and found the sapphire crystal smashed to shards, one hand bent and the other missing entirely, a round dent in the center of the stainless steel face. The aforementioned terrorists had, in addition to losing my phone, destroyed my last watch. This one had been a replacement, a reconciliation gift from Valerie, and was less than six months old. The good die young.

"I'm sorry about that," he said. "You blocked my first blow with your watch."

From her spot on the ground Valerie grunted and shook her head. Kevin gave her an annoyed glance.

He again went to his backpack, the bag that seemed to hold whatever he happened to need at that moment. Hadn't there been a *Twilight Zone* episode like that? He came up with an old-fashioned stopwatch, similar to the kind my gym coach in high school had used. He fiddled with the buttons a little, came over, and handed it to me. The display showed hours, minutes, and seconds in a seriously retro red nine-bar LED format, and as the saying goes, the clock was ticking, metaphorically speaking.

32

The stopwatch was on a rope lanyard, and I hung it around my neck. Not as convenient as a wristwatch, but functional.

"So that's it?" I asked.

He nodded, "Yeah, I think so."

"Simple as that?"

"Simple as that," he confirmed.

"No more rules?"

"Nope," he said with a smug smile.

"OK," I said. Then I hit him.

Six

Given how I had seen him move with Valerie, liquid and quick, I was pretty sure any telegraphing of the upcoming punch was going to cause it to miss. So instead of a John Wayne wind up haymaker, I had chosen to just snap my fist out at him. My shoulder, my elbow, my forearm, my wrist, my fist, his face – simple physics, the Occam's razor of punches. It landed too, but he did something kind of remarkable. He somehow loosened his neck muscles, so instead of meeting hard resistance and flattening out his nose, it was like I pushed his head back, and hitting him probably caused far less damage than it otherwise would have. Still, I'm over two hundred pounds, and I'd like to think a fair percentage of that is muscle, and the distance between us was just about perfect for the length of my arm, giving the punch room to pick up momentum and dump every bit of it into his skull.

The blow stunned him, even if only for a second, and a more experienced fighter would have followed up and taken the opportunity to land more, but I'm not an experienced fighter. And while I didn't go so far as to do a little end zone shuffle in celebration or climb onto the upper turnbuckle and mug for the audience while my opponent recovered like at a WWE wrestling bout, I did sort of stop and watch the aftermath of the punch like a rubbernecker at a car accident. How devastating had it been? Was he coming back for more, or was my job here done?

I also knew my heart wasn't in killing him, not then. The plan in the back of my mind had been to incapacitate him, free Valerie, drag him back to my truck, return to civilization, and let the authorities deal. Even as I watched him blink and give his head a rapid little shake, some part of me understood that had been naïve on my part. Civilization had apparently ended at the weedy entrance to the overgrown parking area. The map here might as well have been labeled 'Lord of the Flies Territory' in ye olde English script.

When he recovered, he slid forward, the damnedest gliding motion, like Michael Jackson's moon walk in reverse. I managed to get my dukes up, a hopelessly amateurish Mohammed Ali boxing stance, like we were fighting using Marques of Queensberry Rules. He responded by slamming his foot into the side of my knee. I was turned slightly, which saved the joint from disintegrating entirely, but it buckled, and as I fell I looked down wondering where the hell my leg had gone. It had been there just a moment ago holding me up just fine, and now I was falling. That, my dazed brain thought, was some fine mystery. I let my guard drop and he hit me with a quick left and right to the face. Or that might have been a right and a left. The two punches were so close together I had trouble telling which had landed first. One of them broke up the clots inside my nose, and fresh blood spilled down across my lips, dripping off my chin and onto the front of my shirt.

While I tottered around trying just to stay upright, he slid back beyond my reach. The whole sequence – in, three shots, out – took place in perhaps two seconds, though I would have needed to check the stopwatch hanging around my neck to know for certain. My own internal timekeeping was fluttering like an old 8mm film with stripped sprocket holes. He gathered himself for a moment while holding a fighting stance, doing his own damage assessment. But far from waiting to see if I was done, I felt him instead dissecting me with a warrior's eye to ascertain what he had already broken and what he would be best served by breaking next.

I didn't recover nearly as smoothly as he had, but I did manage to get my feet under me, straighten up a little, and get my hands back up, though I was seriously woozy and concerned about aspirating some of the blood leaking from my nose. I breathed out through my mouth causing the rivulets on my lips to puff into a fine red mist in front of my face.

He came at me again, that perplexing sliding motion, and I focused as best I could.

He took a swing at my face, and I flinched back. I managed to avoid the punch, which I realized may have been a feint on his part, but I had sort of over-flinched in the process. My center of gravity ended up hanging somewhere way out over my ass and I was in danger of falling over backwards all by myself. He helpfully hooked my ankles with his foot, the same move I had watched him use on Valerie, and yanked the rug out from under me. As I fell, he slammed the flat of his fist against my chest, a blow to my sternum that felt like he had stoved in my chest with a sledgehammer. The blow greatly accelerated my trip to the ground, and I crashed down with a force that rattled every joint in my body like a handful of dice in a cup.

I lay where I landed, blowing bubbles of my own blood, the sickly sweet taste of copper in my mouth.

He took his time unsheathing the knife, and then dropped to his knees straddling me, his shins resting on my forearms. Wasted effort on his part; I very likely couldn't have lifted my arms under my own power even if he hadn't bothered to pin them.

I rolled my eyes up in my head and looked at Valerie upside-down across the clearing. The hopeless look on her face wrenched at my heart. I wanted to tell her that it was going to be OK, somehow, but that was hard to do when I felt him press the knife against the base of my throat. I rolled my eyes back.

He wasn't even breathing hard. There was no emotion on his face I could read. I realized that perhaps, frighteningly, there was no emotion there to read. His was the face of someone about to perform a distasteful but not particularly difficult task, like a farmer about to butcher his ten thousandth hog, and he scared the shit out of me. His pupils were wide open, dark holes I could plummet into, the last eyes I might ever see. I wondered if I would feel the bite of the blade, or if it was so sharp that it would sever my neck painlessly, like stories of the French aristocracy beheaded by the guillotine so quickly that their heads tumbled into the baskets looking back up at the sky and wondering how in the world they had ended up in there. The muscles in his forearm bunched as he prepared to bear down and make the cut. My bowels loosened, and I was surprised that I didn't crap my pants or wet myself.

Then he threw back his head and laughed. It was loud and jovial, a laugh at the best joke ever told. He lurched to his feet and jammed the knife back in its sheath. I rolled onto my side weakly and spit out a dollop of bloody mucus which sat like a gelatinous blob in the sandy soil an inch from my face. My entire body was trembling helplessly, my teeth chattered like I was freezing to death, though I felt overheated and dizzy as though suffering from heat stroke.

"That took incredible balls," he said, chuckling and waggling a finger at me, naughty, naughty. "Really, really amazing." He spun, his arms thrown up in the air joyously. If this was a Disney movie, it would have been the moment he burst into song. After several spins he stopped and came back to me, his path wavering, drunk on his own festivity, his eyes glowing. "This is going to be so much fucking fun!"

37

He dropped easily into a crouch, a move that made my own injured knee sob just thinking about it, and like flipping a switch, the mirth was gone. The emotionless hog butcher was back. Bipolar much?

"Because of your incredible balls," he said, "I'm going to give you that one for free. But that's it; you only get one. When you try again, you bring your A-game, because the next time I put you down, I'm going to cut your head off," he punctuated this speech by drawing out his knife and waving it back and forth above me, as if I had somehow forgotten what implement he planned to use to do the cutting.

He stood, slid the knife into his sheath, and swaggered over to the backpacks. He picked up both and slung them over one shoulder, and then strolled to where Valerie lay, again rooting around inside his pack as he did so. He pulled out a collar, wide black leather with shiny chrome studs. It looked like a sex toy, but maybe was just an ornate dog collar, something a particularly stereotypical biker might have his dog wear. Valerie looked thoroughly shell-shocked and didn't resist as he fastened it around her neck. He clipped on a short leash, one that looked very much like Tonk's, and used it to pull her to her feet and get her moving.

As he led her out of the clearing, she looked back just once sadly and paused. He gave the leash a brutal tug that nearly caused whiplash and she stumbled several steps before regaining her balance. Then they were into the trees and gone from my sight.

Seven

I wanted to get up and race after them. I even pictured doing it: running through the woods, leaping high into the air, driving a flying fist into Kevin's face, doing whatever was necessary to take that shell-shocked look out of Valerie's eyes. I made several attempts to get to my feet, but my limbs refused to respond in a coordinated fashion. To someone watching me, I likely looked as if I were trying to swim a clumsy breaststroke across the ground or maybe like someone making pine needle angels. Finally exhausted, the muscles in my shoulders and back burning, my abused body betrayed me and I passed out.

When I came to, the stopwatch around my neck helpfully told me that I had been dead to the world for about an hour and a half, a smidge under twenty-two and a half hours to go. The sun looked pretty high, at least for December, though the hills all around made it difficult to get perspective or make any useful estimate of how much daylight remained. I knew local sunset was at 4:26; I had checked it online that morning. But with my watch still sprinkling bits of sapphire from its shattered face onto the ground like grains of sand, I had no way of knowing what time it was.

39

Kevin could have come back with Valerie in tow and killed me easily while I was unconscious, not that beating me senseless when I had been fully ready to fight had proved all that difficult for him either. Though grateful, I couldn't understand why he hadn't. Come back, pull out his knife, saw my head off – easy peasy. Who knows why crazy people do the things they do? Taking him at his word, perhaps that wouldn't have been enough fun for him.

I stood up slowly and with a lot of grunting and groaning, but once on my feet I was surprised at how well everything worked. It didn't hurt to breathe, so the blow to my chest hadn't cracked any ribs. My knee was stable and moved without much pain. My face and shirt were stiff with dried blood, but the bleeding had stopped, and I still had all my teeth in my head. I didn't even think my nose was broken. My cheeks were puffy, a chipmunk smuggling acorns, and holy cow was I thirsty. I couldn't remember ever having been so thirsty. I vaguely recalled some link between extreme thirst and internal bleeding from emergency first aid training, but tried to put a hopeful spin on it. I told myself that my thirst was due to exertion and having lost some blood in an entirely external fashion, and my body was craving fluid replacement. There was water in my backpack with Kevin and Valerie, wherever they were, which was about the most unhelpful thought ever.

I crossed the clearing to where they had disappeared into the woods. I meandered in circles examining the ground. Maybe there were some scuff marks to mark their passage, but that was about it. Could I follow them? What happened if they crossed a stream or a granite ledge? I tried to make a big deal out of a snapped branch, guess what it could tell me about the direction they were headed or how fast they might have been moving when they broke it, and then shook my head and threw it aside. I wasn't a tracker, and I had no idea where Kevin might be taking her. Attempting to follow them didn't sound like the smart option. Getting in front of them and laying an ambush I felt certain was the way to go, which meant I needed to get a bird's eye view.

I walked to the base of the hill and looked up at the slope. Had I guessed it was only fifty or sixty feet high? From where I stood it looked taller than a skyscraper. I thought I would have had a better chance shimmying into a pair of Spiderman Underoos and scaling the outside of the Hancock Tower in Boston during a blizzard than climbing this hill. But if there was a better alternative, I couldn't come up with it. A phrase my grandmother used to say came to mind: well begun is half done. Oh, Nana, you have no idea.

There were lots of trees on the slope, and though I had to stop and rest for a moment at nearly every single one to let slow waves of dizziness roll past, I did make steady progress. While I scrambled and huffed and clawed my way up, ripping loose a number of fingernails in the process, I tried to envision some way to beat this guy who was obviously younger and faster and stronger and far better trained to fight than I was, and was carrying a knife that could handily gut a grizzly bear to boot.

I had no cell phone. I didn't have the keys to my truck, though it was waiting patiently for me about a mile away in the parking area. I ran through the stuff that I thought was inside: a small fire extinguisher, a tire iron, and a spare flashlight. A road flare would have made a great weapon and I normally had a couple, and then recalled that I had used my last one at a car accident a month ago. There was a plain white bed sheet I kept in the truck ever since I was the first person on the scene of a motorcycle fatality and had nothing with which to cover the body. Not a weapon, but I could carry it along and maybe Kevin would spread it over me when he was finished.

I shelved the negative thought as soon as I had it.

I remembered that a first aid kit resided in the center console, but had no good idea of what was inside it. Those little, round, useless band-aids? Prepackaged alcohol swabs? Whatever there was, as I rested against a tree trunk about halfway up the slope, I thought I could put it to good use. I took a deep breath and forged onward.

With a little work, I could scavenge the battery. It weighed like twenty pounds and would be a bitch to lug around, but maybe there was something clever I could do with it and the jumper cables. I could also throw battery acid in his face, though I didn't really know how acidic battery acid was, nor how to crack open the case to get at it, nor how I would carry the acid once I got it out. Did I have a cup somewhere in the truck? I didn't think so.

Tired and numb from climbing, my brain fell into performing a simple inventory: ice scraper, dog poop bags, a few lengths of rope, a couple of bungee cords, the spare tire. I knew that, as much as I wished it were so, there was no water or food.

I cleared the lip of the rise and Tonk, his leash tied to a tree branch, lunged at me barking his fool head off. Covered in blood, my face swollen, he must not have immediately recognized me. Shortly, though, he got a whiff of me, a smell he knew, and he hung his head, embarrassed at his outburst.

"Nice to see you too," I croaked wryly as I settled on the ground next to him and worked at untying his leash with my knuckles bruised from the climb up and fingers scraped raw that didn't work all that well. When he was free, the two of us went and stood on the edge of the rocky overlook.

I spotted Kevin and Valerie almost immediately. Actually, it wasn't them I saw, but the hunter orange backpack that Kevin carried, appearing in little glimpses and flickers through the trees. They were a mile and a half away, perhaps two, so they weren't making great time. It probably wasn't easy going leading a woman by a leash with her hands bound behind her back over uneven ground unless you were unconcerned about her falling and hurting herself, and maybe Valerie was putting up

42

some resistance. An alternate reason for their lack of progress was much darker and more foreboding: Kevin was purposely going slowly because he needed me to catch up with them so he could kill me.

This made me consider his selection of backpack color. Was it a choice calculated to make them easy to see at a distance? Just how much of this had he planned out in advance? I dragged my hands through my hair; it felt crisp with flakes of dried blood. Trying to make sense of the convoluted path between some guy ogling my wife's tits backstage at an evening news show and playing hide-and-go-seek, the homicide edition, in the White Mountains of New Hampshire was making my head spin.

I stood there following the bouncing backpack, measuring their pace, and trying to MacGyver the crap in my truck into something useful. No eureka moment had struck as yet, but I decided I really wanted at least the flashlight from the center console so I could keep moving after dark, which happened with startling suddenness in the mountains during winter. It didn't look like I would lose them in the time it would take me to get to the truck and back. I fully realized it was an enormous gamble I was taking with this decision, the possibility of losing their trail and leaving Valerie to that sick puke versus falling off a cliff at night trying to catch up, but I had made the decision and went with it. This was another one of those first-on-the-scene-of-a-bad-call moments, and it was not time to start second guessing every action I took.

I unclipped Tonk's leash from his collar; I had no energy to spare worrying about him getting tangled around my ankles. He probably wouldn't run off, and if he did, it would be in pursuit of a squirrel. Heck, maybe he would catch us some supper.

I took one more look over my shoulder – the backpack was still in sight – and headed off down the trail.

Eight

My truck and Kevin's car sat in the parking area looking almost unfathomably normal, two artifacts from of a civilization that no longer existed. Had it really been less than five hours ago that Valerie and I had been at home where our biggest problem, at least in my mind, was her getting stabbed by a thorn while she crammed the bouquet of roses into a garbage can? The detective part of my brain picked that moment to wonder if Kevin had been watching us that entire time. No, it concluded, he hadn't, because he didn't know that she had thrown the roses violently away or he would have said something about it. So when did he start following us? How had he come to find us here? My brain, devoid of answers, shrugged. Some help it was turning out to be.

I went out to the road, Tonk at my heels, and looked both ways, listened for engine noise. We waited fifteen minutes by the clock around my neck and saw not another soul, heard no distant sounds of a car or truck. This hiking trail was so far out of the way even its access road was rarely traveled. Had we seen anyone, I strongly doubted I could have gotten them to stop and help anyway. The front of my shirt was maroon with dried blood, my face was a mess, and I noticed I had even managed to get some of my blood smeared on Tonk's fur. We looked like members of a crazed cannibalistic hill clan. Anyone driving by would have thought they had stumbled into a sequel to the horror movies *The Hills Have Eyes* or *Wrong Turn*, and promptly mashed their foot to the floor leaving us in a cloud of dust and engine exhaust. Dejected, we returned to the parking area.

I thought about trying to hotwire my truck and going for help. It was brand new, and probably loaded to the roofline with all sorts of high tech anti-theft systems that I couldn't begin to figure out how to bypass. But even if I managed to get it started, where would I go? If I went to the police, their first move would be to put a chopper in the air with a thermal camera or send in a SWAT team. For all I knew the local guys had finagled an armored personnel carrier out of the Department of Homeland Security under the guise of protecting the White Mountains from terrorist incursions, and wouldn't they love to take that baby out for a spin? I had little doubt if that happened Kevin would make good on his threat to kill Valerie as well as his promise to make it hurt. The cops would also want to try and arrest Kevin, which in my mind meant all sorts of opportunities for Valerie to get her throat cut in some botched hostage negotiation.

A second, more promising option was to go to the Dunboro Fire Department. John Pederson, the Chief of the department and an ex-Marine, would hear Valerie was in danger, come out here with his sniper rifle, and liberate Kevin's head from his shoulders from seven hundred yards away. Oh, but that sounded like a beautiful outcome. Getting there and back however would take hours, hours in which Kevin and Valerie would disappear into the wilderness.

It seemed to me, the more I examined it, that Kevin had planned everything out pretty well, and going for help was out.

Without my keys, I had to let myself in through the side window of my truck with a rock. Man, I was hard on cars; my last two had been totaled. I felt sorry for this truck, and all the others I had owned before it. Sibling trucks on the dealer's lot probably held a funeral when they learned one of them was being sold to me.

Once inside, I grabbed the flashlight and was overjoyed to find the LED nearly blinding to look at, the batteries with plenty of charge. It was a Maglite, one of the smaller models. An aluminum cylinder about eight inches long with the promising heft of two C batteries inside, it was practically a weapon in its own right. I slid it into a back pocket of my jeans.

I took a moment to check myself out in the rearview mirror. My face looked terrible: swollen, a mask of dried blood, my right eye a dark hole caked with stuff. The scalp wound looked like it could use a few stitches and had bled copiously as scalp wounds often do. I dabbed at it gently with a Kleenex from a small box I keep in the glove compartment. It had clotted over for the most part on its own and there was nothing I could do about it in any case. I stuffed the tissue into the ashtray and returned to my search.

My second windfall came in the form of two after-dinner mints that I found inside a cup holder, likely tossed there by either Valerie or me after a Mexican meal somewhere. I ate one and gave the other to Tonk. I figured he was missing out on a meal too, and it might marginally improve his breath.

As I searched through my truck, I enjoyed sloshing the minty flavor around in my mouth, banishing the taste of blood that had been there for so long I had almost come not to notice it. A cut in my mouth where my cheek had been bashed against my teeth stung, but it was such a slight pain, it was somehow pleasurable. My energy level climbed a little at even that meager infusion of sugar. I sucked until the mint completely dissolved – no cracking it up with my molars when it was halfway done – and then swallowed, almost coming to tears as the flavor faded.

Tonk, never one to savor a meal, looked to have swallowed his mint whole.

Next I found a partial roll of duct tape in the center console. More than three-quarters gone, there was probably no more than fifteen or twenty feet of tape left. Still, a thousand and one uses, as the book Valerie had bought me several Christmas's ago was entitled. I fitted the roll over my left hand and wore it around my wrist as a wide bangle. For all I knew, kids were wearing rolls of duct tape this way these days.

I discovered my fourth and final bonus in the first aid kit. Beyond an assortment of Band-Aids and small, square alcohol wipes, there were little sealed packets of generic aspirin. I tore one open with my teeth and chewed up the two pills inside. It was a dry, bitter, unpleasant mess, but they went down, though it left me wishing I had found the aspirin before consuming the mint. There was also an ace bandage, pretty old and beat up and with most of its elasticity gone. My knee didn't need support at the moment, but it might come in handy later. I took the whole kit and tucked it into the waistband of my jeans at the small of my back.

I found a portable umbrella, but without rain in the forecast I left it behind.

I located the tire iron. When I was a kid, a tire iron was a serious length of forged steel, almost more weapon than tool. The one in my truck was maybe fourteen inches long. It was probably exactly long enough and no longer than some engineer at Ford calculated the average American male needed to provide sufficient torque to remove the lug nuts. Penny pinching at its finest. It might not even have been forged steel, but annealed cast iron, not that Kevin's skull would notice the difference. Only marginally better than the flashlight, I nonetheless hooked it through my belt loop.

I climbed out of my truck, no more treasures in the offering.

47

My first use for the tire iron was to break a window in Kevin's car. A brief search showed me he had picked it clean, without even leaving the registration behind. Whether that meant he intended to come back to it, had some other conveyance lined up to make his escape after he killed me, or was ultimately planning a double-murder-suicide extravaganza, I didn't care to hazard a guess.

I proceeded to smash out all the windows, the windshield included, which took some doing, plus the headlights and taillights. I flattened all four tires and the spare with the prying end of the tire iron. I gave my rage free reign, let the car become a surrogate for Kevin; if I couldn't destroy him at least I could destroy his car. There was also a more practical purpose to my vandalism: if Kevin intended to try and drive out of here with Valerie tied up and gagged it the trunk, I wanted to make sure he would have to do it on flat tires, and his car would be stopped by any cop who laid eyes on it. I worked up a sweat with all the destruction and stopped to catch my breath when I was finished.

That left me next staring at my own truck, which of course he had the keys to. I really didn't want to beat the shit out of it. The poor vehicle was less than six months old. It still had that new car smell! I opted for popping the hood and yanking all the fuses out of the primary breaker box. A small pile of gem-colored plastic squares, almost like a handful of hard candy, I hid them in a crevice underneath a large rock at the edge of the parking area. That task completed, I slammed the hood and prepared to beat feet, then had one final thought.

His car had followed us into the parking area and stopped short. He had been expecting to find us there, but maybe not right there, which seemed like one of those nagging clues my useless brain is always digging for, and it had already concluded that he hadn't followed us all the way from home. I popped open the hood of my truck again and poked around inside, found nothing, and slammed it shut. I crawled around the undercarriage and again batted zero. Under the dash was where I struck pay dirt, a small box wired into the power for the radio. An antenna wove around in the guts of the dash, and snuck out almost invisibly in the lower corner of the windshield in front of the passenger seat.

Though it didn't have a big sticker on it telling me what it was, it had to be a GPS transponder, something that broadcast the truck's position to a receiver in his possession. He had been following us, tracking me, for I had no idea how long. This was followed by the sick thought that he could have waited until I was out of the house for a fire call, paid a visit to Valerie with his flex cuffs and his ball gag and his dog collar, and kidnapped her easily. I would have returned home to an empty house, and maybe a dead Tonk, with no idea where she had gone or what had happened to her. From that perspective, I was almost glad that he had chosen to do things this way. It gave me a chance, even if at the moment it seemed like a slim one, to do something to save her.

All the supplies I could scavenge in my possession, I closed the truck door, and headed back up the trail with Tonk on my heels.

Nine

By the time Tonk and I returned to the scenic overlook, another hour and a half had passed. Three down, twenty-one to go.

I spied the backpack almost immediately, its vibrant color winking at me playfully through the trees. It occurred to me then that the backpack could have been a misdirection. Kevin could have tied it to a moose or convinced a bear to carry it for him, and I would end up chasing it into the hinterlands while he and Valerie went in some other direction entirely. But I knew that wasn't what Kevin wanted. Kevin wanted to best me in combat and win the hand, as well as the rest of the body, of his lady fair.

It scared the crap out of me that Kevin's reasoning was starting to make sense to me.

They had picked up another mile give or take a little in my absence and were getting quite far away. I would have to hustle to catch up. Doing so would exhaust me, and yet again the genius of Kevin's plan was evident.

I tried to determine the path they were on. I used the spot at the base of the hill as a starting point, drew a line through their current position, and extended it out into the future. Nothing of interest lay along that route that I could see. If Kevin had some fixed destination in mind like a building or a place where he had left another car in advance, I couldn't see it.

I plotted my own route, one that would allow me to stay on the ridgeline. I wanted to keep the bird's eye view advantage as much as possible. If I was mapping everything properly, the two paths would converge near mid-afternoon at a spot I painted a big red X on with my mind. As good a plan as any, I set out.

I tried not to rush and instead set a manageable pace, something I could sustain for hours without a break if necessary. Though I wanted to get ahead of them and set a trap for Kevin, as trite as it sounded, I knew this thing was a marathon, not a sprint. Speaking of which, I'm not a runner of either marathons or sprints, and it was surprisingly hard to find and hold that sweet spot as far as my speed was concerned. Long distance runners must be in tune with their bodies in ways I am not. I devoted fully half of my brain to that task. And the other half? It was causing trouble as always.

"What do you think Valerie told Craig?" I asked Tonk a short time later as we were negotiating the ridge line.

It's not like I didn't have more important things to think about: my wife had been kidnapped, her kidnapper promising to kill me or her or both of us in the next twenty one hours. No, check that, twenty hours, thirty minutes, I realized as I looked at the stopwatch hanging from its lanyard around my neck. My head was throbbing and my mouth was dry and my knee was aching, and given a choice I would have liked to lie down and take a nap for a few hours or maybe a month, which made me concerned that perhaps I did have a concussion, but I couldn't seem to help but keep running over that snippet of conversation between Kevin and Valerie in my mind. She insisting that I'm her husband and she loves me, to which Kevin responded, "How can you, after what I heard you tell Craig?"

"So what did she tell Craig?" I asked Tonk again.

He looked up at me, blinked, returned his attention to the trail ahead.

"That's not a rhetorical question," I added, "You can chime in whenever you like."

He likely already knew this; there are no secrets between a man and his dog, but I wanted him to feel completely free to express his opinion.

"Give it to me straight; I can take it," I told him.

Tonk is a good listener, but not really all that much in the helpful advice department. Plus he drools. He also never wipes his paws when he comes into the house. Occasionally he destroys the Sunday morning paper in the driveway, though in his defense he likely believes himself to be saving us from an IED hurled from the window of a passing car by a terrorist bomber slash newspaper delivery guy. And no matter how much we brush his teeth, his breath is often bad bordering on rancid.

"Now, Tonk," I admonished him, "Let's not make this all about you."

This is so very much like me, I thought bitterly, clowning around, my silly comments and asides. My inability to have a serious conversation even, it seems, with myself; the way I slather everything in a protective layer of comedy. I know this drives Valerie crazy, but every single sentence out of someone else's mouth, my brain instantly looks for ways to make a joke about it. Perhaps this is a defense mechanism, something I've worn like a suit of medieval armor as long as I can remember. Maybe I do it just because I'm bored, or maybe I do it with no clear purpose in mind. It's just a thing I do, automatic, like breathing. Fish swim, politicians take bribes. Processes so finely honed from years of practice that there's no conscious thought involved anymore.

"She might have told Craig about that," I said to Tonk.

If Tonk cared that he was only getting part of the story, that most of it was going on inside my head, he didn't show it.

Seems thin, though, I added to myself. Sure, I'm a pain in the ass to try and have a serious conversation with, but after ten years of marriage could it have built up to a level that would make Valerie not love me anymore? If it were only this, even Kevin, his mental crayoning clearly going way outside the lines, I didn't think he could have reached that conclusion.

I was silent for a moment, both inside and out, as my mind replayed arguments we've had in the past. As home movies went, it was not a particularly joyous one. I mentally tried to change the film reel, play some happier scenes, but seemed unable to locate any in my brain. Sure, we've had warm and loving times over the past ten years of our marriage, but recently? Not so much. Little flashes, like her meeting me with the new truck outside of Tracy's home, but beyond that? Huh. And a lot of the angst felt like it started when I joined the fire department.

When the mass mailing letter from the board of engineers looking for new members to join the department had hit our mailbox, I had asked Valerie if she was OK with me becoming a member. In retrospect we had talked about this pivotal decision surprisingly little. I mean, signing up to be a firefighter isn't like declaring that one is going to become an avid stamp collector or join a knitting circle; there's real danger involved. And while only a handful of the million or so firefighters across the US are killed each year, there's nothing to say that the next tragedy won't strike the fire department in the sleepy little New Hampshire town of Dunboro.

53

Every time my pager goes off, there's really no telling what I'll be headed into. I had read a news story recently about a crew of firefighters, I don't recall where, who had responded to a rather ordinary traffic accident unaware that one of the vehicles involved was a truck illegally hauling ammonium nitrate, an ingredient used in fertilizer and highly explosive. The resulting blast had left a crater in the highway a hundred feet across and tossed their fire truck like a children's toy the length of a football field, much farther than Tom Brady could have thrown a football on his best day. There were no survivors, and damned little left to put into the coffins.

It's stressful – not so much to me, but then again I'm the guy living the dream and having the adventure – but to Valerie whom I leave behind when the call comes.

Initially, when I first joined the department, I worried that my pager would wake Valerie when it went off at night. For a short time it did, but then she seemed to start sleeping through it. But maybe she's not sleeping through it; maybe she's only pretending to. Does she lie in bed awake waiting for me to come home?

As Tonk and I hiked along, I thought about that, her controlling her breathing, trying to lie still and pretend to sleep as I fumble around in the dark for my socks, search briefly under the bed for a missing sneaker, and then I'm dressed and gone.

I responded to a chimney fire last winter at about midnight, spent more than four hours in a crawlspace under the house maybe ten inches high, my face pressed into the dirt and what seemed to me to be an extraordinary number of mouse corpses, like someone had put down a layer of furry, gray carpeting. I didn't get home until well after dawn the next morning. What did Valerie think for all those hours? If she had managed to fall asleep again after I had left, did she wake up during the night to find me still gone? She was up and around by the time I got home.

I had never considered her viewpoint in all of this before, or if I had, I had totally glossed it over. But now that I'd stopped to think about it – metaphorically speaking of course because Tonk and I were hauling ass along the ridgeline – it didn't seem fair.

I've joked with her in the past, asked her if she would like to join the department, become a firefighter, an offer she usually brushes off with a flippant remark, something about ruining her hair or breaking a fingernail. But it doesn't have to be a joke, does it? There are women firefighters all over the place. Sure, Dunboro has only Rachael, but she's a good firefighter, and there's no reason we can't have another one. Valerie is tough and strong and in good shape. She doesn't work, so she is home during the day, and therefore would be a great asset, available to respond to calls when most of the volunteers in the department are away at work at their real jobs. Daytime coverage is a big problem in small volunteer departments, and Valerie could help fill that critical need.

How, then, the shoe on the other foot, would I feel when the pager went off, and if for some reason I couldn't go, but she did? How would I like waiting at home, wondering if she's been crushed by a collapsing building, or hit by a car while working an accident scene?

I stopped walking and stood on the ridge, looking down into the valley spread out below me, the king of all I survey.

"I wouldn't like it," I told Tonk. "I wouldn't like it at all."

Is this what she had said to Craig?

Ten

The ridge was mostly granite ledge and very easy going. Yay for the Granite State. It was flat, and clear of trees, brush, or debris, presumably scoured that way by winter winds. I made great time, better than I had thought I would, and I used my armchair general's perspective of the battlefield to my advantage. I got sufficient glimpses of the backpack to allow me to refine their route and mine, where we would meet in the future. The ease of it made me nervous, made me wonder what additional surprises Kevin might have in store for me.

I had to remind myself that he wasn't omniscient. Though better prepared for a fight than I was, and better trained, and carrying a big honking knife, nonetheless he had to be ready for an attack from any direction at any moment. For all he knew, I had gotten a chain saw from my truck and was preparing to drop a tree on his head. That kind of continual vigilance had to be wearying. Additionally, he hadn't seen any sign of me in hours, and he had to consider the possibility I had chosen to ignore his threats and gone to get help. For all he knew, a squad of Special Forces could be closing in on him at this very moment. On top of all of that, I hoped Valerie was giving him no end of trouble. Woe to him if he had decided to remove her gag. She would have given him such a piece of her mind that he might decide to just surrender without a fight the next time I showed up, the poor bastard.

I could see as we got closer to one another that they were following the route of a small river, glints of the sunlight off the surface of the water sparkled at me like a distant treasure. The mere sight of water reminded me of how ridiculously thirsty I was. I knew that drinking untreated water wasn't the smartest idea with Giardia, E-coli, and all nature of intestinal bugs swimming around in it. Confronting Kevin as parched as I was seemed an even poorer idea, and I figured that coming down with some raging case of diarrhea in a day or two might well be the best possible outcome for me under the circumstances. I looked at Tonk and noticed that the acre of tongue lolling out of his mouth was so dry it nearly had cracks in it, and that decided the issue for me.

I checked their movement and doubled-timed it, jogging along the ridge to get to a particular clearing by the river well ahead of them. I could get a drink, rest a bit, see the lay of the land, and be waiting for Kevin with whatever I managed to cook up by the time they got there.

Luck was with me when I found a slender maple tree that had been killed in a previous winter's frost. It was strong but dry, and I cracked it off near its base with little difficulty. I used my knife to slice off the few twigs that sprouted off its shaft, and then set to whittling one end to a point. It was so peaceful, loping along and whittling, that had I not been fighting for my life, I would have been tempted to start whistling, perhaps the theme from *The Andy Griffith Show*.

I ended up with a spear, a little short, but pretty straight. If I had had some way to light a fire I could have even fire-hardened the tip, but I didn't. Still, not a bad effort for a guy who had never been hunting. Or hunted for that matter.

"Not that I'm complaining," I said to Tonk who swiveled his head up to look at me as I spoke, "but when we were in the humane society adopting you, they had a Rottweiler I thought we should get, but Valerie didn't want a dog that big. I could really use a big dog now, like a German shepherd, some retired police attack dog. Or a Presa Canario, one of those monsters used by drug dealers to patrol their fields and protect their stashes in South America."

Tonk gave a disgusted chuff to indicate what he thought of that idea.

"Not that I don't love you just the way you are," I assured him.

Having traveled along the ridgeline as far as I possibly could, we veered left and headed downhill. I lost sight of them when the woods sprang up around us. My path was blocked by underbrush and brambles, fallen branches choked with dead leaves, some of it thigh deep in places. I scooped up a handful of leaves and they crumbled to dust between my fingers easily. I picked up a twig, and it broke with a dry snap at the slightest pressure. This was what people in the forest fire service call fuel.

It occurred to me I could get help up here, lots of it and fairly quickly, by starting a brushfire. Sure, I didn't have any easy way to light one, and had never been a Boy Scout, but everyone knew how to rub two sticks together. Kevin might think it had been caused by lightning, though there wasn't a serious looking cloud in the sky, but whatever, he might not think I had lit it. Working fire crews wouldn't quite fit with his concerns of snipers in the woods or a helicopter in the sky, and he might delay in carrying out his threat to kill Valerie. Maybe in the ensuing chaos I could put together some kind of rescue, though it was nothing like a sure thing, chock full of maybes and opportunities to botch it. Also, although it had rained not all that long ago, dry fall air flowing down from Canada had sucked the moisture out of everything. Once started, a fire might be difficult to put out.

Wild land firefighting is among the most dangerous activities in the fire service, and I sure as hell didn't want to be responsible for any firefighters who might get injured or God forbid killed working a blaze I had started.

Too risky, I decided. I hefted my spear. It was plan A. If plan A failed and I somehow survived, burning the White Mountains to the ground could always be plan B.

I pressed ahead through the brush, at one point getting the bejesus scraped out of my arms by forging too quickly through some kind of bush that I didn't realize had thorns until it was too late. I kept a grueling pace, one that had me trembling and sucking wind, but I was rewarded when I burst through the last line of trees and into the clearing.

It was idyllic, broad and open, with an even carpet of pine needles. The sun dappled off the stream, giving the light a shifting, living quality, and lit the area in a golden hue. The air smelled rich and alive, redolent with the essences of loam and moss and pine. All that was missing was a pair of deer frolicking at the water's edge and a woodwind section to make the image complete.

I checked the stopwatch around my neck and figured I had to have at least fifteen minutes lead on Kevin and Valerie, probably more, so I sat on a rock to wait for my knees to stop shaking. Tonk ran to the shallows and immediately set about drinking half the stream. That was such a fine idea that I didn't wait long to join him.

The shoreline was wide and rocky, the water running in thin rivulets and sitting in shallow pools among the stones close to shore. I seemed to recall reading somewhere that, when drinking from a river, stagnant water was bad, so I leaned my spear against a tree and carefully crossed the rocks, slick with algae, to where it was deeper and moving swiftly.

I knelt down and scooped up a handful. My first taste of that water was like nothing I can describe. It was frigid and clear and pure, running from some collection of underground springs, filtered through a hundred miles of New Hampshire granite. It tasted like life itself. My brain reminded me that it was probably swimming with germs and would glow at night from all the dissolved Radon. My brain, what a party pooper.

I splashed water on my face, carefully washing off the blood from around my eye and probing gently at the gash in my forehead. I then held my breath and submerged my face until my cheeks were numb. I blew the clots of blood out of my nose and marveled at the simple miracle of having clear nasal passages, the first breath I hadn't taken through my mouth in hours. I became giddy at the luxury of not feeling my nose packed and crisps of blood crackling on my skin. Tonk and I frolicked in the water. I washed my blood out of his fur. I submerged my face again and blew bubbles in the water like a kid.

"I've got to give you credit," I heard Kevin's voice call to me from across the clearing when I came up for air. "You have picked a truly beautiful place to die."

Eleven

I leapt to my feet, better, I figured, than dying on my knees. I shook my head, flinging droplets of water out of my eyes.

How was it possible? I had had a huge lead on them. They shouldn't have gotten here, not for some time.

Valerie's hands were still bound behind her, the gag still in her mouth, and Kevin was still leading her by the leash. He had further wound rope around her upper body, pinning her arms against her, crushing her breasts with the coils. Her cheeks were flushed and she was struggling to draw in enough air through her nose. Strands of hair stuck to the sweat on her forehead. Kevin in comparison looked like he too had been running recently, but for him it had been nothing more than a warm up jog, and he was easily ready for more.

They had raced to cover the gap and surprise me. How could Kevin have known where I was headed and when? Perhaps he had spotted me on the ridge and projected my path the same way I had projected theirs. My jeans were blue and my shirt dark green with maroon patches of dried blood, so I should have been almost impossible to spot. Did he have binoculars in his backpack?

Those questions, fine fodder though they might have been at any other time, seemed irrelevant at that moment with my survival on the line.

Kevin tethered Valerie's leash to a sapling, like tying a dog to a parking meter outside a trendy restaurant. He slung the backpacks on the ground at her feet and approached me. Tonk ran over to Valerie, cavorting around her legs joyously. If only I had been teaching him a useful trick earlier, like how to untie knots or chew through ropes.

I was caught out on the rocks and I had left my spear behind. I glanced at where it leaned against a tree. Kevin followed my gaze, noticed it, and gave me a slow, fuck-you sort of a smile.

How wonderful to be skewered by a weapon I had whittled and crafted with my own hands.

No doubt a big fan of irony, instead of drawing his knife, Kevin moved for the spear.

I raced across the rocks, slimy and treacherous, to intercept him. I was sure I would break a leg or crack my head open like a coconut or quite possibly both and he was going to reach the spear before I did. He seemed certain of that as well, but I surprised both of us by running at a completely heedless and ludicrous speed. Somehow I maintained my balance.

He saw me coming and abandoned the spear, turning to face me, shifting into his now familiar liquid fighting stance.

I had already seen and felt the results of trying to spar with him toe to toe, and needed a different strategy if I wanted an outcome other than getting my neck severed. I threw the Gentlemen's

Guide to Boxing out the window and plowed into him, my head
down, wrapping my arms around him. His stance rooted him to
the earth impressively, but I outweighed him by a goodly margin
and had velocity on my side, and I lifted him off his feet anyway.
I drove him down, my glorious two hundred and five pounds
landing on top with all the gravity I could muster. I regretted a
recent diet Valerie had nagged me into trying that had cost me a
precious seven pounds. The next time she offered me a rice cake
I planned to wolf down a gallon of moose tracks ice cream with
chocolate sauce, chortling like a madman even as it gave me a
brain freeze.

We hit the ground on a bed of deep pine needles, but even so it
had to hurt him. I heard Kevin's breathe woof out of him.

He pounded me on the back, but I had gotten my arms under his
and all the blows went high, up around my shoulders where the
muscle and bone offered plenty of protection. I responded with
several short punches to his sides and stomach. He was rippling
layers of abs there and the punches did nothing more than hurt
my bruised knuckles, but I swore that if we danced like this
again I would have my knife out in advance and do some real
damage. I didn't think I could take the time to dig it out of the
pocket of my pants and get it unfolded now.

That thought reminded me that he had a knife at his hip, and I
reached to take it. It was held in place by a strap which I got
unsnapped easily enough, but the handle had that brass knuckle
feature. I was trying to draw the knife out backwards, with the
grip reversed, and it was extremely hard to get a hold of. He
realized what I was doing and grabbed onto my wrist just as I got
the knife out of its sheath.

His grasp was awesome, paralyzing. If he had been clamping
down on my left wrist, which had a collection of pins and plates
holding it together from a previous injury, no telling what would
have happened. I envisioned screws and bits of surgical steel

flying everywhere. But it was my right, and even so could feel him grinding the bones together with his strength, my fingers going numb, my grip on the knife difficult to maintain. Still I hung on, pouring all my strength into that arm. If I could draw it back and slam it into him just once, maybe twist the blade around a little for good measure, I could finish this insanity.

He tried to roll us with his legs. I wasn't having any of that. I bore down on him with my full weight, imagined that I weighed three hundred pounds. Four hundred. I was Jabba the Hut, and Princess Leia in her gold bikini had a better chance of dragging me around Tatooine than he did of rolling me over.

I had to admit, in the midst of battle, that there was something energizing, primal, and gladiatorial about it, the rush of blood through my body, the pulse of heat on my skin. You didn't have to go back too far, a couple of thousand years at most, to find tribal societies where this was how mates were chosen, were won. Darwin distilled to its essence, where the strong survived to reproduce and further the species while the weak were weeded out, kept from contributing to the gene pool. Though insane by the metric of modern civilization, Kevin may be nothing more than a throwback, a reshuffling of DNA that resulted in an antiquated formula. But out here, out in the middle of nowhere, away from the rules which made his kind obsolete, he had the right skill set to survive, whereas I, with my ability to do higher math and a nearly encyclopedic knowledge of 1980's trivia, did not.

He shifted his grip, got his thumb over some pressure point in my forearm and dug in, and the nerves across the back of my hand caught fire. Despite my best efforts, the knife slithered from my grasp. As soon as it hit the ground he started clawing for it.

I chose to roll us then, grabbing him by the shoulder and flipping us over. He used the momentum to fling himself free of my embrace. That was fine with me. I quickly rolled back and snatched up the knife, scrambling to my feet. He retrieved my spear, and we stood facing each other.

He feinted with the spear and I backed up cautiously. We circled. He had more reach with the spear than I did, and looking at the business end of it, I was impressed with how sharp a point I had managed to whittle. I kept a keen eye on the distance between us. He took another stab and I brought the knife down sharply. The sapling was brittle and the blow cracked the last six inches off his spear. He threw the stick aside in irritation.

He shot out a foot and caught me in the wrist. It wasn't much of a kick, but would have knocked the knife from my grasp had my fingers not been woven through the knuckle holes. As it was, no simple blow was going to make me lose the knife. If he wanted to take it from me, he'd have to break or amputate most of my fingers, not that I wanted to give him any ideas.

He coiled himself for another attack. I anticipated him trying to slam into me, get inside the knife and my defenses and get me off my feet as I had done to him. If he tried, I was going to stab him in the spine, the knife I thought long enough to punch out through the front of his chest like the scene out of Alien.

At that moment, Valerie somehow got her leash untied. She stooped down awkwardly, picked up his backpack by a strap with her bound hands, and ran off into the woods. Tonk trotted along at her heels.

Kevin looked in her direction, and I took the opportunity of his distraction. I scuttled towards him, focused on his abdomen, planning to do some hog butchering of my own.

At the last possible moment he must have seen me out of the corner of his vision, and he threw a wild punch. And it was totally wild, uncontrolled, and desperate, with none of the core of martial arts training he had demonstrated so far. It was also the luckiest goddamned punch of his life. Concentrating as I was on eviscerating him, my eyes were down, and I didn't see it coming until it was just inches from my face. I couldn't duck it, couldn't slip past it, and I had drawn the knife too far back in my attack so his blow was going to reach me first.

He hit me near my left eye, and the shot knocked me off course. The world canted and doubled, and I went down on one knee. I raised the knife, tried to hold it steady, and narrowed my eyes to look as threatening and in control as possible even as the two worlds that I saw converged slowly at best.

It was all wasted effort on my part. By the time I had gathered my meager defenses, he was already off into the tree line after Valerie.

I got to my feet quickly, too quickly, and wandered drunkenly in pursuit as the light turned gray and my vision dimmed. I ended up missing the opening into the woods that Valerie and Kevin had taken and crashed into a tree, the bark rough against my cheek, struggling to hold myself upright. My right hand seemed unable to grasp anything, find any purchase against the trunk, and I peeked around the tree to see what the problem was. I was astonished to find that I still held his knife in my hand.

I looked up and could see no sign of them through the woods. I tried to let go and stand on my own two feet, but my precarious balance told me that I wasn't quite ready for that yet.

"We'll call this one a draw," I muttered to myself.

Twelve

It took me some time to recover, a lot longer than I would have liked. My balance was bad and my thinking was murky. Welcome to concussion city, I thought fuzzily. When I finally managed to stand on my own without the help of a tree I found a new lump, half the size of a golf ball and incredibly painful to touch, rising on the side of my head. Still, I had Kevin's knife, which as far as I knew was the only weapon he had brought to the party, and I had my knife as well. Although this was no game, I couldn't help but feel like I was ahead on points despite the beatings I had taken. My ass was literally the only part of me Kevin hadn't kicked.

I examined the ground where Valerie had run off into the woods with Kevin hot on her heels. The backpack held by a single strap, its weight swinging to and fro, had caused Valerie's gait to become unsteady. She had dragged one foot in a long arc just outside the clearing, a slash through the carpet of pine needles and leaves to the bare dirt below. Ten feet farther on she had dragged the other foot, a short arc this time with a gap in the middle when she must have lurched forward, likely in danger of a face plant, before regaining her footing. This was a trail even I

67

could follow, so I did.

Twenty steps later, her path took her onto a great slab of granite ledge and there were no more marks of her passage. I roamed the slab, trying to find what direction they had gone in, searching for a broken branch, a spot of blood, or a scrap of fabric hanging from a bush, anything to direct my pursuit. I found nothing, and was again reminded of just how poor my tracking skills were, along with my fighting skills and my survival skills in general.

Dejected, I returned to the clearing to collect our backpack, but when I got there, it was missing. I was certain Valerie had only taken Kevin's with her as she fled, yet I couldn't find it. Kevin must have grabbed the second backpack as he took off after her, though I hadn't noticed him do it. Damn. I could have really used a granola bar, and I'm sure Tonk wouldn't have turned his nose up at a handful of kibble.

I decided the clearing was where I would make my stand. Kevin wanted to find me and kill me, and I would make it easy for him by being exactly where he had last seen me. How considerate of me! Of course I didn't intend to make it too easy. Both knives in hand, I stood just at the edge of the clearing. The moment Kevin poked his head through the bushes I intended to become a flurry of blades, a whirling Ginsu reaping machine.

I waited.

I waited some more.

My shoulders were aching from waiting in my ridiculous approximation of a combat stance and I let myself relax, my arms drop to my sides.

Where the hell where they? Valerie couldn't have escaped from him, doddering back and forth like a drunken sailor, could she? Running with her hands bound behind her, trailing a leash, the backpack banging against her legs and sucking air past the ball crammed in her mouth, Kevin should have caught up to her in just a few hundred yards tops. And yet here I stood, time passing, with no sign of them.

Thirty minutes later according to the watch around my neck, I was forced to conclude that waiting in the clearing was a bad decision.

Maybe, having lost his knife, Kevin had decided this wasn't as much fun as he thought it would be. If so, he was likely looking to cut his losses, take Valerie, go back to his car, and leave. He was in for a nasty surprise when he found the condition I had left it in, which might prompt him to leave a nasty surprise of his own for me, such as Valerie gutted like a fish on the hood of my truck. The thought made me nauseous and furious at the same time.

Or maybe Valerie had led him on a merry chase. He didn't know this area. How could he? He had followed us here. And by the time he caught up with her they were both lost and didn't know how to find their way back to this clearing and me.

Or just maybe Kevin had quickly caught up with Valerie. He could have been watching me through the woods at that moment; keeping Valerie pinned on the ground with a knee in her back. He might be waiting for me to do something, and as I wasn't doing anything, he wasn't doing anything.

So many maybes.

This was yet another of those first-on-the-scene-of-a-bad-call moments, and I was getting pretty fucking tired of them. Working through all the permutations, perpetually assailed by my own doubts, was draining. Each choice was more wrenching than the last and I was becoming exhausted. Every time I faced one, I felt my decisions were becoming shakier and less certain, a condition I could ill afford with absolutely everything at stake.

A rustling sound approached me through the woods and I turned to face it, both knives held in front of me, my shoulders tense.

Tonk came bounding out of the brush, as much as a twelve-year-old bulldog is capable of bounding, and ran over to me. I ignored him and watched the woods carefully, figuring he was acting as vanguard, Kevin and Valerie certainly not far behind. Five minutes later my logic again proved faulty as they made no appearance.

I tried to make sense of Tonk showing up alone and couldn't do it. Tonk had somehow lost track of Valerie? Valerie had lost both Tonk and Kevin? Tonk had just become bored and come back to me when Kevin had the food? All those possibilities and any others I managed to come up with were equally unlikely.

Which brought me back to my original choice: stay here, or go back to the cars? That was of course assuming I could find my way back to the cars. I felt pretty lost myself. With some time and a little altitude and enough daylight, I suspected I could retrace my steps and find the way back, but it was far from a certain thing. Kevin with a map and maybe a GPS could make a beeline and leave me in the dust. Racing Kevin back to the cars felt like a losing plan. Continuing to wait had accomplished nothing more than burning up a bunch of time, time I felt I didn't have to burn, and didn't seem like a smart idea either.

A third option suddenly occurred to me: go back to Kevin's original plan. He was carrying a hunter orange backpack specifically so I could spot it and come to them. I could climb to the ridge, see where they were, and away we go. As much as I hated the idea of playing his game by his rules, it seemed by far the best choice. If they were headed back to the cars, they would lead me back to the cars. If they were lost, I would find them. And if, somehow, Valerie had escaped with Kevin's backpack, I would find her. That last one was a slim possibility, but a joyous one nonetheless.

I folded up my knife and put it away in my pocket. I didn't have the sheath for Kevin's knife and was afraid of severing my femoral artery if I tried to put it in my pocket, so I had no choice but to carry it.

Tonk had settled into a heap at my feet. It was a position he often took after a particularly long hike, his way of letting me know that he was done for the day.

"No rest for the wicked," I told him.

I took hold of his collar and tried to heave him to his feet. He played conscientious objector for a moment, leaving his legs limp, refusing to stand on his own. When he realized that I wasn't going to give up and go away, he stood with a huff.

"Believe me, I don't like it any more than you do, but I promise this is the last time we'll climb up a hill."

Tonk looked like he didn't believe me, and he was right of course. If we climbed up and spotted Kevin and Valerie, we would have to climb back down to meet them, and then we'd have to make at least one more ascent to return to the truck.

"OK, you got me. Three more. Just three more times. I promise."

He still seemed unconvinced, but stayed with me as I dragged myself off into the woods in the direction of the ridge. As if he had a choice.

As if either of us did.

Thirteen

The route back up to the ridge seemed a lot tougher than the one I had used coming down. Climbing up is often more difficult than down – gravity is a cruel mistress that way – but I found my path blocked by deadfalls and great hedges of wild roses that I had to take long detours around.

As more time passed, as I ran into more impenetrable vegetation, I grew more frantic. I became utterly convinced that my first instinct had been the correct one: Kevin was headed back to his car, intending to cut his losses, take Valerie, and leave. He would see the destruction I had done to his car, be unable to start the truck, and take his frustration out on her. My experiences in the fire department gave my imagination all the fodder it needed to create a gruesome slide show of the injuries Valerie might suffer at Kevin's hands. I'm not sure how many feet of intestine someone should see in their lifetime, but I'm likely way past that limit.

I pushed myself harder and when that didn't feel fast enough, I pushed myself faster still. Tonk fell behind; I didn't, couldn't wait for him. I became short of breath, lightheaded, and started seeing spots before my eyes. It didn't matter.

Then I stepped on a jumble of small rocks hidden under a blanket of leaves that suddenly shifted on me. I lurched forward and my other foot came down on another unstable rock. My injured knee buckled, and I had a few bad moments scrambling before I managed to come to rest on one foot, one knee, and one hand. I didn't twist my ankle, but I came close, so very close, and it left me shaking, nervous, and all too aware that if I seriously injured or broke something, it was all over. I tried to continue the climb, but found myself shaking like a leaf, so tense and unsteady after my near fall that I had to stop to rest on a boulder.

Stopping made it worse. It allowed my mind to focus on the horrors Kevin could inflict.

I looked around for a distraction, any distraction to break my focus, when I realized that the rock I was sitting on was not some random chunk of stone but part of an arrangement, a structure. It was a rock wall. Over the years many pieces had fallen out of place, but that it had been built and built purposefully was undeniable. It extended left and right from where I was sitting, threading in a more or less straight line through the trees and out of sight in both directions.

I stood and walked beside it, the fingers of one hand trailing along the uneven surfaces of the stones, feeling the patches of lichen and moss, the weather-worn cracks, the curve and texture of the rocks themselves, as if I was reading Braille, as if they had some important information to impart. I had so many more critical things to attend to – I had to figure out how to save Valerie, how to survive – but I was crazed, on the edge of making a fatal mistake. My near fall had proven that, and I needed to take a moment, gather myself, corral my fear, and gain control. To keep rushing headlong as I had been doing was to invite disaster. I let the mystery of this wall consume me, and my exhaustion fell away from me like an old cloak, forgotten.

73

Who built it? When? Why? As far as I knew, these old stone walls, which crisscross the state and number in the hundreds if not thousands, were the result of Colonial farmers tilling the soil. Every time their blade turned up a rock, they would dutifully lug it to the edge of their field and stack them into lines, the walls coming to represent years of farming and rock gathering. They don't call us the Granite State for nothing. Yet as I surveyed the topography of the land around me, I was baffled. I was on a steep slope, no indication of flat, arable land anywhere nearby. Did someone farm here? Why here, and not the more level and inviting land down in the valley alongside the river? I was dozens of miles from the nearest city today. Back when this wall had been built, it might have been a hundred miles or more to the next nearest human being or settlement of any appreciable size. What would make someone live out here?

I found myself fascinated by the stones themselves, here the salt-and-pepper speckle of granite, there a dark gray igneous rock shot through with threads of white quartz like veins. I used to be big into rocks when I was a kid, collecting geodes and chunks of pyrite and shards of agates and calcite, somewhere between my dinosaur phase and when I became obsessed with ancient civilizations after finding an arrowhead down by the creek in my backyard.

The rock wall took on a new dimension, literally, when I came to a corner. I was beginning to get an idea of the shape of the space, a square, rectangle, or trapezoid. The corner indicated that there was an inside to this shape, and therefore an outside.

I turned with the wall and headed up slope. I saw this as a bonus; my examination was taking me in the same direction I had been going originally. Tonk finally caught up to me and followed along, jamming his snout into spaces in the wall and taking deep and probing snorts, searching for chipmunks or mice. If he caught anything, I was so hungry I might have been tempted to share it with him.

I came to another corner, thus establishing the length of the space. As I looked to the inside and outside of the wall, if anything I became more perplexed. The trees on both sides looked equally mature. Where was the farmer's field from which these rocks had been collected? I didn't know. Maybe the wall had been built for some other purpose, the rocks gathered by some other means beyond tilling. I had been secretly rooting for it to have been built by a farmer in hopes of finding some rusty but serviceable tools. An old axe would have been outstanding, but I would have settled for a sickle or whatever the tool used to harvest wheat is called. A scythe? I come from a family of mill workers, not farmers.

I climbed over the wall, stepping and thinking inside the box. I worked my way towards where I believed the center lay. It didn't take long to find the building.

There wasn't much left of it: a cellar hole, three somewhat intact stone walls, a fourth spilling into the hole, forced by an avalanche of dirt behind it. Any evidence of the wood components, the floors or doors or roof, was long gone. What the building had been, what it had been used for, I couldn't guess. A hunting lodge? An ancient flintlock rifle would have been a welcome discovery, even though it probably wouldn't have fired after all these years, and any gunpowder left lying around would have long become inert unless stored in a moisture-tight box. Still, the solid wood stock and the iron rifle barrel would have made a fair club.

I scrambled down into the pit and found myself knee deep in leaves. Tonk opted to stay up top and look down at me. I searched gingerly, careful not to stumble or turn my ankle on something underneath the leaves.

There was a fireplace, or more of a fire pit, and a stub of chimney that hadn't collapsed. There was soot on the stonework – not new soot, but certainly not as old as the building itself. There was also the wrapper from some kind of candy bar, the

75

writing faded beyond readability. I threw it up to Tonk who
gave it an experimental sniff, but it lacked enough residue to
peak his interest, and I once saw him lick a spot on the kitchen
floor where I had dropped a single slice of pepperoni off a pizza
for an entire, uninterrupted minute.

I was oddly, almost unfathomably, heartened by these small
indications of human existence. It meant that other people had
come through here and this hiking area, though isolated, was not
completely so. Sure, no one had been through here in some
time. Was that a discarded Mr. Pibb can lying in the corner?
Could you still buy Mr. Pibb? But people had sat here, warmed
themselves by a fire, and others would do so in the future,
perhaps the distant future. If I were killed, my bones would be
found, eventually. Unless Kevin took the time to bury me.
Unless wild animals dragged them away and gnawed them to
splinters.

"I've gotta stop all this cheering myself up," I said to Tonk, "or
I'm likely to start dancing a jig."

Tonk yawned in response.

As I gained control of myself, I began to worry about the time I
had spent searching the ruins. Still, I spent more time, what was
starting to feel like very valuable time, thrashing around in the
leaves without result. If there had been any useful metal
implements, blades or bars or pipes or anything, they had either
long since rusted away or been scavenged by others before me.

Not rested, nor by any means relaxed, I nonetheless felt capable
of moving again, if more slowly than I had before, so I picked a
direction, and got to work.

Fourteen

I walked more carefully, at a more measured pace, and while I did so, I took a moment to examine the knife, see if there was anything I could learn from it.

It was a real piece of work. The handle was aluminum skinned with a rubberized overmold to improve the grip, the rings of the knuckles left exposed to maximize impact. The blade was light and thin, I thought titanium, with a honed edge that could likely split atoms. I yanked a hair off my head and brought it down against the blade and, son of a bitch, it severed the hair in two. Wow. The knife was in good condition, no nicks or scratches in the finish, nearly new. Maybe he had bought it especially to cut my throat. I was touched by the gesture.

I wasn't sure, but it felt military, and not military like 'let's paint it camo green and sell it to hillbillies who like to go into the woods on the weekends and pretend they're protecting the homeland from Islam,' but genuine Special Forces hardware. Kevin was an assistant to an attorney who worked in Manchester. Where would he get such a thing? And the GPS tracker I had found on my truck – you couldn't buy one of those on Amazon, could you?

Not that any of that mattered. Even with a crazy person trying to murder me and abduct my wife, I was still looking for mysteries to solve. There must be something very wrong with me.

I stopped and asked Tonk, "Do you think there's something wrong with me?"

He didn't answer. He took the opportunity of my momentary pause to settle back into his heap, and getting him moving again was going to be a chore.

I continued to examine the knife.

The butt of the handle ended in a little raised bump, like half the size of a small pea. When I matched it against the face of my damaged watch, I found the bump matched the dent in its stainless steel face perfectly. That was how my watch was broken; Kevin had told me as much. "I'm sorry about that," he had said. "You blocked my first blow with your watch." Then I recalled Valerie had grunted and shook her head.

Meaning, what? Had she been trying to tell me something? That Kevin hadn't smashed my watch with a blow from this knife?

That couldn't be right. The bump on the handle and the dent in my watch were a perfect fit.

I ran a thumb over the bump. It was rounded smooth, but it was so small that in a way it was almost sharp at the same time. I pictured Kevin driving the hilt down towards my head, hitting me with whatever pounds per square inch of force concentrated down into that tiny, tiny fraction of a square inch. Force per area, like they teach women in self-defense classes, stomp down on an attacker's foot with a high-heeled shoe and shatter bones easily. Kevin's blow with the bump on the hilt would have been a devastating impact, punched a hole in my skull, sent fragments and shards of bone buck-shotting into my brain, almost definitely fatal. But he hadn't hit me. I had blocked it, and my watch had taken the brunt of the blow, saved my life as surely as that old story about the guy carrying a Bible in his breast pocket taking a bullet for him.

"But if I hadn't blocked it, I'd be dead, right?" I asked Tonk.

He again didn't answer, but he's a good listener and a great sounding board.

"Kevin didn't want me dead," I added.

Well, he did want me dead, but not like that. He had brought the flex cuffs, rope, and the gag for Valerie. He had wanted to incapacitate me temporarily, tie us both up, lay out his plans, and force me to play my part in his fantasy. One blow and I'm dead doesn't let him do any of that. So, what? Kevin lost his head in the fight and in the heat of the moment took a swing that would have killed me if I hadn't gotten lucky and blocked it? That didn't feel right either.

The sun was past its peak. There were not a lot of hours of daylight left and the temperature was starting to drop. Valerie and Kevin had food and water – our food and water – but by tomorrow morning I would be starving and had nothing to drink but questionable water from the stream. It made sense for me to try and finish this before the sun went down.

I hauled Tonk back to his feet and got us both moving again. The two of us continued what can only be described as a weary stagger up the slope.

As I walked, I tried to play the footage of our first fight at the base of the cliff this morning through my mind. My memories were incomplete, just momentary flashes of action with big gaps in between. It had happened so quickly, and no doubt the blow to my head hadn't helped any, but I did recover two important pieces.

One, Kevin hadn't been frenzied when he attacked me. I wouldn't have called him calm; he was, after all, finally putting a plan into action that he had been planning for I had no idea how long. He was exhilarated, thrilled, practically giddy, but he was in control. The fight was going his way. I had fallen for his trap. He had complete surprise. His shots were precise. He wasn't counting on luck or my good reflexes to keep me alive.

Two, and this one was more of a feeling than a hard fact, I was pretty sure I hadn't blocked any of his blows.

Ergo, Mr. Fallon? I heard the voice in my mind of Dr. Long, the professor who had taught my freshman class in logic and reasoning at Columbia. What can you conclude from these facts?

"If I believe my poor, abused memory, Professor Long…"

I hadn't blocked Kevin's blow with my watch, and he had hit me in the head, but it hadn't been with the butt of the knife because I wasn't dead. Later, when I was already down, he had used the butt of the knife specifically to break my watch, a watch with which he had no previous relationship and, as far as I could tell, had no reason to want to kill. That, I thought, was what Valerie had been trying to tell me. Then, my line of reasoning continued, he had replaced it with the stopwatch around my neck, something else he had conveniently brought in that backpack of his because it played some pivotal role in his plans.

That thought was so jarring that I stopped and lifted the stopwatch. Tonk, shuffling along with his head down or possibly walking in his sleep, piled into the backs of my legs, rebounded, and sat down staring up at me in confusion. Go or stop, his gaze said, but make up your mind.

80

"Sorry," I said, "but this might be important."

I looked at the glowing numbers on the stopwatch face, turned it over and examined the manufacturer's data on the back, patents awarded and pending and such. It looked like an ordinary if somewhat vintage stopwatch as near as I could tell.

Why had he broken my watch? Why had he brought this stopwatch along with him?

Those were some fine questions. I pondered and pondered, but came up empty and finally let the stopwatch drop where it hung against my chest from its lanyard, taunting me with its very existence.

"I have no idea, Professor Long," I muttered as I resumed scrabbling and clawing my way up the hill. Tonk, with a huff, started up after me. "No idea at all."

Fifteen

The going got tough right near the ridge, all loose shale and stones, and Tonk couldn't make it on his own. I had to be seriously off course; I hadn't scaled anything remotely like this on the way down, and hadn't hit the stone foundation either. I wasn't able to build up enough of a map in my mind to figure out where I had taken a wrong turn, didn't want to take time to correct it, and I supposed that I was so close to the top that it didn't matter anyway.

I picked Tonk up, and he's heavier than he looks, close to sixty pounds, and carried him tucked under my right arm like a fat football. He wasn't thrilled at the treatment, and I held Kevin's knife in my right hand which made it a little risky, but I needed a free hand to grasp what handholds I could, many of which crumbled dangerously under my grip. They were a good match to the precarious footholds I managed to find. Tonk did his best to help by kicking me and trying to worm his way out of my grasp.

I banged my injured knee twice, which I could have done without, but we did finally reach the ridgeline. What I saw disheartened me on several levels.

For one, Kevin and Valerie hadn't gone anywhere. If the backpack was any indication, and I could see it clearly, they were maybe a grand total of two hundred yards downstream from where we had last met. In the meantime, I had hiked all the way up here, something like a mile, and would have to hike all the way down. I was racking up some serious mileage while Kevin rested and likely sipped mint juleps on the veranda while waiting for me to come to him.

For another, the ridge on which I stood was starting to cast a shadow into the valley below. All my theorizing and contemplating about spending the night out here looked like it was going to come true. Furthermore the sky was clear, and as anyone in New England will tell you, a clear sky in the winter means the temperatures are going to plunge after dark. It was going to be a cold, miserable night.

And because I can never get enough bad news, the sun at my back meant that I was looking east, and I was 99% certain that the last time I was on a ridge I had been facing pretty much due north. I had thought I was climbing the same hill as the last time, though that clearly wasn't the case, and as I looked around I just couldn't get myself oriented. I was very much lost which meant, even if I beat Kevin and rescued Valerie – the optimist inside me tried to substitute 'when' and I laughed it down – I had no idea where to go after that.

There was, I realized, nothing I could do about any of these problems. Taking it in bite-sized chunks, I was going to have to start by hiking back down and confronting Kevin. I've got all the knives, I reminded myself, and that had to count for something, right? So once again I picked up Tonk and set off, putting him down on his own four feet after we had passed the treacherous bit.

"I've been accused of being an adrenaline junky," I said to Tonk out of nowhere as we hiked. Actually it only seemed like it came out of nowhere to him, but I had been rolling this idea around in my head for hours, unable to let that 'After what you told Craig' comment from Kevin slide.

This was so like my brain, I reflected bitterly, following a hundred lines of thought when what I really needed to do was focus. Sometimes, when I'm feeling especially egotistical, I believe my brain does this because of an excess of processing capacity, that it essentially becomes bored working on only one thing at a time. Other times I feel like I must be suffering from an undiagnosed mental problem, something in the attention deficit disorder spectrum. Valerie typically laughs about it when she finds me simultaneously watching a movie, reading a book, cooking a meal, and researching something on the web. There's likely a narrower line between multitasking genius and scatterbrain than I would care to admit.

"It's not like I'm a firefighter for the thrills," I said to Tonk. If he cared that he was getting only a small fraction of the thoughts whizzing through my head, he didn't show it.

It's not like the majority of firefighting is thrilling anyway. Most of it is very dull, waiting here, standing there. Often it seems to me that the greatest risk to my health that I experience in the fire department is all the sleep I lose. There are, of course, moments. Running into a burning building to rescue a resident, knowing that it may collapse at any moment… Let's just say that's a rush like no other. There's also the very different adrenaline spike I get when I'm the first on the scene of a bad accident. This spike comes with a touch of nausea and a feeling of self-doubt, a momentary overwhelming of my senses at the enormity of the task before me, the lives hanging on my decisions. Then my training kicks in, and it passes.

I understand firefighting is dangerous, though it's not like I spend time dwelling on it during calls. For the most part, the urgency of the calls and the pace of events keep you concentrating on the tasks at hand and not on the bigger philosophical questions of life and more specifically your own mortality. In all my years in the department, I've only worried about getting killed exactly once, though I've been in dozens of life-threatening situations. It was during a call for a horse stuck in the mud – five or six feet of mud – and I found myself standing alongside the horse, chest deep in the muck. I had the realization as we worked to get a sling around the animal, a process that took a good ten or fifteen minutes, that if the horse rolled onto its side and landed on me, I would likely suffocate before I could be recovered.

Years ago I had won a free skydiving adventure in a fire department raffle. Valerie had just about laughed her head off when she heard about it. She saw the prize as a joke, something the skydiving school gave away as essentially free advertising, because how many people were going to decide to jump out of a perfectly functional aircraft just because it was free? She lost that laugh in a hurry when I told her that I was going to do it. How many such opportunities was I going to get in life? Carpe diem, check something off my bucket list, go big or go home, or any other do-something-crazy catch phrase you care to apply. And though we argued, I never felt that it rose to the level of a serious argument.

She went with me to the skydiving site in Pepperell, Massachusetts and sat in on the mandatory class beforehand. There's that old joke about the guy who wants to leave his mark upon the earth, and he does so by taking up skydiving, the mark he leaves being the crater from his impact. They didn't tell that joke during the class, but you could kind of feel it floating around in the air nonetheless. Then at the end of the class I had to sign a lot of forms which read essentially 'you may well be killed or maimed or otherwise bodily disfigured, but our lawyers tell us we're not responsible if you agree to sign these forms of your own free will.'

85

As I was doing so, Valerie said, "I told you so."

"You told me so what?" I asked.

"That's what I'd say to you if you get killed, but since I can't tell you after you're dead, I figured I would tell you now."

I paused in my signing and really looked at her. She had a smile on her face like she was kidding, but underneath that... I couldn't tell. Maybe she was concerned and covering it up with humor. Maybe she was angry at what she saw as more of my pointless, thrill-seeking antics.

After the conclusion of the argument we didn't have, I went through with it, and it was amazing. As a bonus, I get to see the looks on people's faces when I tell them I jumped out of a plane because I had a coupon.

"Maybe I am an adrenaline junky," I admitted to myself as much as Tonk.

And maybe that drives Valerie nuts, and more to the point, away.

Sixteen

The climb down went a lot like the climb up, including all the
deadfalls and wild roses and detours, and I passed the foundation
without stopping. It seemed that in no time at all I found myself
stealthily approaching Kevin in a new clearing, occasional
glimpses of the backpack through the trees leading me onwards.

When there were only a few scant bushes remaining between us,
I knelt. I placed a hand on Tonk's head and he lay down silently
beside me. Nearly directly ahead, ten, perhaps twelve yards
away, crouched Kevin, his back to me as he did something with
his backpack which was splayed open at his feet. The twelve
yards telescoped out like a mile, a trek over naked, open ground,
and if Kevin turned around before I made it across, I was dead
meat.

Kevin was near the water's edge. With time and velocity and
gravity on its side, the water had worn itself a serious channel to
run in, a four or five foot drop from Kevin's location down to the
surface. Here the stream had widened and deepened, tumbling
over rocks, cascading over minor falls, really making a racket.
At least I had that going for me.

Valerie was tied to a tree to my right; though using the word tied was something of an understatement. She stood upright against the tree, coils of rope wound around her at the ankles, knees, hips, waist, chest and shoulders. She was freaking married to that tree. How much rope had Kevin brought along with him?

She saw me and glanced nervously at Kevin before looking back at me.

I pointed at the knife I held in my hand and then at Kevin, which I thought was universal sign language for "I'm going to stab him in the back with this knife."

She shook her head fiercely, blonde hair flying. I didn't know if she disagreed with my plan or had a better one of her own. If she had a better one, I would have loved to hear it, though the gag in her mouth and the noise from the rushing water made that impossible.

She changed tactics, tossing her head, a beckoning gesture. That message I thought was pretty clear: she wanted me to come over and cut her loose instead of stabbing Kevin in the back. The tree she was tied to stood alone in the clearing, the kind of thing Satanists might have secured a sacrifice to and danced around a couple of thousand years ago. It was far from the concealing shelter of the bushes, and not large enough to screen my approach if I tried to keep it between Kevin and myself. Even with Kevin's knife, and it was a good one, it would take me half an hour to hack all the rope away and free her. Unless the thing in the backpack that was holding Kevin's attention was a Sunday New York Times crossword puzzle, he was certain to spot me before I was done.

A bad plan, I shook my head.

She panicked, hurled herself silently against the ropes which held her fast. When she realized her struggles were futile, she stilled, visibly tamping down her terror. She caught my eyes with hers, made sure she had my attention, then flicked her eyes down and stared at my feet, then looked to Kevin.

Translating this was a good deal more difficult. I glanced at my feet, my shoes? Lifted one foot off the ground and looked at the sole, the momentary absurd notion that she was telling me I had stepped in something. I put the foot back down, barely resisted checking the bottom of the other one. Perhaps she meant the ground underneath my feet? Did she want me to throw dirt in his eyes? I gave her a helpless shrug.

We were officially playing the worst game of charades in human history. If we survived, we'd probably joke about this later. Had Kevin been watching this exchange, he would have likely burst out in helpless laughter. I glanced his way though only a few seconds had passed; just to make certain that he wasn't standing there looking at us, his arms folded across his chest, his face flushed with barely-contained mirth. Whatever was in the backpack continued to consume him. Perhaps he was updating his Facebook status from 'single' to 'just kidnapped myself a girlfriend.'

I looked back at Valerie. She tried again – she glared at me, my feet, back to Kevin, back to my feet again.

I wasn't getting it, had no idea what message she was trying to give me. Enough delaying. The element of surprise was the best thing I had going for me. I held up one hand, silencing her already silent protests. I pointed firmly at the knife, at Kevin. That's the plan, and I'm sticking to it. She watched me, her eyes wide with fear.

I snuck into the clearing, slowly and ever so quietly. Ten yards.

The ground was good here, granite ledge, a few pine needles, with no leaves to crunch through or twigs to snap, not that I thought it would matter with the roar of the water nearby. I was pretty sure I could have set off field artillery without him hearing me.

The evening sun was in front of him, sparkling off the water into his eyes, ruining his vision, casting my shadow long behind me where he wouldn't see it.

The water, the sun, the ground: Mother Nature herself was conspiring against him, when it felt like she had been on his side all day. Fickle bitch.

Now only five yards away. Closer. I could have ricocheted a ball of paper off the back of his head or plastered his scalp with spitballs like in elementary school.

I felt lightheaded and paused, realized I had been holding my breath, I think since I had entered the clearing. I took a long slow inhale, yoga style, through my nose, and let it flow out silently through my parted lips. I took another. Fresh oxygen shot into my bloodstream and time slowed, my vision sharpened.

I took another small step. Then another.

Three yards. Two.

Time to pick a target, make it a good one. Not centered, not on the spine. Too great a chance of being deflected by bone, too little chance of sliding between two vertebrae to the succulent, juicy spinal cord within. Left or right, stab with the knife blade held at the horizontal, get between two ribs, hit a lung. Aim for the left, maybe get his heart involved in the party. Worst comes to worst, once the knife is embedded, try and slice around a little, go for a major vein or artery.

But the rib cage is just that, a cage, evolved and damned near perfected over a couple of hundred million years to protect the vital bits, prevent exactly the kind of instantaneously mortal damage I was trying to inflict. The ribs are wide, the slots between them narrow. I've got to be prepared if I strike bone, absorb the shock in my forearm, be ready to raise or lower the knife a fraction of an inch and strike again. I wasn't going to get a third shot at this. The way I've seen Kevin move, I'd be lucky to get two.

Just a yard now. Only a yard away.

I could have reached out, tapped him on the shoulder. I've done that to strangers, as on a train station platform. 'Excuse me, do you have the time?' Or, 'Miss, I think you dropped your glove.' I wasn't doing that here; I was preparing to drive a blade into another human being, all the way to the hilt if I could manage it. I felt suddenly as if civilization had collapsed, and I was trapped in some unfathomable post-apocalyptic wasteland in which this was it, this was how people treated one another to survive, this was the way it had to be. Would my world ever return to normal?

I took another half step closer, got my feet planted.

My heart was thundering in my chest, the power delivered by my blood building up in the muscles of my arm. I shifted my grip on the knife slightly, folded my fingers more tightly through the sockets in the handle. My palm was sweaty, and I was glad for the rubberized grip. The knife was an extension of me, solid in my hand.

A small voice piped up inside, my conscience. It perched on my shoulder like a ludicrously naïve angel from the cartoons. Are you really going to do this, Jack? Stab another human being in the back?

I searched within myself and realized I've got no qualms at what I'm about to do. Zero. I was completely qualmless.

You bet your ass I am, I reply.

Just over a foot away, within easy arm's reach, I raised the blade to strike.

Seventeen

Kevin's leg shot backwards and he kicked me in the chest like a goddamned mule. His foot hit dead center, directly on my sternum, the force of the blow cracking ribs left and right like kindling sticks stressed near their breaking point. I got the wind knocked out of me, became airborne, and flew a good ten feet before coming down on my hands and knees.

The next breath I tried to take simply wouldn't come. My diaphragm quivered like jelly, my chest felt like it had been crushed, and I gasped, spots dancing before my eyes.

Kevin raced over to me at incredible speed. He reached where I had landed only a moment after I did. Without pausing to plant his foot, he snapped a quick kick at my head.

I pushed off with my hands and feet, threw my head back, and tried to roll with the kick, absorb as little of the impact with my skull as possible. My teeth clacked together, but otherwise the maneuver worked perfectly, except that it resulted in an ungainly half backflip, like an uncoordinated child attempting a cartwheel. I landed on my face, my neck twisted at an awkward angle, and continued the rotation, slamming my chest into the ground, stressing my cracked ribs, adding to the damage there.

I had no air in my lungs, none, and probably couldn't have taken in any had I been lying in a hospital bed under an oxygen tent.

Kevin approached again in what looked to me like a blur.

I'll admit it, I was terrified. Flat terrified. And I had no more thought in my head than I had to get away, get some distance, any distance, to recover, regroup, call for a do-over, ask for a timeout. Lying flat on the ground, I didn't even try to get to my feet. I just rolled away from him, over and over, like rolling down a hill when I had been a kid.

I kept going, kept rolling. As long as I was moving he couldn't get a bead on me, kick me again. There are two hundred and eight bones in the human body, and I was desperately, keenly aware that Kevin could break every one of mine and take his time doing so.

My arms tucked tight against my body to protect my ribs from any rocks I might roll across, I turned over and over. My vision was filled with sky and ground, Valerie upside down struggling against the ropes that held her, Kevin chasing me in that fast gliding, liquid motion of his.

Rolling like this used to make me dizzy and a little nauseous as a kid, and it did so now, and at some point I just lost it. My tuck came undone, my arms flew out from my body, and I ended up sprawled out face down on the ground with my arms and legs splayed. I was surprised to find that I still held the knife in my hand, my fingers woven through the handle.

I looked up to find Kevin standing over me; my rolling hadn't accomplished anything at all. His eyes were burning with righteous fury, his smile demonic, inhuman.

He raised a foot shod in a heavy combat boot, a black leather upper and deep waffle tread. He must have changed into those at some point, brought them in his backpack or something, right? If I had seen him jog off up the path this morning clomping along in combat boots I would have noticed that surely, thought it peculiar?

He ended my ruminations by bringing it down on my hand, the one holding the knife.

My fingers, trapped between the finger holes and the ground, snapped audibly, and my world went white. He bore his weight down on that foot, crushing my hand under his boot, breaking more bones, grinding the fragments against each other. I heard Valerie, screaming, high and thin and keening, and then realized that she was gagged and there was no way she was screaming. The person screaming was me, about four octaves above my usual range.

With my free hand I punched him in the side of the knee, the calf, and maybe landed one or two low on his thigh. I had no leverage, and under the best of circumstances my left hand is notoriously uncoordinated, even worse since the plate and screws were put into that wrist. It felt like I was punching a tree or a rock, something hard and completely unyielding. My blows did nothing to unbalance or even distract him, nothing at all.

Kevin shifted his foot, moving it to my wrist, pinning my hand to the ground. He reached down and twisted the knife back and forth, trying to free it from my grasp, and my screams dissolved into wordless jabbering. I was beyond speech, but if I could have formed words I would have told him to stop, that I would give him the knife and bare my throat for him. I recalled my earlier assertion that he would have to amputate most of my fingers to get the knife away from me. It felt like he was tearing my fingers off.

With a final wrenching motion, and the breaking of a couple of more finger bones – I couldn't have told you which ones, but I heard them go – he wrested the knife from me and stepped back, releasing my wrist. I rolled onto my side, my whole right arm on fire. I looked at my hand, the remains of my hand, digits pointing every which way.

Kevin calmly wove his fingers through the handle, admired the way it looked like a man trying on a really comfortable and well-fitting glove. Then he came for me.

Lying on the ground, cradling my broken hand, I had little choice but to roll away from him again, not that it had gotten me anywhere the last time.

Over and over, nausea piled on nausea. Small rocks and sticks poked at me, finding a cracked rib every time. I rolled on my damaged hand and the pain was epic, catastrophic, beyond description. Still I kept going. It was all I could think to do. My one hope, and it seemed a pretty slim one, was that he would get bored of chasing me around and just go away.

But I knew he wasn't going to go away, and I couldn't roll around forever much as I would have liked to. I needed to do something else, anything else, but my brain was too consumed by pain and fear to put a plan together. Every second that passed without Kevin stomping on me or kicking me again seemed like a small, if certainly temporary, victory. I was still trying to formulate some kind of plan when suddenly the ground wasn't there anymore and I was falling.

My brain had just a split second to register surprise before I hit the water. It was frigid, arctic, and the shock would have driven the air from my lungs had there been any there in the first place.

I broke to the surface, sputtering, flailing. My broken hand was in agony. I tried to draw a breath and it felt like the talons of some great, terrible, and ancient creature – a pterodactyl, a dragon, a wyvern – raking across my chest.

Back upstream, I could see Kevin standing on the shore, shaking his head ruefully, looking down at the water's crystalline sparkle. He had had me. He had had me, and I had slipped away. We both knew it.

"You are so freaking lucky, Jack Fallon," he yelled at me as I was swept downstream. "You're the luckiest man alive!"

Eighteen

I didn't feel very lucky. I felt like I was drowning.

I tried to keep my head up, take a breath, but got more water than air.

The stream, really a river at this point, was moving fast and it had me in its grip. From the inside, the channel walls looked even higher, six or eight feet back up to ground level, steep and smooth and impossible to get a grip on. The channel narrowed slightly and the current shifted into overdrive, a pull like being sucked into the intake of a jet engine. The water was dark, dark green, far too deep to see any hint of bottom. It was pale green where it poured through small spillways, frothing white where it churned over submerged boulders like the weathered molars of giants. I was shot through a gap between two of them, rode a small waterfall on the far side, and was plunged into a pool at the bottom.

I again came up sputtering, my second attempt at a breath no better than the first. I looked back upstream, trying to catch a glimpse of Kevin or Valerie, but the falls had left me on a lower level, my line of sight cut off by the rocks and the water.

Something snagged the back of my shirt and I felt it tear. The force of it turned me and something else jabbed me in the stomach. The current was rolling me against a submerged tree, its broken branches poking, stabbing, punching like an angry mob. I was just starting to pick up speed after the falls, and the damage from the tree was limited because of it. At another spot, a faster spot, I would have been impaled, skewered like a cube of beef on a kabob. As it was, it all felt superficial, though the frigid water was turning my skin numb, and I really couldn't be certain.

From the top of the channel Tonk barked, racing furiously, bounding from rock to rock. He dodged around trees, plowing through bushes and weeds, trying to keep up with me as I was dragged downstream.

I tried to collect my wits about me, what felt like herding a large flock of cats, and tried to concentrate. Among all the craziness in the fire service, flood waters are among the most dangerous thing we deal with. It might be the most dangerous thing; it's certainly in the top three. You can get pummeled by debris, stabbed by nearly anything with even a mild point. You can get wedged in a strainer – a collection of rocks or flotsam that the water can pass through but you can't – and trapped there, pinned by the force of the water which can reach dozens of pounds per square inch, until you drown, or are overcome by hypothermia, or crushed to a pulp by something bigger coming downstream in your wake.

After getting caught last year in the collapse of Baxter's Dam, swept away, driven through a drainage culvert, and narrowly rescued by Tank, I had taken a class in water survival and rescue techniques, what the fire service calls swift water training. Know thy enemy, right? Though it also struck me as something like closing the barn door long after the horse has been sent to the glue factory.

The training had taken place only six weeks ago, the beginning of November, and I remember standing, shivering on the shore of the Merrimack River just south of the 101 overpass. The thin Maverick dry suits we wore were no match for the biting wind and the tiny ice-like snowflakes that spiraled out of the air to abrade our exposed faces, pelt against chapped lips and needle frosted cheeks.

Learn to read the water, the instructors had told us. Rapids may look violent and chaotic and random, churn and foam and froth, but they are in fact nearly constant and provide a map of the river bottom for those who know how to read it. Pools, eddies, upwellings, rip currents, whirlpools – they are driven from the structure of the riverbed and the rocks underneath the water. If you can understand its language, the water will tell you where you can fight to gain ground, where it is safe to rest, and places to avoid or die. They then gave us a grave warning: this may be a class, but this is also a real river. If something goes wrong, we can't shut the water off.

What followed was two days of the most grueling training I have ever undertaken in the fire service, sixteen hours in the icy water with breaks where we would cling to mossy rocks in the even colder air.

Taught by my father to swim almost before I could walk, I loved the water. I had thought I knew the water from more than thirty years of frolicking in placid lakes and tiny creeks. I quickly learned that is not water. Though we use the same word for it in the English language, those peaceful lakes and burbling streams are like water's kindly aunt, a matronly woman who visits children with a purse full of butterscotch hard candies and perhaps pinches cheeks overzealously, but rosy cheeks were about the worst you could expect to suffer. The water I was introduced to over those two days was relentless, powerful, unforgiving, and merciless. It was a bully who shoved and pushed, injured and maimed and killed without thought, without anger, if you failed to show it the proper respect. I thought that perhaps like the Eskimos, who I've read have dozens of different words to describe snow, we should adopt more words for water.

The class concluded with videos of failed swift water rescue attempts. Sometimes taken by a shaky cell phone held in someone's hand, but more often steady, crisp imagery filmed by a professional news crew, these videos showed teams of firefighters or cops or bystanders trying to rescue someone from being swept away in a swollen drainage culvert or trapped in a car caught in a flash flood. When they went badly, they went apocalyptic, resulting in the deaths of the victim, the rescuers, sometimes a bystander who just got too close to the action.

The final video they showed has stuck with me to this day. It was aftermath news footage from somewhere in Texas and told the story of a young teenage boy playing with a friend in a drainage ditch along the roadway in front of his house. It was a nothing ditch, less than three feet deep and only fifty or so feet long with a corrugated steel pipe buried at each end. His mother said that when he went out to play, the flow was a sluggish trickle, almost more mud than water. Then a thunderstorm miles away dumped millions of gallons of water into the drainage system, and in the blink of an eye that trickle became a torrent. The boy was washed off his feet, slammed against the drainage pipe, folded in half, and forced inside. A nearly grown boy was driven into an opening smaller than a basketball. The news footage ended with the picture of the excavated ground and the hole that had been cut into the pipe hundreds of feet along its length to recover the body.

That's the water I had been taught to respect, and also to read.

I looked downstream and saw a spot where the water spilled over a broad rounded boulder. On the far side I knew there would be a small pool, and the water pouring into that pool would well up from the bottom and create a spot where I would bob like a cork with no effort at all on my part. I angled for it and let the water wash me over the boulder. I had a momentary instinct to try and cling to it, but I knew near the surface the top of the rock would be slick with algae and the force of the current was stronger than I was.

I conserved my energy and gulped some air, holding it as I rolled over the lip and plunged into the icy depths, deep, deep down. I kept my eyes open and watched the light fade: green, dark green, a nearly lightless gray that was the absence of color, and then deathly pitch black. I hovered, blind in the darkness, holding my breath, waiting for the upwelling. Had I been wrong? Was my waiting akin to that of an acolyte awaiting the return of a savior who had abandoned him for his sins? No, the physicist in me counseled, water is an incompressible fluid. For every drop of water that rolls over that boulder and falls into this hole, a drop already in here has to go somewhere, and if I am patient the current will take me with it.

Still, it felt like I wasn't moving, and my lungs began to burn from lack of oxygen. I imagined myself somehow in an underground tube, a natural pipe system that might not resurface for two or ten or twenty miles. It seemed like as good a time as any to panic, and so I did. I twisted and thrashed, reaching out, probing with fingers and toes to find an edge, a wall, some surface to check my motion, guess at which way might be up. There was nothing. It was an abyss, an airless void indistinguishable from deepest space. I floated, a stranded astronaut, weightless, freezing, suffocating, and dying.

Then I noticed the water around me was no longer black, but an ever so slightly less black, call it charcoal gray. I picked the direction I thought was lighter still and kicked towards it. I was rewarded as the radiance took on color, the green of the absolutely deepest forest shade. I kicked again and the green became rich and vibrant, the color of life. I swam and clawed at the water, my lungs feeling as though they would burst, the instinct to take a breath nearly overwhelming.

At last I broke through the surface, took great, whooping,

choking, heaving gasps of air. I was dizzy, and the sun that dappled off the water, spearing into my eyes, was disorienting. I lay limply in the water and tried to recover, my fingers and toes going numb, extremis frostbite.

I found when I collected my wits that I hadn't moved downstream at all. The current held me in the lee of the same rock, gently, turning, swirling. I had been right, I had read the water correctly, but the hole had been deeper than I could have guessed.

I lightly tread water, examining the river around me for a safe path to shore.

It didn't look good. The river had widened and the channel walls had flattened, and if I could get near land I could probably drag myself out of the water, but the rapids here were brutal. Given a choice I wouldn't have tried to forge them in a kayak. My hand a twisted claw, I'd have to swim sidestroke – not my strongest stroke – and would need to rest frequently. Waiting in the lee of that rock, hoping for some kind of geological upheaval to come along and change the course and character of the river wasn't an option either. I was already well on my way to hypothermia, my entire body shivering and trembling like it was trying to shake itself apart. Still, shivering was good; when I stopped, I knew I was in real trouble.

There was another rock downstream that was halfway between my position and the shore. It was smaller than the one I was hiding behind, and though I didn't have a good angle on it, I thought it would offer another shelter where I could rest.

I took a deep breath, which actually felt not awful because all the nerves in my chest were frozen numb, and set off. It was hard going, fighting the current, my broken hand slapping at the water ineffectually, and when I got there I found that another even smaller rock was in the spot I had been hoping to sneak into.

The current grabbed me while I was considering my options. It dragged me another hundred yards downstream at an incredible speed. I had this weird moment of dislocation, the uncanny feeling that it was the shore that was whipping by me like a speeding freight train while I was standing still. I foundered in the water thinking, 'Wait, I want to get on board.'

I narrowly missed a massive strainer, two submerged trees, some branches, and about three tons of sodden leaves sprawling like a giant net. Past that was a row of boulders laid out as a natural breakwater. A wave crushed me against the first rock in the line, battering my bruised and cracked ribs, eliciting a grunt from between my clenched teeth. The moment one wave subsided, another came and slammed me against the rocks again. I managed to get my shoulder into it, and push off with my good hand, averting the worst of the damage, inching my way down the line. Again and again, the water pounded me, smashing me against the rocks. It felt like I was being worked over with a meat tenderizing mallet.

At the end of the line, I found myself only a few dozen feet from the shore, the current beaten and sluggish, much like myself, as it made its way past the breakwater. I switched to a breaststroke and swam like mad, my broken hand clawing at the water like a rake missing half its tines. I felt my knees scrape against the bottom and stood up, stumbled back to my knees, and crawled the last few feet.

I dragged myself onto shore choking and coughing and spitting. I sprawled out just above the waterline, my chest heaving, all my ribs feeling somehow wrong. There, a rock propped underneath my head like a pillow, I lay face down and was still.

Nineteen

I rested there; I'm not sure for how long. Given my druthers I would have stayed there all day, lingering, as though nesting in the finest featherbed, even as the rock I was using as a pillow mashed the ear on one side of my head flat. I was having a dream, though perhaps dream is the wrong word as I teetered in the twilight realm between sleep, delirium and unconsciousness. In this dream I was a teenager again, living at home, lying in bed and late for school. My mother, trying to rouse me, licked my face unceasingly.

"All right. All right, mom I'm getting up." I pushed my mother away, who of course turned out not to be my mother at all, but Tonk.

His job done, he obediently retreated. I ran a hand down my face, wiping off a glistening layer of dog saliva. "I don't think that breath mint helped at all," I told him.

I felt feverish as I struggled to my feet and took stock. I looked like the quintessential castaway on a deserted island. My shirt was literally in tatters, strips and streamers. Both knees of my jeans were out and there was a long gash in the denim on my right thigh, but miraculously the thigh beneath was unscathed. The sole of one shoe had become detached at the toe and flapped like a loose tongue. I had lost the tire iron somewhere in the water and the flashlight, but I still l had my knife, the first aid kit, and the roll of duct tape was still around my wrist and still sticky. That stuff is incredible. I had also somehow managed to keep the stopwatch on its lanyard around my neck and it was still running. Good old 1970's technology.

I tore off a length of tape with my teeth and wound it one handed around the toe of my torn shoe. I hobbled around a little, and it held firm. Good enough.

Shrugging off the scraps of my shirt, I was shocked at the sight of myself, painted like an overcrowded canvas with swaths of red and blue and purple, a patchwork of livid bruises and small cuts. My back, which naturally I couldn't see, felt even worse.

I opened the first aid kit and found that it was not designed to be waterproof. I poured out the water that had accumulated inside during my afternoon dip. The band aids and gauze pads inside were sodden and ruined. The alcohol swaps were too small to be of any use. There were two packages of aspirin remaining, still dry because their little envelopes were foil-lined. I tore one open and chewed the tablets up then and there, and put the other in my pocket, saving it for later. I took the damp ace bandage out and threw the rest of the kit aside, not as useful as I had hoped.

I've taken some first aid classes, mock bandaged an injured wrist or ankle in class, never anything about cracked ribs that I could recall. I squelched the water out of the ace bandage and wound it around my chest. Maybe I was doing some good; maybe I was making a complete hash of it. I secured the end with another strip of tape. I took an experimental breath and it hurt a lot, but seemed better than without the bandage.

That left the mess of my hand, my broken fingers misaligned and pointing every which way.

Back in college I recalled breaking a finger while playing ultimate Frisbee. I had set the break myself, taping the finger to a stub of pencil as a splint. That probably wasn't the best approach to medical care I could have taken, but you can't imagine what college student health services were like in those days – some bored senior with no medical training whatsoever sitting behind a desk as part of a work study program that offset financial aid payments. The majority of their care consisted of telling you whatever you had going on didn't look too bad, even if it did, and sending you on your way. For those unable or unwilling to leave their office under their own power they would call an ambulance that would take you fourteen blocks north to some hospital in Harlem, the innerest of inner city hospitals, where you could hang out with gunshot and stabbing victims in the emergency room, pushed repeatedly to the bottom of their triage list unless you were lucky enough to be shot or stabbed yourself. Ten hours later you might have earned class credit for urban studies, and scored just about any illicit drug known to man from one of your fellow emergency room denizens, and maybe even witnessed another shooting or stabbing like some kind of macabre floor show, but received nothing approaching medical care. Believe me, I was better off with the pencil stub.

The way my hand looked, had I been standing on campus at that moment, I might have been willing to take my chances with health services.

I certainly couldn't run around with my hand as it was and had few options open to me. I let the physicist part of my brain take over: my fingers were bent, and I would straighten them. Simple solutions for a simple problem. Straight fingers were better, right?

I submerged my hand in the water until I couldn't feel my fingers anymore, then lay it palm down on a flat rock and used the thumb of my other hand to press them back into line. They made little snapping noises as I did so, a damper and cracklier version of cracking my knuckles. The cold water had worked; this didn't hurt nearly as much as I had expected it would. My index finger was bent to one side and no gentle pressure seemed capable of pushing it back into place, so I put a knee on the back of my hand and leaned on it. It set with an audible snap that knocked me back on my ass and had me howling at the sky in pain, clutching my injured hand at the wrist with my good one. When it subsided, I found that my hand, though swollen and not precisely the right shape, looked sort of like a caricature of a human hand which I took as a good thing.

I opened my knife – a maneuver that required me to use my good hand and my teeth – and cut strips from the remains of my shirt. I wound the strips around my hand and secured it with tape, all the fingers out straight like I was about to perform a karate chop. I found the thumb worked and wasn't broken, so at least I was still part of the opposable thumbs crowd. That was the best I could do, though what my hand might look like in a couple of hours I didn't care to speculate.

As the pain in my hand diminished to a dull roar, my knee reminded me that it too was in need of some medical care. I didn't have another ace bandage and there was too little left of my shirt to use, so I would have to learn to live with it as it was. I limped around, got a feel for it, thought about the advice of my little league coach to rub some dirt in it, wondered if it would hold me up or fold like a lawn chair when I needed it most.

At a minimum I needed about a day of bed rest. Optimally, I would have found a hospital and checked myself in for a week. Instead what awaited me was another long hike followed by a beating at Kevin's hands. All my gallivanting around, all my effort, had I even put so much as a scratch on him? I didn't think so.

"This isn't going very well, is it?" I asked Tonk, who of course had no answer for me.

I folded the knife up against my hip and put it back in my pocket. The roll of tape was down to just a few turns, six feet of tape total, maybe less. I had so few possessions and the tape had done so much for me already, I was in no position to toss even a small amount away as trash. I fitted the roll over my hand; let it rattle around on my wrist. After considering the scrap of my shirt on the ground, not much remaining but the collar, I left it where it lay. My meager supplies collected and collated, it was time to get moving.

I took my first look around since climbing out of the water and realized that I had no idea where I was. That wasn't particularly surprising. Not only did I not know this area, but to my weekend hiker's brain every tree, every rock, looked like every other. Upstream was to my right, but how far had I been washed downriver? Was it even in a straight line? I didn't know.

The land in front of me sloped upwards and there was the suggestion of darkness up ahead, the rise of land partially blocking the sky. I was exhausted and battered, and though it wasn't dark yet there were only a few hours of daylight left. Lacking the flashlight, the best plan I could come up with was to retake the high ground while it was still light, find somewhere to rest for the night, and tomorrow morning try and spot Kevin and Valerie from the ridge. Go from there.

A part of me couldn't believe I was going to yet again climb this goddamned mountain, though I realized it was not actually the same mountain. In my mind this region of New Hampshire on a map looked indistinguishably green and all held the label White Mountains. There are people who can name every major hump of rock in the state and recognize them from their shape, keep spreadsheets on their strategy for climbing them all. I wasn't one of those people.

Tonk beside me looked as tired as I felt. Bulldogs, whatever they had been bred for, hiking wasn't it. They really aren't working breeds at all. Short legged, big headed, old – he looked just about done in.

"I could have adopted a St. Bernard," I told him, "They're used all across the Alps as mountain rescue dogs. I think they even come with that little barrel of scotch underneath their chin as standard equipment."

He yawned, letting me know he didn't find me nearly as amusing as I found myself.

"I'm sorry," I said, "Mommy and I love you just the way you are. If there's a McDonalds at the top of this mountain, the chicken nuggets are on me. How about that?"

He seemed to think the chances of that were slim and none, and, as the saying goes, slim had already left town. He rose to his feet, slowly, his hips giving him obvious discomfort. That bit about each human year being equivalent to seven dog years isn't based on great science, but as rules of thumb go it's pretty good. Tonk, at twelve years of age – it was like I had been dragging an eighty-four year old around in the mountains all day, put him through a forced hike of ten or twelve miles.

"I know, it's not fair, but I'm doing the best I can," I said to him as we staggered off into the failing light.

Twenty

Tonk and I climbed through the thickening gloom. It was often hard to see my feet, and I risked tripping on a rock or an exposed root and sprawling or turning an ankle in my blindness, exhaustion, and desperation. Still, I forced us both to keep a fast pace. The darkness pursued us from below. I imagined it to be a sentient creature, some kind of nocturnal predator hungering for a meal. I thought I could hear it snuffling over my own labored breathing, imagined I could feel its exhalations on my back, warm and humid and tinged with the odor of rotting meat.

My irrational fears got the better of me, and I scrabbled up the hill in a panic, skidding and sliding back, my arms scraped by branches, my hands cut by stones, fingernails torn out as I clawed for purchase. Tonk's hackles went up, though I don't think he understood why.

As soon as I cleared the ridgeline, I was bathed in the full light of the setting sun. I climbed onto a rocky outcropping and stood, squinting, and willed my racing heart to slow, felt icy sweat drying on my bare skin. Though not exactly warming, the sun nonetheless felt good upon my chilled flesh, and I closed my eyes to face it, watching the blood pulsing in my eyelids.

After taking several deep breaths, or at least what passed for deep given my cracked ribs, I turned and looked down into the valley below. Though bright and sunny up where I was, it was full dark at the bottom of the bowl, difficult to discern even the meandering path of the river. I attempted to follow it back, often losing track of its glimmering silver against the velvet black of the trees. I couldn't spot Kevin's backpack as it was too dark, or maybe I had been washed farther downstream than I had thought, and they were too far away. I tried not to become disheartened at that, tried to tell myself that in the bright light of a new day they would be easy to see. I only halfway succeeded.

I watched as the sun set, the valley vanishing in a rising tide of black, as if filling up with ink. I didn't want that darkness to touch me; I was afraid to let it lap over my toes. I couldn't put a name to my fear: whether I was afraid of Kevin coming at me from out of the darkness, or nameless creatures capering in the darkness, or the darkness itself, I didn't know. My heart raced anew, and I had trouble catching my breath.

I turned away and gazed at the last orange slivers of the sun, scorched corneas be damned. Perhaps I was becoming delirious from hunger, thirst, or pain, but I had to get a grip or the night would drive me bonkers. I felt as if, had someone been kind enough to deliver a queen-size featherbed to me, I would be unable to sleep in it for fear of the monsters lurking underneath. I shook my head and forced myself to turn back, staring into the featureless black heart of my enemy.

The light faded, and whatever dwindling confidence I had that I might come through this alive faded with it. This would be my last night on Earth. I would die of exposure overnight, or Kevin would kill me tomorrow. Those seemed the most likely outcomes. The thought of being alone out here in the last dozen hours of my existence, in the dark, only the faint red glow of the stopwatch on the lanyard around my neck, was more than I could

111

handle. As the last of the light and color leeched from the land, my heart thundering, blood pounding in my ears, I blinked, and then squeezed my eyes shut. I couldn't do it. I couldn't face my fear.

I felt silly and childish. I run into freaking burning buildings as a hobby, yet here I was afraid of shadows like a six year old.

When I finally worked up my nerve to crack my eyes open again, something miraculous happened. It wasn't dark! The sky was alit with millions upon millions of stars, and their light limned everything with silver. The nearest significant source of light pollution in Dunboro is a tractor and heavy equipment distributor miles away in Milford, and I had thought we had great, unobstructed views of the stars, but what I was looking at was incredible. I could see the red tint of Aldebaran, the eye of Taurus the Bull, perpetual target of Orion, recognizable by the three stars in his belt. I marveled at the myriad of constellations, shapes as old as time itself.

I might well have stayed there all night, dazzled by the night sky, but with sunset came a cold and biting wind. Shirtless as I was, it sliced through my ace bandage wrapping and drove me off the ridgeline. I found a crevice a little ways off the peak and packed myself inside. The temperature felt like it dropped below freezing and I cuddled up around Tonk's little body for warmth. At least it didn't snow.

Even with the sweatshirts from our backpack, Valerie was in for a rough night, provided Kevin untied her long enough to let her put one on. Born and raised in Kentucky, she has always been more susceptible to the cold than I am, and I was freezing my huevos rancheros off. Still, I wasn't going to freeze to death. My adolescent and teenage years in the North Country, where the temperature might not get out of the single digits for the entire month of February, had thickened my blood. In high school I had gone snowmobiling and overnight camping with friends in the snowy wilderness with little more than a thin, nylon pup tent for shelter. I'd be fine almost no matter how cold it got. Maybe if Kevin was citified, born in Miami for all I knew, I had this edge on him.

On the other hand it was possible that Kevin had planned this all out and had elaborate camping gear, cold-weather sleeping bags and tents and the makings for S'mores, stashed for their use. I even hoped for Valerie's sake that it was true. It was, however, highly unlikely. Kevin had wanted this confrontation to take place in the wilderness where he and I could fight out his twisted romance fantasy to win Valerie's love undisturbed, but he had no way of knowing this particular piece of wilderness would be the location in advance. He also likely had not been thinking that it would take this long to kill me. Perhaps he had expected to be home with Valerie as his prisoner by lunch. I was terribly sorry to have disappointed him.

I shifted my position on the hard ground and felt my jeans, frozen with a thin skin of ice, crackle. It was going to be a long goddamned night. I hoped Kevin's need to remain constantly vigilant should I try and attack was allowing him to get as little sleep as I. A nocturnal assault might have been a smart idea. Oh, the joy of stealthily catching Kevin fast asleep and bashing his head in with a rock. But I was beat, and my shattered hand was too painful – the two aspirin I had chewed up hadn't made a dent in it at all. It was also too dark, and I had no idea where they were, or where I was for that matter. I told myself again that come first light I would be rested and I would regain the high ground and find them. Again, only halfway successful.

I felt Tonk shivering against me; the cold was miserable for him as well. I hugged him closer.

"I ever tell you about the time the fire department got called out for a dog bitten by a beaver?" I asked Tonk.

He stilled and pivoted his head around to look at me, snuggling in for my bedtime story.

"It's true. I don't know how it works in big cities, but when you call 911 in the boonies there's a dispatcher with three buttons to choose from: police, fire, ambulance. They have to make a decision on the fly as to which one to hit. Health emergencies go to the ambulance. The police deal with crimes. Sometimes it seems to me that the one for the fire department might as well be marked 'other.' So we got a call for a dog bitten by a beaver."

"A guy had gone walking with his dog off its leash in the woods, and they came to this area where the woods ran into a bog. A beaver lived in that bog, but at the moment they passed, the beaver was on the shore gnawing at a tree. On land, the dog, a big Rhodesian Ridgeback, had a distinct advantage, and he gave this poor beaver a run for its money until they hit the water."

Screams suddenly echoed up to us from the valley below. I thought it must be some kind of night bird, but it sounded just like that, like a woman screaming. Not Valerie, much higher pitched. The echo and the cool night air made the sound travel, gave the impression that the source wasn't all that far away. Tonk and I listened as it swelled and faded, and then swelled again before dissolving into a low sobbing moan that raised Tonk's hackles. His and mine both. Then the moan faded until it was swallowed up in the background noise of the wind whispering through the trees and the occasional hoot of an owl.

Gotta be a bird I told myself, reciting it like a prayer. It's gotta be. The creatures of the night have a myriad of calls, and I'm far from an expert in them. I've heard porcupines having sex, and believe me when I tell you that it sounds like a person being slaughtered with a dull knife, not that I'm an expert in what that sounds like either. And yet, listening to two porcupines go at it, there's something about it, some element missing, you somehow know the noise is not human. What I had just heard, as I played it back in my mind, I couldn't tell.

In the aftermath, surrounded by what my experience told me were normal night sounds, I had difficulty convincing myself that I heard it at all. Still I sat motionless, breathless, my blood pounding in my ears, waiting for more, but nothing came. Finally, I continued my story in a graveyard whisper. "In the water, the beaver holds all the cards. All the dog can do is paddle around, but the beaver can dive and surface, hold its breath, sneak into its den and pop back out again."

"The dog was totally befuddled, and the guy was standing on the shore yelling for his dog to come back, and the beaver was having a grand old time, but the beaver eventually tired of this game. He dove down, came back up underneath the dog, and took a big bite out of one of its hind legs, a piece the size of an ice cream scoop. The dog was actually pretty lucky with this bite; the jaw of a beaver can generate a lot of force, and probably could have broken a bone and amputated a piece of the leg instead of just taking a pound of flesh."

Tonk started to snore softly. I liked to think that he could hear me even in his sleep and that it was comforting to him. I lowered my voice and continued.

"Suddenly this wasn't much fun for the dog either and it headed back to shore. Once there, it turned out it couldn't carry its own weight. The dollop of missing muscle was too much, and it was bleeding like a stuck pig. The guy took off his shirt and wrapped it around the bleeding leg, staunching the blood flow. Then he had the problem of getting a hundred and twenty five pounds of dog back down the two miles of trail to home. He started out trying to carry it, but two miles is a long way to go, and that was when we got the call."

"We're better equipped to transport injured hikers, but we've got all kinds of tools, and the difference between and dog and a person is pretty insignificant in the transportation game. We go out there with a UTV and a Stokes basket. I'm sure you've seen that basket. They use it in every fire department TV show and movie ever made because it looks so professional and has a distinctive shape. Anyway, he had given us good directions of the trails he had taken, and we found him right where we expected to."

"I don't really know dog anatomy all that well, but I figure a person at a hundred and twenty five pounds and a dog of the same weight probably have about the same blood volume, and while this dog had bled plenty, it didn't look like a life threatening amount to me. The dog was alert, appeared well-hydrated, and was surprisingly calm. We loaded him up in the basket and drove him on the UTV to the nearest road. A firefighter met us there with his personal pickup truck, and we put the dog in the basket into the back and raced right to the vet hospital with lights and siren. We radioed dispatch who called ahead to the doctor, and she was there waiting for us when we rolled up."

"I understand the dog needed some stitches, but it turned out OK. Score another save for the Dunboro Fire Department. Hurray."

Tonk stirred in his sleep, his hind legs pumping as he ran in his dream, I hoped in some sun drenched meadow chasing butterflies and not from a bloodthirsty nightmare beaver.

"It turned out OK," I repeated softly. I stroked his flank with my good hand and he quieted. "It's somehow all going to turn out OK."

Twenty-One

I can't say for certain whether or not I slept that night. I don't think I did. Tonk had dozed off in my lap during story time, and his weight against my thigh caused my right foot to go to sleep, but I didn't want to move for fear of waking him. The poor little guy needed all the rest he could get.

From our cramped nook I kept watch on the stars, naming as many of them as I could, which wasn't nearly as many as several of my college friends who were serious astronomy nerds. Then sometime later clouds rolled in and snuffed them all out, and it was just me and Tonk and a darkness so absolute it felt as though I had gone blind. Perhaps my line of sight was blocked by the terrain, but I couldn't even see the halo glow of distant cities. At some point I would have become convinced I was blind, if not for the glowing numerals on the stopwatch, though as they were counting out my time left on Earth, that wasn't much of a morale booster. If Kevin lit a fire that night, I never saw it.

I shifted minutely, tried to get blood flowing down to my foot without disturbing Tonk. No dice. I'd probably have to amputate come morning.

117

Though I couldn't make them out, I could somehow sense the mountains around me; picture in my mind their silhouettes as I had seen them in the fading light. Their resilience, their gravity, by their very presence, they were a comfort to me. They endured, they survived, and somehow in their proximity I would too. Though nonsensical, it somehow felt right. That's one of the beauties of exhaustion and starvation and dehydration induced delirium; it doesn't have to make sense.

Time seemed to pass quickly, so maybe I dozed, or maybe I just zoned out. The next morning dawned gradually, a million shades of gray, dull and damp, my absolutely least favorite weather.

Tonk roused himself at first light. He climbed slowly, creakily out of my lap. He shook himself, doddered about on leaden legs, and shook himself again. He then snuffed around, looking for his food bowl, seemed to remember where we were, and sat down dejectedly.

"Sorry," I told him, "no breakfast for either of us."

I would have given nearly anything to take the sad look off his face.

It required a couple of tries for me to pry myself out of the niche and a couple more to get to my feet, dew frost crackling on my jeans. My maladies were legion. I was cold. My ribs ached, my hand throbbed, and my knee seemed disinclined to hold my weight. One eye was partially swollen shut, and a bruise on my scalp that I hadn't even remembered getting hurt like a mother. Also, my eyes stung for reasons that I couldn't understand and I had a dry, hacking cough that I couldn't seem to quiet. Perhaps a touch of the flu coming on, as if I needed another malady added to my list.

Once upright, I staggered around as though I was drunk. I reached out to steady myself against a tree using my broken hand, which, all things considered, was a more effective wake-me-up than a quart-sized espresso, though involved a lot more groaning.

Just a few moments later, a dull pain in my abdomen progressed rapidly to cramps, and from there to diarrhea, of which I'll spare you the details. Botany not being a particularly strong subject of mine, there was a real risk of wiping my ass with poison oak, but I selected a plant as non-threatening looking as I could find nearby and hoped for the best. How come this kind of thing never happens to James Bond?

I sucked so badly at this survival stuff. I was probably surrounded by all manner of edible plants and insects and barks, but I had never been a boy scout and didn't know diddly from squat. There was a bush nearby with some tasty-looking bright red berries on it, tasty of course being a relative term given my current state of starvation, but I seemed to dimly remember some book I had read which advised against eating brightly colored berries. Or maybe it was the drab ones that should be avoided. Strawberries are bright red, and we eat those, right? I thought about picking some and seeing if Tonk would eat them, wondered if he had some ingrained survival instinct, perhaps something inherited from wolves that would keep him from ingesting poison. Who was I kidding? Tonk was so domesticated and trusting that he would hoover up gravel if I poured it into his bowl, and I had no desire to risk poisoning my dog. There were not very many berries on the bush anyway, certainly not a meal's worth, so I left them alone.

I rubbed at my stinging eyes and found myself wondering if Kevin knew any survival skills in addition to his combat skills. Valerie and I had put only a little food into the backpack, some granola bars and a couple of baggies of dog kibble. We hadn't been planning to spend the night out here when we packed, and I couldn't imagine that Kevin had thought it would take this long to kill me, so how much food could he have brought along with him? If we were both starving, was Kevin with his washboard abs and his low body fat percentage at a disadvantage? My love handles may come in handy yet.

I hobbled around, hoping to loosen up the things that should be loose and tighten up the things that should be tight, then did a lot of coughing and a little stretching – nothing dramatic, just some twisting at the waist and bending to touch my toes. I immediately became lightheaded and stopped. I hoped it was from low blood sugar, but could have been due to a small concussion, hypothermia, internal bleeding, or any of a number of superb possibilities.

My thinking last night had been that things would look better in the morning. In the dismal light of this new day, I couldn't imagine what had led me to believe that. The basic problems – kill Kevin, rescue Valerie – remained from yesterday, only now I was a collection of cracked and broken bones and strained muscles. Plus, if I allowed myself to honestly assess my situation, I was also hungry, dehydrated, and I'd lost everything I had retrieved from my truck except the few feet of duct tape remaining on the roll, plus I still had my small, practically useless, pocket knife.

"But no reason to get all negative about it, be a Gloomy Gus, as my mom would say," I told Tonk.

The time had come to climb back to the ridge, spot the backpack, and do whatever it was I was going to do, but Tonk looked to have grown roots. With some difficulty I sat down next to him and stroked him with my good hand.

"I've got nothing," I admitted. "No good plan, no new ideas."

I was reminded of the definition of insanity, doing the same thing over and over again and expecting a different outcome. I kept going to Kevin, getting the tar beaten out of me, and narrowly escaping. Except for the narrowly escaping bit, I was totally playing his game by his rules. But had I ever had a chance to play by my rules, whatever they might be? Could I have gone somewhere, gotten help? Now, with only a few hours left on the stopwatch, no, but yesterday at some point, maybe. Instead of climbing up here last night and cramming myself into a hole and stargazing, I could have used those eight or so hours to drag my carcass back to civilization and called in the Marines. A wasted opportunity, I could have been there and back by now.

I reminded my brain that this kind of hindsight being twenty-twenty thinking wasn't helping any. I needed innovative ideas for a new day. My brain ignored me and kept grimly grinding along this line of reasoning.

How did Kevin know I hadn't gone to get help? He hadn't laid eyes on me since late yesterday. For all he knew, I could be dead. I really should be dead. Broken handed in that icy river, it was only a little bit of skill and a whole lot of luck, my recent completion of the swift-water training class, that had kept me alive, but Kevin had no way of knowing any of that.

How had Kevin seen this whole thing going anyway? In his fantasy, had we slugged it out toe to toe until I lay dead at his feet? If so, why give me twenty four hours? Perhaps he had seen this scenario in some movie, woven it into his plans, but Kevin wasn't completely crazy and he had to understand the difference between reality and fantasy. In real life, unlike some action movie hero or villain, he had to sleep. Twenty four hours virtually guaranteed some big chunk of time, possibly several of them, when I would be out of his sight, during which I could have hiked all the way to the State Police barracks in Concord.

He also had no way of knowing that I would be willing to play along. Kevin knew my marriage was on the rocks and maybe, faced with the choices of either dying at his hands or killing him, I would choose option 3, just let him keep Valerie as a sex slave chained up in a dungeon somewhere. Most normal people would consider such an alternative abhorrent and inhumane, but as Kevin had already proven pretty substantially, he was far from a normal person. He might believe my most likely choice would be to turn tail and run, and consider myself lucky to be done with Valerie. If so, would he have camped up here with Valerie tied to a tree, waiting for me to show up, and when I didn't would he take her and leave? Twenty four hours of waiting didn't seem to be in Kevin's chemistry from what little I knew of it. My mind balked at such a possibility.

What initially might have looked to Kevin like some grand adventurous romantic gesture quickly fell apart in the details, and Kevin, planning the ambush and bringing the zip ties and the gag for Valerie and the collar and leash, was a guy who kept track of the details. So, my brain reiterated, how had Kevin seen this whole thing going?

I had no answer for it. I stopped petting Tonk, who had fallen asleep again, and looked at the stopwatch, saw time slipping away. I urged my brain, if there was some conclusion to be drawn from all of this rumination, that it had best reach it quickly.

I waited, but my brain had gone silent. It had followed that logic, if such could be called logic, as far as it could go.

It was time to get moving. I stood, a little surprised that my knee, instead of being unable to support my weight, was now unable to bend. Things seemed bleak for our hero, unless I was lucky enough to stumble across a weapons cache hidden by some doomsday prepper.

Tonk woke, and looked up at me with tired eyes. The thought of what would happen to him if I were killed suddenly occurred to me. It seemed unlikely Kevin would let Valerie keep him, and he wouldn't survive up here on his own. I pictured him sitting loyally by my body, gradually succumbing to the elements. That image was more depressing than I could handle. I rubbed at my stinging eyes, but didn't shed any tears; maybe I was too dehydrated for that, which was a scary thought in itself, but my eyes continued to burn and I rubbed at them as I hacked and coughed.

I'm almost embarrassed to say how long it took me to understand why my eyes were burning, and me, a firefighter, but after all my choking and squinting, my nose brought a familiar scent to my brain – smoke.

Twenty-Two

It took me some time to find the source.

I followed my nose, the smell of smoke. Stronger this way? No, weaker. Then stronger again.

It was frustrating. Human beings are so poorly equipped for this kind of thing. Tonk could have led me to it instantly, but he had no interest in finding where the smoke was coming from. He was looking for breakfast. Indeed, he seemed to lose patience with me as I frequently paused, sniffed the air, backtracked, sniffed, and then backtracked again. If there had been a pizza within two miles of us that would have been an entirely different story.

We get calls like this sometimes in the fire department. "I smell something burning in my neighborhood," or "There is the odor of propane outside my house." With no more specific information than that we load into trucks and drive grid patterns through the streets, the windows down, our heads hanging out into the breeze like bloodhounds.

"Could have adopted a bloodhound," I told Tonk.

I had meandered at least two hundred yards more or less downhill, and it seemed for a time that I had lost the scent completely. I stopped in the spot I was certain I had last smelled it and waited. The shifting direction of the wind wasn't helping any, and I was conscious of the fact that I was wasting precious time. The stopwatch around my neck told me that I had less than four hours, and I had no idea where Kevin and Valerie were, and I should have been climbing up to the ridge to get a look around, and yet I couldn't let this go. I didn't know why it was important, only that it was.

The wind shifted again and I got a nose full, acrid and dry. It was burning hardwood with some leaves mixed in. My time in the fire department has made me a connoisseur of smoke, swirling it within my nasal cavities, teasing out hints of cherry and maple and oak. I could also tell that it was close, very close, seemingly coming from the direction of a hedge of brambles. I paced left and right like a caged animal trying to find a way through or around, and finally lost my patience and just bulled myself a path. The thorns clawed at me, tore at my jeans and ace bandage. drew bright beads of blood from exposed skin, conspired to keep me from finding out what was on the other side. I pressed forward, Tonk on my heels, and finally burst through into kinder, gentler vegetation.

There I crouched down. I placed a hand on Tonk, and he settled silently by my side. The two of us peered through the leaves at a small campsite tucked in among the close trees, a campfire near its center. Whoever had built the fire was conscious of the risk of brushfires. They had dug a deep hole and ringed it with stones carefully fitted together, as if they were building a rock wall, something intended to last for ages. Even a stiff wind would have been unable to steal embers from that pit.

Down in the hole, the light from the fire would have been invisible until you were right on top of it, which was why I

125

hadn't seen anything even though this campsite was only a few football fields from the cranny where I had spent the night. The morning dew had settled on the banked fire, and it was smoking heavily, big puffy, steamy white as if they were electing a new Pope. It was only because it was so smoky that I had been able to detect it.

A blue tent was pitched to one side, the front zipper open and the fabric flapping lightly in the breeze. It looked just large enough to hold two people sleeping side by side if they were friends, close friends. A brook babbled and chuckled to itself somewhere nearby.

Was this Kevin's campsite? His gear? I waited and listened, but heard nothing.

I then noticed something just past the edge of the tent. A controlled curve, a shape not of nature. Something manmade. I moved carefully, slowly, quietly to my left. My new perspective revealed more: a hiking boot, a smidge of ankle of someone lying prone behind the tent. It wasn't Kevin's shoe, not what I recalled him wearing, or Valerie's either. I advanced, holding my breath, didn't make a sound.

It was a man, young, mid-twenties, athletic. His head was misshapen, had been bashed in, the weapon a rock the size of a softball on the ground nearby, the jagged granite surface matted with blood and clots of hair. He was so obviously dead, but I couldn't help myself. I placed two fingers against his throat. No pulse. His skin was ice cold, sheathed in a thin layer of dew frost; he had been lying out in the open all night. He had taken a blow to the neck, maybe the first blow that incapacitated him before Kevin went into a bashing frenzy, and I could feel the broken crockery of his spine underneath the skin.

I withdrew my hand and stayed crouched by the man's side.

This was my fault.

If I had somehow managed to kill Kevin, or allowed him to kill me, this would never have happened. Kevin wasn't planning to have this take all day, and whatever else was in that backpack of his, he had lacked camping supplies. Then he had happened upon this poor soul, someone who unwittingly had picked a truly beautiful place to die, and for the price of a little murder Kevin had first class accommodations.

I thought then of the sounds I had heard last night, what I now knew were screams. I closed my eyes and replayed them, listened to them in the light of this new understanding. They were definitely the screams of a woman, not a man. Not Valerie, though. Valerie's voice is deeper. I've joked with her that she has a voice meant for the news anchor desk on television, like Diane Sawyer. The one from last night was higher, reedy, a pitch Valerie could not possibly have achieved, even in abject terror. Who then?

I checked the tent and found only the wadded up bulk of two sleeping bags and a few fragments of leaves and pine needles. Then in the corner I spotted a glint of gold, a ring, Valerie's wedding ring. She must have worked it off her finger and left it as a message: she had spent the night here. I picked it up and held it, watched the sharply-slanting morning light play off the facets of the diamonds. I put it in my pocket, and backed out of the tent.

Kevin and Valerie had spent the night only a few hundred yards away from me. I couldn't make any sense of it; the coincidence was beyond comprehension. I had been washed I had no idea how far downstream, a mile or more was certainly not out of the question. Kevin had seen me go. He had untied Valerie from the tree, clipped on her leash, and hauled her along until they came to where I had managed to get out of the water. They would have been able to find that spot because the remnants of my shirt were lying on the bank.

From there they had headed inland. Why? Had they spotted or

127

heard something that led them to this campsite, something that I hadn't seen or heard? As always, I had no answers.

Circling the campsite, I located the brook, a meager thing meandering in puddles between mossy rocks. Then I found a path, branches snapped off from the bushes at both sides of its mouth, the deep impression of a man's boot in the soft soil, the direction pointed outbound.

I pushed into the path, afraid that at any moment I would come across Kevin hunched over another body, this one a woman. In my mind he had been transformed into a horror movie monster. I would find him feeding on her, his hands full of torn pieces of her flesh, his teeth stained with her blood, rivulets running down his chin.

I didn't run into zombie Kevin or vampire Kevin, but what I found wasn't much better. A woman lay across the path face down. Like the man, she was in her mid-twenties, likely young twenties, athletic. Toned thighs and calves extended below the line of her denim cutoffs. I felt her neck. Her skin was cool, but not deathly cold. I discovered no catastrophic spine injury, and carefully rolled her over.

She cried out as I did so, a weak and pathetic whimper that died somewhere in her throat. She didn't open her eyes; she couldn't. Both were swollen shut and her face was a mass of bruises, two broken teeth visible between her parted lips. Kevin really went to town on her, took his time, spent his fury with his fists and his feet.

Her mouth moved and she made small sounds. I leaned in close to catch them.

"Please, no more. Don't hit me again," she sobbed.

She couldn't see, thought I was Kevin coming back to finish the job.

"I'm not him," I told her, "he's gone." Even as I said that last however I wondered if it was true. Kevin could have been watching me from nearby as he pressed Valerie's face into the dirt to keep her quiet. I whipped my head around, tried to catch a glimpse of his neon backpack somewhere, but I saw nothing.

Her body, tense in fear of another beating, relaxed when she heard this. She took a breath preparing to speak, wincing as she did so. Her ribs were in worse shape than mine. I leaned in again to listen.

"My husband?" she asked.

I noticed then the thin band of platinum on her finger.

There are probably psychology classes I could attend through the fire department about how to handle this kind of thing, though I've never taken one. Still, I've been in this situation before: bad car accidents in which I've wheeled the sole survivor to the ambulance on a stretcher, telling them that, yes, their spouse or their child who was riding with them is fine, just fine. Everything is going to be fine.

Is that the right thing to do? I don't know. I really don't. But it's what I do, and I did it again now.

"He's OK," I told her. "You're both going to be OK."

Even with the minimal expressions she could make with her battered face, I could tell she didn't believe me. Tears leaked from her swollen eyes, and she cried softly, though it caused her obvious pain to do so. I rested my good hand over hers, made ineffective and pathetic shushing noises like I'm trying to calm a baby who has lost its binky.

Her tears ran their course and she asked, "Water?"

"I'll get some," I said.

I hobbled back up the path to the campsite. I didn't have anything to carry the water in and performed a quick search, but if they had brought canteens or cups or anything, Kevin had taken them with him, along with any food or tools or medical supplies they may have had. Pretty much all he had left behind was the tent and the sleeping bags. He wasn't going to need those; this would end today.

I went to the brook and found a puddle between two stones just wide and deep enough for me to submerge my cupped hands. I returned to her, losing ninety-nine percent of the water between my broken fingers that simply wouldn't form any kind of seal.

"Open," I told her, and let ten or so drops of water fall from my hands into her mouth.

She choked on them, each cough punctuated by a cry of pain. She tried to roll onto her side and I helped her, and she coughed the water out along with some blood, and then slumped onto her back, spent.

Her shirt had rucked up on one side, and gently I lifted it further to get a look at her abdomen. The bruising on her right side was bright and fresh and spreading underneath her skin even as I watched. Something was seriously ruptured inside her, her liver or her kidney, and she was bleeding out internally at a terrible rate. I thought that maybe moving her had made things worse, and I had yet another of those first-on-the-scene-of-a-bad-call moments, but the decision to move her was in the past, and there was nothing I could do to change it. I was going to have to live with it, even as I was certain she wouldn't. If there had been a Life Flight standing by, a team of trauma surgeons with half a gallon of cross-matched blood to transfuse, maybe she would have had a chance. A small one. In the wilderness with only me to count on to save her, lost, alone, cracked-ribbed, broken-handed, with a crazy man trying to kill me, no way. No effing way.

I couldn't think of anything to say to her, nor apparently she to me, and so we sat quietly, and I listened to her labored breathing and watched her get paler as her blood left her circulatory system and pooled in her abdomen, distended her stomach grotesquely. Tonk settled down at her side with a whimper, his head resting on his paws, his liquid eyes watching her closely.

I don't know how long I sat there. I could have checked the stopwatch, but I didn't. I owed her that much. It would have been like looking at the time while you waited beside someone's deathbed, as if you had somewhere more important to be.

"Water?" she asked again sometime later, even more softly than the first time.

I traveled back to the brook, cupped my hands, lost another ninety-nine percent on the way back. By the time I returned, she was dead.

I wiped my damp hands on my cheeks and forehead, and then rested my face in my palms. I mourned for this woman I had never known and couldn't help, her and her husband both. Innocent people caught up in the shit show that is my life.

No more. Not one more person.

I was going to put an end to it.

I was going to kill that motherfucker.

Somehow, most likely with the loss of blood, the swelling in her face had gone down and her eyes were open. They were a perfect baby blue, a warm and friendly and guile-less color, and it chilled my soul to think of Kevin staring into them as he beat her to death. I tried to close them, but they snapped back open again like faulty window blinds. They gazed up at me, accusing. That was of course just my mood. She was dead, she wasn't gazing at or accusing me of anything, and in any case they

131

weren't pointed directly at me. I think they were looking at my left arm, or maybe over my shoulder. The eyes are terrible pointing devices.

I reached forward to try and close her eye again and froze.

The eyes are terrible pointing devices.

And that was when I put everything together.

Twenty-Three

Valerie had looked at me, right at me, stared pointedly at my shoes, and looked back at me. She had done it repeatedly, two, three times. Each and every time I had misunderstood.

She had shaken her head when Kevin had said I had blocked his blow, and that's how my watch was broken. She had been trying to warn me.

I left the woman's side, hobbled my way back up the trail, my thoughts racing, the pieces coming together rapidly. All the inconsistencies, all the things I couldn't explain when they happened, now they made sense.

He and Valerie had hustled to catch me at the first clearing, the beautiful place I had chosen to die, when he couldn't have possibly known that I was there. I had been quiet as a frigging church mouse as I crept up behind Kevin planning to stab him in the back with his own knife. The river had been loud, and my shadow had stretched out long behind me, and yet he had known I was coming, known exactly when to kick backwards and catch me in the chest. Seriously, how many clues did I need?

And beyond all of that, Kevin's car had been empty, stripped clean. How the hell had I overlooked that?

Back at the campsite, I found a flat rock on which to work and took the stopwatch and its lanyard from around my neck. I placed it on the surface face down and sat awkwardly next to it, my injured leg laid out straight in front of me.

I had asked myself repeatedly how. How did Kevin know I was playing his game by his rules? How did he know I didn't go to the cops? How did he know I hadn't been killed in the river, my corpse well on its way to wherever the current would take me, be it Lake Winnipesaukee or the Merrimack River or the Atlantic Ocean?

I fumbled my knife out of my pocket, clamped it between my teeth, and used my left hand to lever out the Phillips head screwdriver. My hand shook as I tried to fit the tool blade into the screw head on the back of the stopwatch, but whether from exertion or hunger or excitement at the possibility of being one step ahead of Kevin for the first time since, well, ever, I didn't know. I removed the screw from its socket and placed it on the rock next to the stopwatch, and put my knife down next to that.

I turned the stopwatch over one more time to make a note of the time. Less than two hours. If taking the back off caused the batteries inside to lose contact, I wanted to be able to set the watch back to near the current time so I would know how much I had left.

I worked my thumbnail into the gap between the front and back halves of the plastic case and worked it around the circumference. Little plastic tabs popped free as I did so, and finally the back came loose. I removed it carefully and set it aside.

The insides of the watch had been heavily modified. The display was possibly original. Beyond that, it was all new. The time keeping circuitry in the mid-1970's, when the watch had been built, would have been made of discrete electronic components like resistors and capacitors and inductors and would have filled most of the inside volume. It had all been replaced with a tiny monolithic chip held in place with a few wires, fine as human hairs, and a small dot of clear adhesive. The nine volt battery that would have powered such a device had been replaced with a dense stack of lithium button batteries, like the kind used in hearing aids, wrapped in electrical tape. The kicker was a little black box and a coil of antenna, a not-too-distant cousin to the tracking unit that had been planted on my truck.

The eyes are terrible pointing devices. Valerie had been looking, not at my shoes, but at the stopwatch hanging from its lanyard around my neck. Kevin had broken my watch intentionally after I was unconscious, so he could give me this one, so he could track me. Valerie had tried to tell me. Did I get it? Did I understand? No, Valerie, I'm sorry. Not until this moment I didn't.

I knew he had used a GPS device on my truck to follow us here, but had found nothing in his car, no tablet computer he could use to access the tracker. I had been looking for food or tools or weapons, but it hadn't occurred to me to wonder where that computer might have gone. He was carrying it with him, using it to track me. That was what he had been looking at in his backpack while I crept up behind him. That was how he knew exactly when to kick me.

With shaking hands – this time it was definitely excitement – I reassembled the stopwatch. I checked the LED display; it was still running. I folded up the knife and put it back in my pocket and then got up. I left the watch where it lay and stepped away from it.

For the first time Kevin didn't know where I was, even if at the moment the error in his knowledge was only ten feet or so. It's hard to describe the sense of freedom I felt, as if the weight lifted from around my neck far surpassed that of the watch. I could move, plan, act without him keeping track of me.

Oddly what I also felt, in addition to elation, was anger. He had ambushed me, kidnapped my wife, smashed the bones in my hand to smithereens, cracked my ribs, murdered an innocent couple whose only crime was camping in the wrong place at the wrong time, and he made my dog miss breakfast, but somehow the fact that he had been cheating throughout made me the angriest of all. If that seems weird, in my defense I was half-starved and almost certainly had a concussion at the time.

I wanted to climb to the ridge and yell 'Cheater!" out into the valley. Counterproductive, I know, but the urge was there nonetheless. I felt it, building in my throat like a growl, and gave it a restrained voice as an impressive string of muttered curses, like I would hear my father utter when he would bash his knuckles while working on the car. Dad, you taught me so well.

The urge thus quenched, I began to pace. I always think better when I'm moving, and I realized that I had to think everything through carefully. This was all I was going to get, the only chink in Kevin's armor I was going to find, and it wasn't so much of a chink as a seam, a nearly invisible slit, and whatever plan I came up with, it would have to be a good one. Kevin was uninjured whereas I was doing my impression of the walking wounded. I needed an idea, a really great one.

My first instinct was just to leave the stopwatch where it lay. Indeed, the thought of picking it up gave me a hollow feeling of dread, what Valerie must have felt as Kevin locked the collar around her neck. The thought of putting myself back into Kevin's game on his terms, doing so willingly, I could hardly get to compute. I would have rather picked up a rabid fisher cat and shoved it down my pants. Also, if Kevin wasn't tracking me, I could go and get help. If I knew the direction in which help lay, which I realized I didn't, and if I had the time, which the stopwatch informed me I didn't. If I had figured all this out last

136

night, or better yet yesterday, I could have. Now? No. Finally, depending on how accurate Kevin's tracking hardware was, and how often he looked at it, he would come to realize that the device was no longer moving, which might lead him to believe that I had figured out his game or lost the stopwatch. Either way, it would put him on high alert. I didn't need him on high alert. I needed him on low alert, non-existent alert, comatose alert. This meant he had to believe everything was working just as he had planned it. The stopwatch had to keep moving. I looked around to see what might help me there.

I could tie it to a branch, let a breeze wave it around, but not only was there no appreciable breeze, but I didn't think such a simple back and forth motion would fool him for long.

Somehow attached it to a wild animal, a deer, rabbit, or bird perhaps, presented an interesting possibility, though a deer might run faster than possible for a man, and a rabbit might scamper into a burrow hiding the signal entirely, and a bird would report my position as hundreds of feet up in the air. How would I even go about catching one long enough to attach it? Nothing useful lay down that line of reasoning.

For a long time I became fixated on the idea of the river. I could build a little raft, set it afloat with the stopwatch on it. The more I considered the idea, the smugger I became at my own brilliance. The water would keep it moving indefinitely. Then I began worrying about the stopwatch not being waterproof enough. Sure, we'd taken a dunk together, but perhaps I had gotten lucky, and maybe by taking it apart and putting it back together again I had damaged the seal. I also worried about the raft getting hung up somewhere and stopping, and if Kevin's GPS had geographic information, it would tell him that I was back in the water, which seemed farfetched. It would also go wherever it was the river was going, and once the stopwatch was a couple of miles downstream with no indication that it was ever coming back he would become suspicious.

I stopped my pacing, closed my eyes, and tipped my head back. I gave myself a little shake to loosen up my muscles, which made both my ribs and hand hurt. I took a few deep breathes to clear my mind.

"OK, brain," I said. "You're going to have to do a lot better than that."

I opened my eyes again to give the world a fresh look, gain a new perspective, and come up with the idea that was going to save the day.

And I saw it. It had been right in front of me the whole time. Sitting there right in front of me.

Wagging his tail.

Twenty-Four

I hated my plan almost from the moment I conceived of it, and I hadn't even finished half-baking it yet. Tonk – loyal, trusting, octogenarian Tonk – was going to be my diversion. When I attached the stopwatch to his collar, he would keep moving, keep Kevin distracted, while I did whatever it was I was going to do. And if Kevin caught up with Tonk, discovered my ruse, Tonk would bear his ire. And if I failed, Kevin would use the GPS to track Tonk down and kill him. There were many other alternatives I could envision, and no doubt others I could not. Pretty much all of them led to Tonk dying, except that one small sliver of all possible futures in which I won, a probability which I saw as so slivery it was hardly worth mentioning. By attaching the stopwatch to his collar, I would be welding our fates together.

I looked at Tonk and knew that I was going to do it; he was my only option.

Time was short. I had a lot of things to do, not the least of which was figuring out where Kevin and Valerie were. I retrieved the stopwatch and looped it again around my neck. No beast of burden in recorded history every hated its yoke so.

Tonk and I climbed to the ridge. As we did so, my knees started to shake. I was tired and weak and cold and hungry. I had walked too far and scaled too many mountains, and even though the day was just beginning, I was dangerously close to the bottom of my tank.

The view from the top was spectacular as always. The sluggish, cloudy dawn had matured into a stunning day, the sky cloudless, a blue so sharp you could almost cut yourself on it, the forest the deepest possible green, a green so dark it was nearly black. The cold, however, had hung around. The air had a frigid bite that chilled my sinuses and sucked the moisture out of the back of my throat.

The backpack was immediately visible. Neon orange was a great color where visibility was concerned.

Kevin after spending the night nearby, rather than lay in wait at the campsite, had retreated to a more distant spot, and I thought I understood why. He liked clearings, the room they gave him to maneuver, a place where he could use his speed to attack and slip outside my grasp without the risk of getting tangled up in trees or bushes, without the risk of me getting a hold of him and using my size and weight to my advantage. I could almost picture it: flat, level, open, Valerie somehow immobilized as Kevin waited, pretended to be engrossed in something, perhaps something in the backpack again. It had worked once, so why not use it again? But what he was really doing was watching the GPS, drawing me out into the open even as he tracked my movements. He had one hell of a surprise coming if I could pull this off.

I knelt down, took a hold of Tonk's head and turned it, pointed into the valley towards the backpack. I don't know if Tonk understands the concept of pointing. I've pointed out a piece of popcorn I've dropped on the floor and he seems to get that right away. So maybe he understood. But maybe he couldn't see the backpack. For one, do dogs have color vision? I didn't know. Also, at his age, maybe his far vision was terrible. Maybe he needed glasses. As I pointed, he didn't perk up or nod his head sagely or give me a wink. I was only guessing that I was doing any good.

Next, I hunted around in the deadfall near the ridge, the remnants of small trees too frail to survive the brutal winter winds. I found and discarded a number of pieces as too short or too thin or structurally unsound until I came across one that strongly resembled a baseball bat. It was the same length, and pretty straight, and tapered at one end to a hand grip. All it lacked was the little knob on the end and Louisville Slugger imprinted on it to make it genuine. It had been weathered smooth and gray over the years, the grain fine and nearly imperceptible, and therefore I had no idea if it was oak or maple or what. I didn't much care, as long as it was solid, which it was, and pretty heavy to boot.

I ran into my first problem as I tried to swing it. I couldn't. My left hand wasn't coordinated enough to get up any kind of momentum. I had never batted lefty, and couldn't seem to figure out how to put my shoulders and hips into the swing, let alone aim the blow. My right hand with all its broken fingers could hardly hold onto it. I thought if I really focused, I might get one up at bat, but would drop it as soon as I hit anything.

I considered giving up the bat, setting it aside regardless of how perfect it looked for that purpose, and trying to whittle myself another spear. Then, while again searching the deadfall, I reconsidered. Did I think my left hand was going to be magically better at stabbing, which required higher finesse? Did I think my right would have any better luck grasping the slender shaft of a spear than the grip of a bat? No on both counts. I had to hope that when the time came a rush of adrenaline would allow me to swing the bat as I needed to. Even as I had that thought, I realized it was a false hope, and I began to doubt. Doubt risking Tonk's life. Doubt even the possibility that Kevin could be surprised.

I wracked my brains looking for an alternative and came up with other plans that were even worse than this one, if you can believe that.

This was it, the plan I had, the plan I was stuck with. I wanted to scream in frustration. I tried a few more experimental swings with my right hand, and they got progressively worse. My hand was getting weaker, my abused ribs complained more stridently. Practice was definitely not making perfect.

What was Kevin thinking at that moment, his GPS reporting my lack of motion while my time dwindled down to nothing? Was he becoming suspicious? Would he come looking for me? Neither possibility allowed me to use the slim element of surprise I had going for me.

I was going to have to make my plan work, somehow.

The police are prepared to deal with crimes. The EMTs are the perfect solution for health emergencies. We do all the other stuff, all the things that fall in the margins. Every fire, every car accident, offers its own special circumstances. Firefighters ad lib. It's what we do, what we're good at, making it up as we go along. It's why people call us when all hell breaks loose. We find a way.

I removed the lanyard from the stopwatch and used six inches of duct tape off the roll to attach it to Tonk's collar. There were only forty-five minutes remaining in Kevin's imposed twenty-four hour timeline. I marveled at the way these things always seemed to come down to the last possible minute in television shows and movies, the guy who defuses the bomb with two seconds left on the timer. It lent an uncanny unreality to my very existence, the feeling that I was living out some script, and frankly I'd have liked to ask for a rewrite.

I also found myself wondering what Kevin would do the moment the twenty-four hours were up. Would he hightail it out of the woods immediately or would he give me a grace period? He really wanted me dead, so that suggested a grace period would be in order, but I didn't want to test that theory if I could avoid it.

After some internal debate, I opened the blade on my pocket knife and taped that to Tonk's collar also, carefully, so he wouldn't injure himself. I didn't think I would get an opportunity to use it, and Valerie might be able to cut herself free while I had Kevin distracted and get away. I looped the tape back upon itself, creating a little tab, something I hoped Valerie could use to grasp and pull the knife loose without too much difficulty, but attached well enough that it wouldn't fall of while Tonk was on the move. These activities left another couple of feet of tape still on the roll. I couldn't think of anything to do with it, anything else that I needed to secure, but waste not, want not, I fitted the roll back over my hand and let it rattle around on my wrist.

I checked that everything was firmly attached to Tonk's collar, and then rechecked it. I was on the verge of checking everything for a third time when I recognized it for the delaying tactic it was. It was time to do this.

I sat Tonk down, looked into his eyes, tried to form a mind-meld with him. My hands resting on his flanks, I could feel the muscles under his skin bunched, tense. He knew something was going on, even if his walnut sized-brain didn't allow him to understand what.

"I know I've told you a lot of times that you have a walnut-sized brain," I told him. "I also told you I wished you were a Rottweiler and a Saint Bernard and a German Shepherd and a Presa Canario, and I think that's just today. But I want you to know that I love you just the way you are, and if you can just do one thing for me, I promise I'll feed you sirloin for a week."

143

Tonk seemed to be getting bored with my speech. He wasn't much of a win-one-for-the-gipper guy; he was more about getting down to business. At least I hoped that was the case.

Something scuttled underneath the leaves off to our left and his ears perked up, his head snapped in that direction. With difficulty I pulled his head back towards me, but his eyes remained focused on the leaves. I snapped my fingers in front of him, and grudgingly I regained his attention, tenuously.

I spent an inordinate amount of time trying to pick the right tone for my voice. Demanding, cajoling, pleading, fun? In the end I settled on just speaking to him.

"Go to your mommy, Tonk. Go to your mommy."

Twenty-Five

I released Tonk and waited. He did nothing. Well, he sat and scratched himself behind one ear, and then spent an inordinate amount of time licking himself in a manner I won't delve into, but otherwise nothing. When he was done grooming he turned and looked up at me, the expression on his face conveying something to the effect of 'were you talking to me?'

My heart sank. I didn't have any treats to bribe him with.

I imagined Kevin in his clearing, looking down at the GPS, seeing me parked out here in the woods, wondering what I was planning, what I was waiting for. How long would he wait? Surely not indefinitely. Would he eventually come out here to confront me? I didn't know, and didn't know if that would be better or worse for me. I was too exhausted to try and reason it out. This was the plan I had; I had to follow it through.

Tonk continued to sit and do nothing. I was considering giving him another pep talk, maybe putting some alpha male rumble into my voice, when he stood up. He shook himself, glanced in what I judged to be Valerie's general direction, and looked back at me.

"Go," I whispered and made small shooing motions with my
hands, afraid of derailing whatever train of thought was
gathering steam in his mind.

He huffed. This is a remarkably, almost human, sound he makes
sometimes to let me know when he is impatient or displeased. In
this instance I took it to mean that while he was a willing
participant in my plan, he didn't see it as a good one. You and
me both, I thought in reply.

He shook himself again and trotted off, and at that moment I was
committed. Whether or not Tonk went to Valerie, at some point
Kevin would realize that his tracking device was on my dog and
not me. The fresh idea hit me then that if he found Tonk
sporting his tracking device, he might choose to take that out on
Valerie. I had to end this before that happened.

I picked up the bat, fit it as best I could into my right palm, and
took two steps. The bat fumbled from my grasp and clattered to
the ground. I tried again, but couldn't even close my fingers
around the handle. My practice swings on the way down must
have exacerbated my injuries, caused blood to flow down to my
hand, turned my digits into little better than swollen sausages.

I took a few experimental swings with my left. Terrible. Utterly
without accuracy or velocity. I couldn't even get it to whoosh
through the empty air. Should I go at Kevin empty handed? Try
kicking him as he had done to me? Close my eyes, and hope that
when I opened them this would all turn out to be a bad dream?

Whatever I was going to do, I had to do it. Tonk could have
been at Valerie's side already. Kevin wouldn't remain fooled for
long. My brain, ever helpful, showed me a scene in which Kevin
picked Tonk up, held him and threatened to break his neck
unless I came out of the woods and offered myself for sacrifice.

Fine, empty handed it was. If things got desperate, I could always bite him. That strategy had worked for me in the past.

I put the bat down, and was just about to move out when I saw the remnants of the roll of tape rattling around on my wrist. There wasn't much left, only a couple of feet, but I thought I could work with it.

I peeled the last of the tape off the roll. I felt as though I should give the empty cardboard spindle a proper burial, like honoring a fallen soldier, a comrade who had stuck by my side through thick and thin, but with time running short I simply tossed it aside.

I again fitted the bat into my palm. I wound the tape around my hand and the bat. Perhaps I got the tape too tight. My hand began to throb immediately, but any attempt to correct it would result in the tape torn to pieces, and I didn't have any more.

I took a few experimental swings. Wow, that really hurt. It stressed my fingers, felt like it might dislocate my wrist, but I could get the stick moving fast enough to hum as it moved through the air. I wasn't in the slightest danger of dropping it now. With it taped in place, I couldn't put it down if I wanted to.

I started moving as silently as I could manage. That was surprisingly hard to do with a three-foot stick taped to my hand. I held it down alongside my leg, but it was heavy and long enough that it would drag on the ground if I let it, which I tried my darnedest not to do. I hoped Kevin was a creature of habit, that the layout would be the same as before: an oval space of open, him crouching big and obvious in the middle of it, Valerie restrained a little off to one side. If the geometry were different, say him in the middle with Valerie at his feet, things would go to hell quickly. Tonk would come trotting out of the brush to Valerie's side, and one look at the GPS, which would show him standing right on top of the tracker, would be all it would take.

The brush discernibly thinned just ahead. I faded to my left

147

because I thought Tonk had gone off more or less to the right. I kept hidden in the tree line, even as I tried to get some sense of the clearing I was skirting, some idea of where Kevin and Valerie were within.

I was finally rewarded with a spot that showed me what I needed to see, and it was about how I had envisioned it, the same as last time without the nearby river. Kevin crouched in the middle of the open space, the backpack open at his feet. From my angle I could see the tablet computer he held in his hands. He made a swiping motion, looked to his right, did the opposite of the pinching thing with his fingers, looked to his right again.

I shifted over and could see what he saw.

Valerie lay on the ground some distance to his right. There was no tree in this clearing, so to restrain her Kevin had forced her down onto her stomach and tied her ankles. He had then run a rope between her hands and feet, pulled it taught, drawing her back into a bow, her fingers brushing against the soles of her boots. Even for a woman as flexible as Valerie, that position had to be uncomfortable.

Tonk joyously capered about her, darting in to lick her face and then springing back. Bound, she was unable to escape his tongue. Already both cheeks and her forehead glistened.

Kevin gave the tablet a few swipes and pokes in frustration. He stood, turning full in the direction of Valerie and Tonk, which coincidentally put his back to me.

"No fair, Jack," he called. "You can't claim the prize before you've won the game."

He took another look at the tablet, was maybe starting to get the idea that something wasn't right.

"Jack?" he asked.

I chose that moment to strike, lurching out of the bushes, my stomach a boiling knot. No tiptoeing around; subtlety be damned. I would have taken the shock-and-awe approach, run into the clearing screaming my head off or perhaps yelling "Freeeeeedom!" like Mel Gibson in *Braveheart*, if I thought Kevin was the kind of guy capable of being shocked or awed. I didn't, so while I didn't yell, I came into the clearing as fast as I could, unwilling to trade speed for stealth.

I hit an uneven patch of ground and my wounded knee threatened to fold under me. I came within a hair's breadth of doing a face plant. I recovered, sort of, but found myself stumbling forward, running on my toes, my momentum totally out of control. If I hadn't already considered myself completely committed to whatever course of action I intended when I came within striking distance of Kevin, I was now. I couldn't have stopped if I wanted to.

I almost saw that as a good thing. It was time to push all my chips into the pot. There was no point in saving anything in my tank for later as there would likely be no later in which to use them. It wasn't as if I was holding back some great inner wellspring of strength and endurance anyway, but I gathered myself, collected the scraps, and leaned forward another smidge more.

I was looking at the back of his head as I approached. Close. Closer. Closer still.

His attention divided between the screen of his tablet computer and the world around him, I was pretty sure he heard me coming, but his brain was unprepared to parallel process the information. I've seen teenager drivers wrap their cars around trees and telephone poles doing essentially the same thing. Then it was like a light turned on in his mind, and he started to turn. I went from looking at the back of his head, to the edge of one ear, to most of one ear, to all of one ear full on. A slice of his cheekbone appeared like a crescent moon, and the tiniest edge of

149

an eye followed.

I found myself wondering just how good his peripheral vision was, because I was going to test that, and unless he failed that test, I was going to pay dearly.

Twenty-Six

I raised the club high, intending to drive him into the ground like a railroad spike, a tent stake. I was concerned that a Babe Ruth swing-for-the-fences could be ducked or dodged, while a downward strike was almost guaranteed to hit something, an arm, a shoulder. That would be good enough. It had to be. And if I hit him in the head I might get lucky and kill him with a single blow. Only yesterday I had been considering knocking him out and turning him into the police. Oh, what a difference a day makes.

The branch struck him dead center on the top of his head. His scalp split wide open, and like many scalp wounds it was a gusher. His reflexes were truly superhuman, and even as the blow landed, he let his lower body go limp, the tablet slipping from his hands, his knees and ankles folding up to lessen the impact. The downward arc of the attack reduced the effectiveness of this strategy, but it did keep me from crushing his skull outright.

The vibration back up the shaft to my broken hand no doubt hurt, but I was cruising along on pure adrenaline by that point and all that pain was distant and muted, my nervous system swaddled in thick cotton batting. I used the momentum of the blow to get my speed back under control, get me solidly on my feet.

At the bottom of his crouch, Kevin redirected his motion into a roll away from me. The branch glanced off his shoulder as he did so, but only managed to tear his shirt a little bit. I pursued him. He finished the roll with an athletic, almost graceful, jump and spin that set him back on his feet facing me. The effect was spoiled as he staggered unsteadily. Blood poured down his face, ran into his eyes, and he shook his head like a dog to clear them, flinging droplets everywhere, some of which I felt dot on my face like warm rain.

He drew his knife from its sheath hastily, raising it up even as he finished weaving his fingers through the knuckle holes. I curled my swing downward, drawing the momentum of the branch in a circle, like a batter warming up in the batter box, and rotated my shoulders into a backstroke. It caught him in the hand, breaking a few of his fingers and sending the knife flying from his grasp and off into the woods. Better and better.

I stepped forward, my foot coming down on something that felt solid, but then yielded with a glassy crunch. I managed to keep my balance and didn't let whatever I had just broken distract me. Reversing the swing at the bottom of travel, I brought it back towards him again. It wasn't a great blow; my hips were turned square to him and my injured ribs couldn't take the stress and my shoulders didn't have the strength to create the kind of acceleration I would have liked. Also, despite the tape, I was losing my grip on the wood. Still, it slammed solidly against his ribs, likely cracking a few.

He clamped his arm down, trapping my weapon against his side, and pivoted his body, dragging me towards him. As I approached, he hit me in the chest, but my ace bandage wrapping absorbed most of the punch.

152

I continued to stumble forward until we were entangled, like
ungraceful dancers. I reached out with my left hand and grabbed
a hold of his right hand, crushed down on his broken fingers like
an over-aggressive jock at a high school reunion. His eyes flew
open wide and his mouth was a big 'o' of surprise and, I'd like to
think, pain.

And just like that, I seemed to be out of limbs to hit him with. I
couldn't get the branch free of his grip or my hand free of the
tape, not that my broken hand would have been good for much.
I wasn't going to let go of his right hand, stop grinding those
bones together, even as I knew on some level that wasn't going
to win the fight for me. He wasn't going to die of broken
fingers. I didn't have any good ideas.

But Kevin's training gave him one. He stamped down rapidly on
my foot twice. It hurt enough that I felt it, even through my shoe
and the adrenaline haze, and he might have smashed some toes
with his combat boot.

Impulsively, I head butted him. I didn't aim it and we were
about the same height, so we just met forehead to forehead, like
cracking two bowling balls together. It was a terrible idea, and I
can't imagine what possessed me to do it, but I was desperate to
find a way to do him some damage, and damage him I did, he
and I both. The agony blasted through the adrenaline, an agony
like my skull was splitting open. The whole world wavered.

When my vision cleared and cognition returned, we were in the
same position as before, and I was afraid of him breaking my
toes if he hadn't broken them already, so against all better
judgment I head butted him again. I tried to turtle my neck, see
if I could get my forehead to meet his nose, and he did the same
thing, and again our foreheads collided. There was an explosion
that annihilated all rational thought. It felt as if my head was
going to come off, and I was torn between the fear of that
happening and relief that if it did, I would get some distance
between the rest of my body and the pain. I actually heard

church bells ringing.

I lurched backwards like I was reeling from a stroke. The tape
tore loose and I lost my grip on the branch and fell onto my ass.
I found myself staring up at Kevin, a position I had been in far
too often lately. I had some trouble focusing and my thoughts
were running thick and muddy and chaotic. I needed to get to
my feet, but my mind was consumed with concern over the fact
that I might have left the headlights of the truck on yesterday
while I was searching it, and if so the battery was going to be
stone cold dead when we got back to it.

Kevin swayed and blinked almost sleepily. Streaks of blood ran
from his split scalp down his face, dribbled off his chin, stained
the front of his shirt. I could feel dampness on my forehead,
maybe his blood, maybe mine. Did it really matter at this point?
He seemed to come to himself suddenly, noticed the branch
trapped in his armpit, and did a neat little motion where he
flipped it free and caught it in the same hand, fully brandished,
ready to brain me. A slow, lopsided grin split his bloody lips.

The message from my head to my feet to get moving was caught
in a backlog of traffic consisting mostly of childhood memories.
The one I was stuck on at that moment was of the time when I
was six and made popcorn myself in an old hot oil popping
machine, and how I had used way too much oil. The resulting
popcorn had been saturated, like little greasy sponges, and nearly
inedible, so naturally I ate it all, and later threw up on the rug in
the upstairs hallway.

Kevin began raising the branch to strike, then thought better of it
and cast it aside. I guessed that he didn't want the unsatisfying
experience of bashing me to pieces with a stick when he could
get up close and personal and do it with his bare hands and feet.
He took a deep breath and steadied himself, shifting into his now
familiar fighting stance.

I lay slumped on my back, my cognitive processes too short

circuited to put up even a meager defense. It looked like my last thought on earth might be, 'Man, I ruined that carpet.'

Then I saw Valerie come up on Kevin from behind, pieces of rope wound around her wrists, the ball gag still in her mouth. She gave an animalistic grunt and stabbed Kevin in the back of the neck with my pocketknife.

Even as wounded as he was, I marveled at his athleticism, the efficiency of motion as he pivoted from his hips, through his waist, up to his shoulders. He built up astonishing rotational speed all the while keeping his feet solidly rooted. At the peak of his angular momentum his fist shot out and struck Valerie in the side of the head. She literally left the ground, as if hooked by a cable attached to a speeding car, and flew at least a dozen feet to land in a heap. Tonk raced over to check on her.

As Kevin rotated back I noticed my knife still embedded in his neck. It was stuck off to one side. Another inch to the left and she would have missed him entirely. The fingers of his right hand broken, Kevin reached back awkwardly with his left and grasped the handle.

I've been taught in the fire department and learned firsthand that embedded foreign objects can be a tricky business. I've seen people impaled on pipes and skewered on bits of cars, stabbed with big pieces of plate glass. We're not talking about removing a splinter and you don't just rip them out willy-nilly. The knife was in all the way up to the hilt. Sure, the blade was only three inches long, but the neck is a complex structure, crowded with muscles and tendons, critical nerves, and the big pipes that feed blood to the brain. Were it my neck, or my accident scene, I would have packed the knife handle in gauze and tape to stabilize it and let the staff in the ER do their thing, but frankly I was kind of past giving Kevin helpful advice.

The angle was bad for him, and as I've mentioned I kept the knife sharp, and Kevin pulled it out cockeyed, the blade effortlessly slicing through the meat of his neck along the way like the proverbial hot knife gliding through butter.

The fountain of blood began instantly, and the warm gush made him instinctively drop the knife and clap a hand over the wound. He looked around, but I'm not sure for what, perhaps an ambulance. Whatever he was looking for, he didn't find it, and he turned back to me. I would have said his face flushed with anger, but very little blood was getting to his head, certainly not enough to flush anything. I guess I would have to say his face paled in anger. He took half a step forward and kicked me in the thigh. It was a nothing blow, probably less than ten percent of what he would normally be capable of delivering, and so came just short of snapping my femur. It definitely resulted in a bone bruise I would hobble around on for at least a month.

Valerie had recovered well enough to struggle to her knees. She worked on the strap holding the gag in place, managed to wrench the ball out of her mouth, and threw it into the bushes. She breathed heavily and spat, likely trying to get the taste of rubber off her tongue.

Kevin looked like he was going to kick me again, but he didn't have it in him. He slouched, appeared to be on the verge of collapsing, but somewhere within himself found the strength to stand up straight. Then his face went blank, and he toppled over straight, like a falling tree.

Twenty-Seven

Kevin died, but not quickly, and not well.

He lay on his back gasping, his hand clamped grimly to the side of his neck as his blood seeped out between his fingers, first in little, red, high-pressure pulses, then more sluggishly as the puddle in the dirt around him grew.

Valerie sat on a rock nearby, absentmindedly rubbing at the raw spots the ropes had left on her wrists, and watched it happen with no expression on her face at all. I would have been more comfortable had she displayed a little hatred or anger. The nothingness, as though she were watching paint dry, and not even a color she particularly loathed, was unsettling.

I did manage to get one brief blip of emotion out of her when I stepped forward to try and render aid. Even for Kevin, who had spent the last twenty-four hours trying to kill me, I couldn't just stand there and watch him die. That's likely a firefighter reflex of some kind. With only a single step in his direction, and not actually an entire step but just a small fraction of a step, a miniscule fraction, the tiniest iota of a leaning towards, Valerie's head snapped around like that scene from *The Exorcist* and she growled, actually growled, a low rumbling emitting from somewhere deep in her throat. Without word or argument I backed off, and she went back to watching.

After more than an hour, far longer than I would have thought he would survive, Kevin seemed pretty far gone. His eyes were glassy and his breathing was shallow, though he still managed to keep his hand pressed to the wound for all the good it was doing him. Waiting, expecting each breath to be his last, watching as he writhed weakly on the ground like a dying animal, became unbearable for me. I wanted to leave, but didn't have the crane that I thought I would need to move Valerie, who looked bound and determined to see the entire show right up until the final credits rolled.

Thinking of credits rolling made me think of movies, which made me think of movie snacks – Jujubees, Junior Mints, Good N Plenty – which reminded me of just how hungry I was. I crossed the clearing to the backpacks and rooted around. I found my car keys and pocketed them, and then turned up a granola bar. I began unwrapping it, but the wrapper crinkled so loudly that it seemed to me an obscenity to eat it while Kevin was busily bleeding out, like noisily smacking chewing gum during a funeral. I figured I could survive just a bit longer without it, and put it away unopened. I did take out a bottle of water, quietly cracked the cap, and drank half of it in one go. Propriety has its limits. I offered water to Valerie and was rebuffed, gave some to Tonk, and then polished off the bottle myself.

I opened a sandwich bag of kibble and dumped it on the ground. Tonk, who probably would chew gum at a funeral without a care in the world, rocketed over and gobbled it down in record time, and came back looking for more. I began searching for the other bag that I knew must be in the backpack somewhere, unless Kevin had eaten it or fed it to Valerie, when I looked up and saw Kevin reaching for her.

It wasn't an aggressive move; he didn't have the strength for that. But Kevin, who should have by all rights already died, had turned his head and held a quavering arm out to her just an inch or two off the ground. "Valerie," he said in haunting tone, his voice crammed with the absolute maximum of anguish and sadness and loss that one word could convey.

Valerie, in response, stood up and stepped toward him, planting her left foot as she came, delivering two solid kicks to the side of his head with her right. She did this entirely without hesitation, with none of the pulling-it-up-short that I thought would be natural when kicking a completely defenseless human being lying on the ground in the side of the head. She had gone for the absolute maximum damage she could inflict. She kicked him with such force, like she was going for the Super Bowl winning field goal from the fifty yard line, that I was halfway surprised his head didn't come clean off his shoulders or that her hiking boot didn't cave his skull in.

The momentum of the kicks rolled Kevin partly onto his side before gravity rolled him back. His arm flopped to the ground. He was knocked out cold and his hand came off his neck, but only a small rivulet of blood flowed. His blood pressure must have truly been in the basement.

Afterwards she returned calmly to her seat.

Maybe, just maybe, with whatever Kevin had done to her, something had been seriously broken inside my wife.

And still, somehow, Kevin lived on, though he never regained consciousness.

I passed the time by sitting until my ribs would start to throb, and then getting up and pacing until I was dizzy and my knees ached, and then sitting down again. The waiting with nothing to do was making me aware of the significance of my own injuries. There was no position that I found comfortable for more than ten minutes at a time.

While wandering around I came across Kevin's tablet computer. I vaguely remembered stepping on it during the fight. The screen was cracked and the body was bent into a shallow vee. I tried to turn it on anyway, leaned on the power button until it put a little dent in my fingertip, but was unsurprised when it failed to boot up. I got not so much as a flicker out of the screen. I shook my head and tossed it aside.

The sun slid behind a nearby peak, and the light was so cleanly and abruptly sliced off by the granite edge that it was like someone had flipped a switch in our little valley. The sudden darkness was better, and it was worse. I couldn't see Kevin anymore, but I could still hear him breathing, or at least what he was doing which passed for breathing. The darkness seemed to amplify it, echo it, so that it doubled and redoubled around us until I couldn't hear anything else. It was a sound I was certain I would hear in my nightmares forever. I squeezed my eyes closed and tipped my head back, then opened them and looked up at the stars, wondering if Kevin could see them with his dying eyes.

It seemed like hours but could have been minutes later that Kevin finally gasped and rattled and stopped breathing entirely. The silence was absolute, even the breeze hushed. I heard the crunch of Valerie's boots as she got up. I could just discern her outline as she approached.

"Give me the flashlight," she said flatly.

I dug one out of our backpack and turned it on and placed it in her outstretched hand, and then followed her back to where Kevin lay. She shined the beam on his face. His mouth hung askew – her blows had broken his jaw – and his eyes were open, drained of their life, two lusterless marbles.

She stood watching him in silence for some time. She breathed in, breathed out. I tried to read some emotion into that – relief or sadness or something – but in the end decided that I was reaching to find something that just wasn't there. She was only breathing.

"Let's go home," she said at last.

"Yes, ma'am," I replied.

Twenty-Eight

It turned out that we didn't really know which way was home.

Valerie set off in one direction and I in another, and then we both stopped when we realized we weren't headed the same way. My internal compass was completely frazzled by that point; beyond being pretty certain we were still somewhere in northern New Hampshire, I had no idea which way was north. I was somewhat relying on gravity just to keep up and down in good working order. I was aware there were people who could chart a perfect course from here to Santa Barbara, California using nothing but the stars. Alas, with my PhD and all the pointless skills and minutia I have crammed into my brain, I was not one of them. I didn't know how we would find our way home.

Tonk stood between us, looking back and forth, before trotting off in a third direction. He seemed to go with such purpose, such certainty, that we both followed him.

Valerie and I must have looked like refugees fleeing a war zone. I hung on her, she on me; we supported each other as best we could. My hand was a swollen mess, my chest cavity felt like it was lined with shards of broken glass which scraped against my lungs with every breath. Valerie's external injuries appeared minor, but inside, where it counted, Lord only knew what was going on. Her gaze was fixed, her lips pressed into a thin, determined line.

We walked, or perhaps staggered would be a better word, through the night. My hunger returned, as did my thirst, and I thought of the backpacks both she and I had neglected to pick up. At least, I consoled myself, I had my keys, and the flashlight whose beam shone bright and true. Yet I was aware of the irony of starving to death lost in the wilderness after all that we had survived.

Eventually we crested a hill and were greeted by the muted, cloud-shrouded glow of the coming dawn at our backs. Somehow we had walked all night.

In the morning light I could see the bruise where Kevin had hit her. It was big and dark, encircling her eye, encompassing part of her cheekbone and flowing down to her jaw line. The eye on that side was swollen closed to a slit.

Our heading was roughly west, which in my mind meant, if nothing else, we would run across Interstate 93, the major north-south roadway in NH. How could we miss it?

Then, a few hours later, I was starting to debate with myself just how we could have missed it. What the next north-south road and how far away from Vermont were we? I was wondering if it was possible to accurately navigate from the fuzzy ball of brightness that was the sun swaddled in clouds and how much dimly-remembered Euclidean geometry I would have to recall to do so, when suddenly we stumbled out of the woods and into the deep grass of the parking lot.

I took a shallow, painful breath and let it out in a huff, which was about as close as I could come to jumping around and screaming

"Yippee!" at the top of my lungs. But trust me; inside I was dancing a jig.

We climbed into the truck. Tonk had to be helped, and he collapsed as soon as he hit the seat. How he had walked ten or maybe twelve miles during the night, maybe twenty or even thirty over the last day, on his little legs, I had no idea. Other than completely exhausted, he seemed OK. Valerie buckled herself into the passenger seat, but gave no other indication that she was really aware of her surroundings.

As I clicked my own seat belt, the shoulder strap felt like it was crushing my lungs against a bed of nails. I had to reach across my body and the steering wheel to turn the key with my left hand, but even left handed I trusted myself more than Valerie in her condition to drive. I turned the key and got a dashboard full of indicator lights but not a peep from under the hood. I leaned forward and groaned in frustration, then groaned again because of the shoulder strap cutting into my chest. Then I recalled that I had pulled the engine fuses earlier.

"Fuses," I muttered to Valerie, who gave no sign she had heard me.

I got out and found the fuses just where I had left them, and took a moment socketing them back where they belonged. The truck caught on the first try, but some smoke puffed out from the vent slots at the bottom of the windshield. I must not have gotten the fuses back in the right places, and one took more current than it was rated for and gave up the ghost. Probably the AC wouldn't work or the emission controls were offline. I didn't give a shit; it was running.

I put it in gear and headed for the nearest hospital. On the way I tried to engage her, asked her how she was feeling, if she was hurt. I got nothing.

It should have been smooth sailing from there, relatively

speaking of course, so naturally a tire blew just as I merged onto 93. I managed to limp my truck into the breakdown lane on the side of the road and put it into park. Changing the tire wasn't an option. For one, the tire iron was lying at the bottom of some river, but even if I'd had it, no way was I changing a tire one-handed. I flipped on my hazard lights and stood on the side of the road waving my good arm.

Morning commuters whizzed by me with eyes locked straight forward. Some drank coffee; others futzed with their phones, put on makeup, styled their hair. One had a newspaper spread out across the steering wheel and dashboard. No one paid any attention to me or stopped to help, though I'm sure being covered in dried blood wasn't helping.

I was just about to give up, wondering if I was up for another long walk to the nearest police station or hospital or whatever I might find, and if I should try and drag Valerie and Tonk along with me or if I should let sleeping dogs lie, when a Littleton firefighter on his way to work pulled over. He looked so much like the stereotypical firefighter, beefy, with a shock of red hair and a waxed handlebar moustache that I busted out laughing. Stress will do that.

He took one look at me and radioed for police and ambulance, and then came over. "Are you OK? What happened to you?" he asked. The fire department lights on top of my truck were likely the reason he was treating me so casually, because the whole scene must have looked hinky as hell: bloodied guy laughing like a lunatic, catatonic woman, nearly unconscious dog, truck with a smashed in window.

"You wouldn't believe me if I told you," I said, trying to quell my laughter as I hunched over, my broken ribs a shifting mass of pain.

While he didn't seem to be satisfied with my answer, he didn't ask me any more questions. Instead he kept his eye on me and went and checked on Valerie. He got no more response out of her than I had.

The ambulance arrived, and we were loaded in back. I sat on one of the side benches while Valerie straddled the gurney with Tonk between her legs, which I'm sure was a huge violation of sterile protocols, but no one was going to take him from her. He was the only thing she had shown the slightest reaction to. She cupped his sleeping head where it rested against her thigh, and occasionally petted him with short, slow strokes.

The EMT took one look at my hand, realized that it was going to take a lot more to set it right than he could do in the back of an ambulance, and wrapped it in gauze and padding until it was the size of a basketball. He then went to work on my scalp wound.

His partner treated and bandaged Valerie's wrists examined her face and swollen eye, all the while murmuring soft questions to which Valerie gave no answers. She looked to me to be getting worse, all pale skin and shallow breathing.

A state police cruiser arrived and parked behind the ambulance, the lights on its roof popping and flashing, painting patterns on Valerie's bruised face.

"What's her blood pressure?" I asked the EMT.

"One hundred over sixty," he answered taking the stethoscope out of his ears, rolling the blood pressure cuff off her arm, "Is she usually that low?"

"No."

"What happened to her?" he asked.

I thought about that for a long time. "I don't really know."

The troopers stood talking to the Littleton firefighter between the fender of the cruiser and the guard rail. The firefighter gestured in our direction, then at my truck, and then shrugged. One of the troopers was taking notes on a pad.

"I need to take off her, uh, necklace," the EMT working on Valerie said to me.

I turned and looked. The EMT was just being polite. It was a dog collar and it looked like nothing other than a dog collar, and I had somehow not noticed she was still wearing it.

"Let me," I said.

I got up awkwardly, cradling my bandaged hand close to my body, and sat sidesaddle on the gurney facing her, Tonk between us. I gently put a hand behind her head and pulled her towards me. She moved stiffly, all her muscles locked up. It felt like I was posing a mannequin. I fumbled at the catch one handed, finally managing to get it open, leaning her back as I took the collar off her neck. It had left a ring of abrasion around her throat.

She tilted her eyes down minutely to look at the collar dangling from my fingertips, or maybe that was just wishful thinking on my part. I half turned and threw the collar out the back of the ambulance. It rattled off the hood of the cruiser, and then skittered along the pavement before coming to rest in the breakdown lane.

Both troopers and the firefighter stared at it where it lay. One trooper turned back to us, looked like he was about to say something, and then thought better of it. His partner went and collected the collar and put it into an evidence bag.

I turned back and looked at Valerie, but found only a shell that looked like my wife.

"Val?" I asked.

167

Nothing.

Her hands were resting on Tonk and I rested my good hand on hers. They were cold, so cold. Not a human temperature at all.

"We're taking her to the hospital," the EMT working on Valerie announced.

"The cops are going to want to talk to her," his partner warned.

"Then they can talk to her at the hospital," he replied. He leaned out and grasped the door handles and pulled them shut, then leaned back and banged a fist on the dividing wall with the driver's compartment. "Let's roll! Lights and siren!"

And with a lurch we were on our way.

Twenty-Nine

God bless the clumsy skier.

The Littleton ER was state of the art. They jammed an IV in my arm within minutes of me coming through the door. A first-rate trauma team that had my hand X-rayed and the bones set straight and the whole mess encased in plaster in only slightly more time than it had taken Kevin to smash it.

The nurse who helped me roll off the ace bandage gasped when she got a look at my chest, which meant something coming from a person who had likely seen the worst damage high-velocity skiing accidents had to offer. I couldn't blame her, though. I was a mass of blue and purple and red and black bruises, a sadomasochist's rainbow.

The doctor frowned at my chest X-ray thoughtfully before informing me, "You've got six cracked ribs, but the good news is that nothing is completely broken. The bad news is that it's going to hurt like a son of a bitch while we wrap you up, but you'll feel better afterwards."

He wasn't kidding either. I saw spots and very nearly passed out as they wound me in ace bandages from my armpits to my belly button far tighter than I had wound it, tight enough that it was a little difficult to breath. Once they were done, I had to admit it did do a wonderful job of holding everything together and in place.

All that remained after that was a few stitches in my scalp, and I'm an old hand at stitches. If they had handed me the needle and thread, I could have done them myself. I've had enough stitches to make 'Jesus Loves You' throw pillows for every trailer park in Arkansas.

Littleton police officers showed up and bagged my jeans and ace bandage as evidence. The hospital staff gave me a johnny in exchange, which didn't seem like a fair trade. The officers examined my wallet, my keys, and the granola bar they found in my pocket, didn't seem interested in those, and handed them back to me. Lacking a pocket in a johnny, I held these items in a clump in my one good hand. I had to put them down to sign the inventory sheet left handed. My signature looked like little more than a spastic scrawling that, maybe if you squinted, you could just make out the 'J.'

While they were wrapping up I asked the nurse if she could get me an update on Valerie. She jogged off to do so with a sense of urgency that I appreciated. Bobby Dawkins found me in the outpatient lobby waiting for her to return. I sat there like a refugee from some cataclysmic, natural disaster, all my worldly possessions piled in my lap.

"What are you doing here?" I asked him.

"The Staties pulled the registration out of your truck, saw the Dunboro address, and called me. I drove right up. They've already told me what happened. Are you OK?"

"As always, it's nothing that won't heal."

"Is Valerie alright?"

"Yes. No. I don't know," I told him.

The nurse arrived then. "Mr. Fallon, your wife is in Examination Room 3." She pointed down a nearby hallway, a little curl to the end of her finger indicating we should take a right where it hit a T intersection. "She's with a doctor right now, but you can see her as soon as they're finished."

"Thank you," I said.

She nodded once and dashed off, no doubt needed elsewhere. And it wasn't even ski season.

The walk down that hallway was the longest fifty yards of linoleum in my life. What was I going to find at the end? What condition was my wife in? Bobby lumbered along at my side, companionable, silent. And while I appreciated his lumbering presence, this was one of the rare occasions when I could have used a little conversation, mindless banter, anything to take my mind off the empty look in Valerie's eyes after I had removed the collar.

As I neared the end of the hallway, I'll admit I was afraid. Deep down core afraid. My wife is a strong person, but I'm aware there are limits. In news footage of people fleeing bombings or mass shootings, you can see it in their eyes. The belief that the rest of us walk around with, that despite all the terrible things that happen, the world is essentially a safe place; they've lost that. It's lost, and for some of them it's never coming back.

The doorway to Examination Room 3 was closed, a Littleton police officer stationed in front. I let out a sour breath that I hadn't been aware I was holding. Bobby led me a little farther down the hallway to a place where it widened into a small sitting area, four cheap plastic and chrome chairs, two shabby pine coffee tables, a plastic ficus in a plastic pot; an out of the way nook that hadn't seen the same renovation as the rest of the hospital.

He pushed me down into one of the chairs, crouched down to look at me at eye level. I could feel the cold plastic of the chair against my back where the johnny had gapped open. "Valerie is getting absolutely the best care possible. While we wait to hear from the doctors, can I get you something to eat? When was the last time you ate?"

I opened my mouth, and then closed it again when I realized I didn't know the answer to his question. Did an IV count? Had I eaten anything for breakfast yesterday morning? I couldn't conceive of planning to take a hike without breakfast, yet could only seem to vaguely recall drinking a cup of tea. And dinner the night before that? Chicken? Fish?

Absentmindedly I looked at the granola bar I held, uncertain what to do with it. The bright foil wrapper, the festive lettering on the front, my brain couldn't connect the dots. The thought never crossed my mind to open and eat it.

I was still staring at the granola bar and pondering Bobby's question when we were approached by two Staties, crisp uniforms, almost comically shiny shoes. They were built like fireplugs, walking side by side. Between their width and swagger and all the crap hanging off their equipment belts, they nearly filled the hallway. Certainly anyone trying to sneak a gurney past them was shit out of luck. In the sliver of light between them I could see a skinny man following behind dressed like Ranger Smith from Yogi Bear, right down to the funny hat he held in his hands.

Bobby and I stood and introductions were made all around. The guy in the back turned out to actually be a forest ranger. Who knew New Hampshire had those? Between Bobby, tall and wide, the two fireplugs, and the skinny forest ranger, I felt like I was surrounded by funhouse mirrors.

The troopers got right down to business. They listened to my story, which took far less time in the telling than I had thought it would. When you actually boiled it all down, it amounted to little more than Kevin had tried to kill me, and Valerie had killed him first. Her statement, when she was capable of giving one, would likely be much more complicated.

The forest ranger slid a stack of laminated maps from a canvas tube that he carried on a strap over one shoulder. The troopers pushed both tables together and the maps were unrolled on their surface. We grouped around it like football players in a huddle. The ranger pointed out the parking area where Kevin's car had already been found, marking it with a blue X using a grease pencil. A dashed line marked the trail up to the overlook. He then handed me the pencil, encouraging me to mark the rest of our travels, like a particularly deadly and convoluted panel from a Family Circus comic strip. Here's the dotted line showing the route Dottie's body was dragged by rabid wolves.

I marked the path down to where Kevin had faked his injury and laid his trap, back up to the ridge, to the cars, then back to the ridge. The line wavered along the ridgeline, but where did I climb down? Had Kevin and Valerie intercepted me in this clearing, or that one? Did I climb the same ridge again, or a different one? Where was the foundation? Then back down to the stream. The same stream? How far downriver had I been washed? Which peak had I stood upon to watch the sunset? Where had I spent the night? Where was the couple's campsite?

The trail became more and more uncertain, conjecture heaped upon speculation piled on top of estimation. By the time I marked the clearing of our final confrontation, the spot where I thought Kevin's body lay, everyone realized it was little more than a guess, and not a particularly educated one at that. Kindergarten. First grade, tops.

They consoled me. They would go out immediately in a helicopter with thermal imaging and send out K-9 search units on the ground. My directions could be off by miles, and they assured me they would still find the body. Nonetheless, I felt deeply frustrated as they thanked me and left. Not that it mattered to me if they found Kevin's corpse. He could rot out there nibbled on like carrion for all I cared, but I thought Valerie would want to know, would want proof of death.

I was still grinding my teeth, envisioning the maps in my mind, already questioning the path I had marked, when the door to Examination Room 3 yawned opened on its pneumatic hinge.

A doctor poked his head out. The room lights behind him were dimmed, and he squinted in the bright hallway fluorescents like the first groundhog of spring. He was short, bald, stood with kind of a hunch in his back, but that might not have been his age, just bad posture. I could see Valerie through the opening sitting on the exam table. Tonk lay by her side snoring loudly enough that I could hear him now that the door was open.

I moved for the doorway and the doctor stepped out to block my path, the officer shifting his position in support. As I debated pushing past them both, the door sighed shut behind him and I couldn't hear Tonk snoring anymore.

"Your wife has been through a terrible ordeal," the doctor began in a calming voice.

"I kind of didn't need you to tell me that," I interrupted, perhaps with more hostility and sarcasm than I had intended. Perhaps not.

He looked flustered, "Yes, well," he began.

"Can I take her home?" I pointedly interrupted again.

The doctor took a moment to collect himself. "As I was saying, Mr. Fallon, your wife had been through a terrible ordeal. She's dehydrated, with ligature marks, abrasions, and bruising on her wrists, ankles, and throat. Also, although she doesn't have a concussion, there is an oblique fracture of the orbit of her left

174

eye. But her physical injuries tell only part of the story."

Here he adopted a professorial tone, describing in cool, clinical terms her mental state. My sister, an oncologist at Sloan Kettering in New York, has told me some doctors fall back on jargon as a defense mechanism, a way of insulating themselves from patients and cases they feel will have a bad outcome, while others do it because they lack the ability to simplify complicated medical concepts, without any intended portents. As I didn't know enough about this doctor, I didn't know if this conversation should be scaring the shit out of me or not. I did know that as he spoke of her degraded response to stimuli, verbal, aural, and tactile, I felt as though I was losing a small piece of myself, perhaps of my soul, up, up and away, never to return.

"Given her condition," he continued, "I don't want to give her a sedative, but I'm going to provide a prescription in case she becomes agitated later. I advise you to seek psychiatric-"

His dialogue halted as the door to the room swung slowly open. Tonk came out, stood in the hallway looking at our silent gathering, and looked back over his shoulder. Valerie came shuffling out of the room, her eyes downcast. She fell into my arms. No tears, no words, just exhaustion, or so I hoped.

She was wearing a hospital johnny, a twin to my own, and some kind of disposable paper-like undergarments that crackled when I hugged her to me.

The Littleton cop cleared his throat, caught my eye. "We, uh, had to take her clothing for evidence."

I nodded like this was alright, though it wasn't alright at all. I couldn't see alright from where we were standing with the Hubble telescope. My clothes? Fuck it – I'll parade around the hospital au natural for all I care. But Valerie, after what she's been through, very much not alright. Indignities heaped upon indignities; how many more did she have to withstand? How many more could she withstand? Bobby glowered at the officer in my stead, which I appreciated.

The doctor wanted to keep her overnight for observation. I could see the words coming together, forming a sentence behind his eyes as though I could read his mind. I wasn't going to let that happen. A night of insomnia lying on an unyielding foam mattress between scratchy sheets underneath the cold fluorescent lights of a hospital room was not how her healing would begin. She was going to spend this night at her home in her own bed.

"I'm taking her home," I announced. "Let's go home," I murmured to her and began an awkward sideways crab walk down the corridor, Valerie glued to me.

The officer reached out and touched my arm. Maybe he was going to tell me that we couldn't leave. I felt my adrenaline rising, preparing for a big ugly fight if he chose to instigate one. As I did so, I found myself wondering just what the capacity of my adrenal gland was. One gallon? Two?

Instead what the officer said was, "We, uh, had to impound your truck." He ducked his head a little as though I might strike him and added, "Evidence." If I could have lifted my arms, I might have. Bobby, though I'm sure he knew all the rules of evidence, looked just about ready to hit him anyway. Good thing we were standing in a hospital; the other cop was about to need one.

Having seen enough violence for one day, Valerie defused the situation. "It's not important," she said to Bobby softly and slowly, her eyes closed, as though she was drugged, though the doctor has said she wasn't, "Just take us home."

Bobby, ordinarily a guy slow to anger and then even more difficult to calm, took one look at Valerie's face nestled in the crook of my shoulder and melted. "Your chariot awaits," he said.

Thirty

By the time Bobby got us home, December had reasserted itself
with a vengeance. The sky was a flat, iron gray spitting snow
and there was a cold, biting wind. We moved as quickly as we
could from the car to our house, which amounted to little more
than a broken shamble. I gasped as the wind knifed through the
thin johnny, dug icy fingers into the exposed skin above and
below the ace bandages. Bobby had pulled a Mylar blanket from
some emergency pack in his police cruiser glove compartment,
and I had wrapped it around Valerie. As she shuffled along, the
blanket crinkling like wrapping paper, she gave no indication
that she felt the cold.

Inside, I pointed her at the stairs and told her to go up to bed
where I would bring her food. She went, docilely, not like my
Valerie at all. Her head hung, she hobbled up the stairs like an
eighty year old, one hand white-knuckling the banister.

Bobby took a seat at the kitchen counter while I dumped a

double serving of Kibble into Tonk's bowl. He mashed his face into the food so excitedly that kibble went flying everywhere. He chewed and crunched like a wood chipper.

I retrieved a can of chicken soup from the pantry. Chicken soup, like Valerie had a slight case of the sniffles, a cold coming on, as though a hot bowl of soup could solve all. Opening the can took some doing. I clamped it painfully between my cast and my ribs, the opener awkward in my left hand. Bobby looked like he was going to offer to help, but intuitively knew this was something I wanted to do for myself, a small piece of the world that I could try and control.

Five minutes later it looked like the can had been gnawed open by beavers, but I managed to get it poured into a pot on the stove to heat without an enormous mess. I peeled off the label and rinsed the can and put it upside down in the drain rack to dry.

I had thought doing these things, little bits of routine, would help me feel more normal. Instead they highlighted my discomfort, like I couldn't quite connect to them, as if someone else was doing them. Everything felt unnatural and at a distance.

I stood, watching, waiting for the soup to boil, trying to relate with the world around me.

"You want to talk?" Bobby asked.

"What's to talk about?"

He shrugged, picked up the salt shaker from the counter and turned it in his hands.

"Should I talk about how I just spent the last twenty-four hours narrowly avoiding getting killed by some guy who had the hots for my wife? Or that my semi-catatonic wife is upstairs after spending a day tied up and beaten and," I had almost said raped, come oh so close. Of course she had been raped. Spoils of war.

Raping and pillaging is a time-honored tradition of mankind going way back, to before the Romans. But I couldn't bring myself to say it out loud, couldn't do it, as if doing so would somehow make it more real, so I concluded lamely with, "and whatever."

Bobby knew what I was talking about without me having said it. He put the salt shaker down, spent far more time aligning it precisely to the pepper shaker than necessary. He scratched at one eyebrow. "I just want you to know that I'm here to talk if you need to, or vent if you want to. For whatever." He realized that he had used the same word, whatever, that I had used, though obviously with a very different meaning. He frowned, reached for the salt shaker again, then withdrew his hand instead and folded both of them on top of the counter in front of him.

"Any idea when can I get my truck back?" That question was far down on my list, not really even in the top ten, or twenty for that matter. But it seemed like a safe and simple question, something that might lead me from where ever I was currently residing back to planet Earth, or if not there at least to a haven without conversational pit traps or land mines.

The question relaxed Bobby. It was something actually in his job description, something he could address. "Kevin is dead so they won't need evidence for a trial. They'll run it through their lab just as a formality. I'll make some phone calls and see if I can't get it bumped to the front of the line, speed up the process."

And just like that, we had run out of safe conversation. I couldn't think of a word that could pass my lips that wouldn't risk taking me somewhere I didn't want to go.

The soup was boiling and I poured it from the pot into a bowl. I gathered a spoon and napkin and carried them upstairs. Valerie was in bed, the covers pulled absolutely all the way to her chin. The paper johnny from the hospital was in a ball in the vicinity

179

of the wastepaper basket in the corner. I put the soup and accoutrements on the nightstand, picked up the wad and stuffed it in the trash. The paper underwear was in the wad, and I couldn't help but notice there were fresh bloodstains on them. My wife was bleeding, down there, not badly, but still.

I watched Valerie, her eyes closed, her breathing even. She appeared to be sleeping, or maybe she was pulling that trick kids do and faking being asleep.

"What did he do to you?" I breathed.

She gave me no answer.

I decided not to disturb her and left, closing the door softly behind me.

The soup had smelled good, set my own stomach rumbling. Back downstairs I opened a can for myself, again gnawed by beavers, poured it into the same pot on the stove. I did the same shtick with the soup can, and it felt no more natural than the last time.

Tonk, starving and exhausted, had eaten half of his food and fallen asleep with his face in the bowl, snoring softly, a ring of uneaten kibble scattered around him. The scene reminded me of watching one of my nieces or nephews eat, decimating a plate of food. Half goes in their mouths, half on the floor.

"There are resources available," Bobby said, the salt shaker one more in his hands. "Counselors and support groups for Valerie if she wants them. For you too. I have all the information at the station."

I nodded but gave him nothing more. Perhaps some time in the future I would be in a place where I could use that kind of help. Where ever I was at the moment, it wasn't in that place.

Bobby put the salt shaker back, carelessly this time, and stood, smoothing the wrinkles out of his uniform slacks with his hands. "I'm going to get back to the office, call about your truck. Whatev-" He had been on the verge of saying whatever again. Would that word forever hold such connotations for me? He withdrew and rephrased. "Anything you need, call me."

He turned, went to the front door, put his hand on the knob.

"Bobby?" I asked.

He paused, "Yeah."

"What will they do with his body?"

I'm not even sure why I had asked that question. In the back of my mind I thought maybe I would like to see him cold on the slab in the mortuary with my own eyes, and though I'm not a violent man by nature, maybe I would punch his corpse in the face for good measure. I grimaced inwardly at that thought, concerned about my own state of unhingedness.

"They'll look for next of kin. Assuming he has any, the State will release the body to them for burial."

At the word burial my brain perked up a bit, filled with a vision of me pissing on his headstone. I could see myself doing it: bringing a picnic lunch and a bottle of fine tequila, desecrating his grave, making a day of it. Maybe it would become an annual event.

Maybe I should ask Bobby for the phone numbers of those support groups.

Instead I held my tongue until he left, and went back to watching my soup boil.

Thirty-One

Three weeks passed.

The search for Kevin's body consumed a lot of money and a lot of man hours. Helicopters flew dozens of sorties and K-9 units ran through the mountains for days on end. Newscasts led with fifteen second video clips of their efforts: search and rescue teams traipsing through the hills carrying long poles they would use to stir up suspicious-looking piles of leaves or jab down into a narrow crevices looking for the body, otherworldly imagery from a helicopter-mounted thermal camera as it flew a grid pattern, a man in uniform hiking in the forest with a sable German shepherd cadaver dog, the dog racing to and fro, sticking its snout into holes and under logs.

Forest rangers stopped by the house several times to ask me more questions, show me more maps, grease pencils in hand. We would sit at the dining room table for hours, the corners of a maps weighed down with coffee mugs, as they offered suggestions. Did I remember climbing this ridge? When I had found the remains of the stone foundation, had it been this one or that one? Here or there? My memory had not proven all that great when fresh, and time had only made it worse.

Everything paused in early January for the first big nor'easter of the season, finally giving the ski resorts a solid base they could build upon. It raged for two days during which Valerie and I hid inside and talked to no one, not even each other, the world outside our windows a blinding white that was painful to look at. When it passed, though greatly hampered by the snow, the search started up again.

They found the remains of the other couple in the fourth week. The news reported their names as Mark and Laura Hopewell, newlyweds from Colorado. Their friends described them as warm and kind, avid outdoors people who had been waiting their whole lives to hike and camp in the White Mountains of New Hampshire, an experience they had saved for their honeymoon. They were in the ninth day of a planned twelve-day trip when Kevin came upon their campsite and killed them both.

I was glad they had been found, glad that their families had been given closure. I was even happier as it meant my directions were not worthless, that they would be turning up Kevin's hopefully vermin-gnawed corpse any day now.

That lonely, abandoned trail became one of the most-traveled in the region, hiker selfies festooning Facebook pages like badges of honor. So much for our own secret hiking spot. Someone organized a campaign to rename it after us – created an online petition and collected signatures and everything – which was a horrifying thought. Jack and Valerie's Near Death Experience? Death takes a holiday stroll? I couldn't imagine what was going through their minds. Thankfully the idea died quietly in some committee in the State House.

Late in January the helicopters and K-9 teams called it quits. The story had gained a little nationwide traction, and the decision to end the search for Kevin's body resulted in the Governor of New Hampshire holding a press conference. "My fellow New Hampshirites, as much as we would love to find the corpse of this sick fuck so Jack Fallon, one of our greatest hero firefighters, can punch it in the face, I can no longer justify the expense in light of the fact that the green fees at my country club are due."

OK, that's not precisely what he said, but I could read between the lines.

Volunteer hikers continued to wander the trail system, but at a much lower intensity level, and I began to think that Kevin might never be found.

I'm not concerned.

There's a lot of wilderness out there, and Valerie and I had wandered through the night and probably gotten turned around a couple of times, even with Tonk leading us. Trees all look alike, at least to me, and trails all look alike, and in the dark every rock looks the same as every other. The snow, when it came, obliterated every footprint, every drop of blood, every trace. Maybe in the spring, when the snow melted, he would turn up. Such had been the case before with missing hikers.

And the woods are full of hungry critters: coyotes, wolves, several species of large cat: cougars and lynxes and mountain lions for all I know. And bears, oh my! Ranger Smith could likely name them all. Maybe Kevin had been eaten, and might never be found except as an unrecognizable pile of bone chips mixed in with bear excrement.

But I'm not concerned.

I've been in the fire department a lot of years and I've seen a lot of dead. I've smelled dead. I've laid hands upon dead. Car accidents and suicides and machinery mishaps. Kevin was dead. Capital D Dead as I call it. It's not like he's a comic book super villain who is vaporized in an explosion in one issue only to reappear in the next with some cockamamie explanation why he wasn't vaporized, likely as not involving wormholes or time machines. I know that he's dead. I also know that his body might never be found. The White Mountains, ancient, patient, really know how to keep a secret.

Sometimes, when I lie at bed at night, my hand not hurting too badly and having found a position where my ribs don't ache, I have trouble believing that Kevin was human. Lacking his corpse, it is surprisingly easy to see him as an evil spirit, the embodiment of a curse I have brought upon myself and my wife. I know that sounds nuts, and by the light of day, as I'm sitting at the kitchen counter with the winter sun streaming through the window and turning my mug of Earl Gray tea a glorious amber color, like a fine aged scotch, it seems as ridiculous to me as it no doubt does to you. But at night, the silver moon hovering in a midnight sky and snow lying peaceful over the land, vast ships of painkillers cruising slowly, languidly through my bloodstream with their sails aloft, my mind runs in horror movie circles and creep show eddies.

I've had nightmares, a lot of nightmares, in which I come home and find the front door ajar. With a sense of dread I enter, certain I'll find Tonk beaten to death at the base of the stairs, but he's fine, joyous, capering around my ankles. I go upstairs, relaxing, relieved. The open door didn't mean anything, just a silly oversight. In our bedroom I find Valerie, the old Valerie, vibrant and happy, waiting for me and smiling. I come closer and we clasp hands, my broken one giving me no problems. Up close I can see that her smile is wrong, a rictus, frozen, and her eyes, there's fear in her eyes, and I don't understand why. Before I can ask what's wrong, Kevin comes out of a closet behind me. Our bedroom doesn't, can't, have a closet there as a hole cut in that wall would open out into the stairway, but dreams don't have to follow real-world geometry or architecture, do they? I try and turn but in her panic Valerie has clamped down on my hands and I can't get loose. Kevin draws his knife and drives it into my back. His knife is larger in my dreams,

185

elongated like a sword, and it punches right out through my chest and into Valerie. We stand like that, skewered together, bleeding, dying, as I watch the light go out in her eyes.

And that's one of the better ones. In others, I writhe in sweat-soaked sheets as Kevin floats above me, a ghost, a vampire, the blade of his knife held against my throat.

I kept expecting some big shock ending. Hollywood has conditioned us all to anticipate that the moment when life returns to normal is when the guy we all thought was dead turns out to not actually be dead, pops up in the back seat of a car, and cuts the hero's throat. I imagined Kevin doing that, and let me tell you I checked the back seat of every car before I got in, and occasionally popped the trunk and looked inside there too.

Did I say I'm not concerned? Because I think I'm damned concerned.

I haven't told Valerie yet, that they haven't found his body; she's having enough trouble sleeping nights as is. Maybe at some point in the indefinite future, when she's ready.

When we're both ready.

Thirty-Two

Bobby made a habit of coming over most mornings for breakfast, brought some paperwork with him and hung out for about an hour. We'd talk about how Valerie was doing or what was going on in my head or nothing at all. Maybe he was playing bodyguard, or maybe psychiatrist. Whichever, I appreciated the company and the little slices of normalcy he brought with him. When it was just Valerie and I at home, which was most of the time, the atmosphere got weird and heavy with all the topics we avoided and the things we left unsaid.

On one particular morning I was busily making eggs. With my right hand in a cast, I was learning to do a lot of things lefty. I could feed myself. I could wipe my own butt. I could even wash my hand between those two activities. But for the life of me I couldn't flip an egg over easy without destroying the yolk.

Bobby sat at the kitchen counter ignoring a cup of Oolong tea I had steeped for him in a Lake Winnipesaukee mug – he had refused my offer of anything more substantial to eat – sorting through a manila folder containing a heap of documents which lay open in front of him.

187

"His name was Kevin Mercer," Bobby said.

"You mean is," I corrected him.

"Huh?" he paused in his paper shuffling, a sheaf of pages held in each hand, and looked up at me.

"Is," I said, "His name is Kevin Mercer."

"He's dead, Jack."

"Anyone found a body yet?"

Bobby made a face like I was being ridiculous, and went back to his papers.

We'd been going around and around on this point ever since the search for Kevin's body had ended. Sure, I'd watch Kevin bleed out a couple of quarts of blood, and stop breathing, and shined a flashlight in his face, peered into his eyes. I'd certainly thought he was dead, but the lack of an actual corpse was maddening, and it was making me start to doubt myself. It had been dark. I had just wanted to get the hell out of there and go home. Had I rushed it? Maybe I hadn't looked closely enough, and maybe he had been holding his breath. I should have checked his goddamned pulse, I chastised myself, provided Kevin didn't have some monk superpower which allowed him to slow his pulse below the point of detectability. Where Kevin was involved, I wasn't willing to rule anything out.

"Fine. His name is Kevin Mercer," Bobby grudgingly allowed. "Mean anything to you?"

"Not a thing."

And I couldn't think of a reason why it should. Kevin, was – is, I corrected myself – the assistant to an attorney my wife had been having an affair with. Kevin and I had no direct relationship at all. At least now I had his whole name, for whatever that was worth. Thoughtless of him to have spent the day trying to kill me without formally introducing himself first. What was civilization coming to?

"Should we ask Valerie?" Bobby offered.

"She's sleeping," I said, but didn't add that she spent a lot of time sleeping. She got up late, skipped a lot of breakfasts, sometimes went to bed early, skipped a fair number of dinners as well. She looked to have dropped about ten pounds. For a woman who had been born with a good metabolism and attended yoga and Zumba classes regularly, it was ten pounds she didn't quite have to spare. You could see it in her face, her eyes retreating deeper into their sockets, cheek bones so pronounced they made Angelina Jolie's face look chubby in comparison.

Bobby glanced at his watch, and then at me, gave a concerned frown. He looked like he was about to say something about Valerie and her possible overuse of the snooze button, but then thought better of it and shrugged, "It's just a little wrinkle. It doesn't matter. His name was all over the paperwork with the rental car agency, and the attorney, Craig Lerner, confirmed that Kevin and Valerie know each other."

"Did Kevin ever happen to mention to Craig that he was planning to kill Valerie's present husband, namely me, and keep her as a captive bride?"

"No," Bobby said quietly.

And that little wrinkle did very much matter, because with two dead hikers and lacking Kevin's body to corroborate our story, Valerie and I actually looked pretty good for their murders. Sure, the rental car was a problem with that theory, but another way to look at it was that we had lured Kevin up there on some pretense, and when he arrived in his own rental car we had killed him for reasons unknown and done something as yet

189

undiscovered with his body, making us guilty of not two but three murders. The icing on that evidentiary cake as far as the detectives were concerned was that I had Laura Hopewell's blood on my clothing from when I had tried to help her.

Meanwhile the Hopewell friends and relatives were becoming quite vocal in their questions, both online and in the media, about why we weren't under arrest. I had to admit that from their point of view things looked pretty grim.

If Valerie had displayed any interest in watching the news, I would have had to find a way to dissuade her. On top of everything else, she hardly needed to be accused of murder several times a day by overly cheerful newscasters and pundits.

On an almost entirely separate topic, the rental car company was none too happy about me beating the living shit out of their property with a tire iron, though in the scheme of things that problem was so far down my list it was in the noise.

"Anything on the knife?" I asked.

Bobby shook his head. Along with Kevin's body, the knife was nowhere to be found, as well as our backpack. They had found Kevin's backpack two weeks after locating the Hopewells, which meant they were looking in the right place. His backpack had contained zip ties, rolls of duct tape, and about a mile of rope, everything the enterprising bachelor needed to immobilize the object of his affections. Where Kevin's body, the knife, our backpack had all gone was a fine and disturbing mystery.

Bobby picked up the folder and turned it around, lobbed it so that it landed open in front of me with a weighty thud.

I probably shouldn't be looking at this stuff given that it might end up as evidence in my own murder trial, but Bobby didn't doubt our story for an instant. For all I knew it was his confidence that was keeping me out of jail. My reputation with the State Police was decidedly less stellar, and if it were up to them I suspected I'd be receiving three hots and a cot at the State's largess already.

On top of the stack in the file folder was a thick pack of pages bound with a heavy clip. I turned off the heat under the eggs and looked through the papers, studied the progress of the investigation into the origin of the knife I had claimed was in Kevin's possession. The report listed it that way: "claimed as being in the possession of..." On the one hand, I allowed that it was accurate, but on the other it would have been nice to have at least one small facet of my story accepted as fact.

My initial impression, that the knife was genuine military issue, turned out to be in error. Over a dozen commercial companies, most in China, made knives like it with only small variations in blade length or handle material or paint color to differentiate them. My description of it, which I had thought would nail down at least the manufacturer in no time, turned out to be insufficient. Who knew such a weapon, which as far as I could see had no other designed purpose than to gut human beings, would be so popular? Again, what was civilization coming to?

As I reached the end of the pack, I could see that although the police hadn't given up on it, the search for where Kevin had gotten the knife might well come up dry without the knife itself to work from. Too bad; his ownership of it would have bolstered our story.

"Damn," I said.

I flipped through some more papers in the folder hoping to find some good news.

Notes from the investigation showed the detectives had no idea what to make of the GPS units found in my truck and the modified stopwatch. Made by a high-end electronics manufacturer in Taiwan, there seemed to be some disagreement as to whether they were only sold to foreign military or could be purchased by anyone. Regardless, they weren't easy to get a hold of, and their presence didn't mesh well with the narrative of Valerie and me as a Bonnie and Clyde couple joined by marriage and our mutual love of mayhem and bloodshed. If anything, they supported our version of events, so score one for the good guys.

Other paperwork indicated that Kevin rented and lived in a loft apartment in a mill building in Manchester that had been converted into trendy living spaces. An inventory of the contents of his apartment was unremarkable. A search of the files on his laptop was still pending at the State lab. Interview reports with various neighbors turned up nothing significant. He had no current significant other anyone knew of, nor close friends. Co-workers knew next to nothing about his personal life, reporting that he rarely if ever took part in office social events. His family – both parents, divorced, and one brother – had not heard from him recently, though found nothing unusual about that; they were not a particularly tight-knit or chatty family. The man had passed through his existence like a wraith. There was a watch on his bank account and credit cards, but both were idle, at least as of five days ago, the last time the report had been updated.

I came across forms for incorporation.

"Hey," I mentioned to Bobby, "he opened an LLC."

"I noticed that. The State Police put a request in with the forensic accountants in Concord to see if they can track down anything about it. They're so backed up with mortgage fraud cases from the housing collapse, they tell me they'll get to it in about a year and a half."

"Let's see what we can find out about it," I said.

I spatula'd the egg out of the pan and onto a plate. In my left-handed awkwardness I broke the yolk. Normally at home, not a slave to etiquette, I would lick the plate clean. With Bobby here, I planned to resist, or at least wait until after he left. I grabbed a napkin and fork, and we reconvened in front of my laptop at the dining room table.

According to the forms and state websites, the incorporation had occurred a little over ten years ago. The sole contents of the LLC seemed to be another LLC founded at the same time in Vermont, which in turn held only an LLC established in Maine. Not everything I did to find the information was strictly legal, but Bobby either didn't care or wasn't able to follow everything I was doing, perhaps both. The paper trail led me through ten more states. It had been deliberately set up like a maze. Damned lawyers, and I supposed I should include lawyer's assistants in that condemnation by association.

The final link in the chain appeared to a second LLC established in New Hampshire for the sole purpose of owning a piece of land in the North Country. Lacking an address, the piece of land was identified only by GPS coordinates. I punched them into the computer and found a satellite image of uninteresting hills and dales with no apparent structures on the land that I could see.

"Where is that?" Bobby asked looking over my shoulder.

"North, way north. Dix's Grant."

"Where?"

The geopolitics of New Hampshire are surprisingly complex for such a small state. It is a conglomeration of two hundred and twenty one essentially independent towns, thirteen cities, and twenty five unincorporated places with pleasantly old-timey appellations like grants, hamlets, and settlements. Locations in that last category have no established form of local government, and often no population to govern. Wikipedia informed me that as of the 2010 census, Dix's Grant listed one permanent resident, though that wasn't necessarily Kevin. Lacking full time landowners, the area was riddled with little seasonal hunting cabins and campsites and whatnot. This was likely what Kevin owned, though why he felt the need to hide it behind a bunch of legal mumbo jumbo was beyond me. If I had to venture a guess, I would say nothing good.

Just for the heck of it, I mapped directions from my house to Dix's Grant and found that the drive would take a little over four hours.

"You want to go check it out?" Bobby asked me as he peered over my shoulder.

No, I dearly didn't want to go check it out. In retrospect, I shouldn't have even mapped the directions, and I wouldn't have if I had thought Bobby would suggest actually going there. But Bobby wanted to go; I could hear it in his voice. The curiosity monkey was riding him hard. I had to admit, I wanted to see it too, but my curiosity monkey was tempered by the nagging feeling that we might come across a very much alive Kevin, which could lead not only to our deaths, but to very embarrassing ones such as those that clueless and braless teenage girls have been blundering into since the slasher flick was invented. I could see it now, the movie of my life, with the audience shrieking "Don't go in there! Don't open that door!"

But this was where I put my foot down, metaphorically speaking. Kevin was dead. I had to believe that; I demanded that of myself. To believe otherwise would have me checking the back seats of cars for the rest of my life, and I wasn't willing to live like that. I just wasn't. Kevin was dead, I repeated.

I found it funny how the more I said that to myself, the less I believed it. On second thought, I didn't find it funny at all. On third thought, I found it the exact polar opposite of funny.

If any of these anxieties showed on my face, if Bobby had any inkling of my hesitation, he wasn't letting it dampen his enthusiasm for the road trip. He had been behind the curve on too many mysteries that I had solved, and here he was on the forefront of this one, and he wasn't going to miss out on being there at the end. And who could say no to his big, eager, puppy-dog eyes?

So against my better judgment, I said "Let me get my coat."

Thirty-Three

I did more than just get my coat.

For one, I put on a pair of thick socks and sturdy boots. Who knew what the terrain was like up there? I also put on heavy denim jeans with flannel lining for warmth. I would have liked to change my shirt – all I was wearing was a short-sleeved T-shirt that read 'Coed Naked Firefighting' – but the bandage for my cracked ribs had been changed recently, and the new one was much looser and easier to breathe with, but contained more than two inches of padding. The T-shirt, a gag gift sized 3XL, was the only shirt I owned that fit me over the bandage. From the back of the hall closet I dug out a huge, puffy ski jacket, one that is designed to be worn with three or four layers underneath it in sub-zero conditions. With a little struggling, I just barely managed to get it zipped up over everything. I had more than a passing resemblance to the Michelin Man.

I left a note for Valerie to let her know that I would be home in time for dinner, and that I loved her. I didn't think that she would read it. Mostly when she got out of bed she drifted around the house like a restless ghost, maybe ate something, and went back to bed again. Healing, I reminded myself, is a slow process. I also knew that she had an appointment with her psychiatrist that afternoon and that she never missed one, so she would not be alone for the whole day.

"Ready to go," I told Bobby when I came back into the living room. He wore a greatcoat made of dark blue wool, the kind of thing that, given his blonde hair and blue eyes, would have let him fit right in standing on the conning tower of a German U-boat plying the waters of the Bearing Sea.

We took his patrol car. I checked the back seat of the car before I got in, and came within an iota of asking him to pop the trunk for me. The passenger seat wasn't all that comfortable; perhaps it wasn't intended to be used. The center console contained a keyboard and display that horned in on my personal space, especially considering my present bulk. Still, it was that or ride in the back seat behind the Plexiglas shield while sitting on the vomit-proof plastic upholstery, so I bore my discomfort stoically if not joyously.

We each kept our own council for the first hour or so. Bobby finally broke the silence with, "You want to talk about Valerie?"

To which I responded, "I'd rather sing a billion bottles of beer on the wall."

Reading between the lines, he seemed to take that as a "No" as I had intended. "OK," he replied, and I thought for just a fraction of a moment that he was going to break into song, but he didn't.

An hour later we were driving through the Notch, and somehow, though the mountains themselves had not changed, my problems no longer seemed small and insignificant in comparison. Echoes from the earlier trip Valerie and I had taken set up a resonance in my head. I felt my heart pounding at a dangerous rate and sweat coated my skin. I opened the window and let in an arctic vortex which dried my skin even as it set my teeth chattering. When I couldn't take the cold anymore, I closed the window again and glanced over at Bobby, who was studiously concentrating on the road and pretending he wasn't driving around with a basket case in the passenger seat.

"They'll find him, right?" I blurted out. I had not realized that I was going to ask that question until it had already left my mouth and found my lungs weren't ready for the utterance. As a consequence, my voice was thin and high and squeaky, a teenager hung up in puberty, as if the question itself didn't make me feel pathetic and helpless enough. But I had to know. I had to know he would be found, or my life would be forever altered.

Bobby made a face like I was being ridiculous. I'm not sure he realized he was making it, but it didn't help my self esteem any.

"Sure," he said, "you two wandered around during the night and the terrain is a challenge, and I'll admit that it is taking longer than I thought it would, but it's just not that big an area as searches go. Someone may stumble over him during the winter, but if not he'll turn up with the spring thaw. Of course they'll find him."

It was a nice speech, and I had been through the search and rescue training classes so he wasn't telling me anything I didn't already know, but at my core a seed of doubt had germinated and was spreading tendrils and creepers of uncertainty throughout the entirety of my being. A shiver ran up my spine, what my grandma used to call feeling someone walk across your grave. I fucking hoped not.

I tried distracting myself, avoid thinking about what, or more to the point who, might be lying ahead, setting traps, plotting our dismemberment. I flipped through the folder some more, even though reading in a car always makes me vaguely nauseous. I borrowed a pen from Bobby and made some notes, then found myself making sketches of knives dripping blood and explosions, mushroom clouds, and the like on the inside face of the folder, so I forced myself to set it aside and put the pen away in my pocket.

I closed my eyes and tried to pretend that I was asleep, see if my brain would fall for it. It didn't. The edge of the center console display was jabbing me in the hip, plus the seat wouldn't tip back at all because of the modifications that had been made to the car to mount the Plexiglas shield.

Finally my mind dragged me kicking and screaming back to the subject I had been avoiding. This. This was what Valerie had told Craig. This is what drives her crazy. That I go off against my own better judgment to do whatever the hell it is that I think I am doing, while she waits, and wonders if this will be the time I don't come home. I could have told Bobby to take one of his deputies, or call the State Police, or the Canadian Royal Mounties, and to leave me out of it. But I didn't. I was here for reasons I was finding difficult to articulate, even to myself.

I wanted to help. I get that. Lots of people want to help, the other members of the Dunboro Fire Department to name just a few. They're not here. Only I seem to be willing to risk life and limb in my pursuit of Batman-esque justice. Why do I feel that I have to do it?

Why?

I was still pondering that question, my eyes still closed, when I felt the car slow and then stop.

Bobby, likely thinking that I had fallen asleep reached over and shook me gently. The very idea that someone could fall asleep on a drive to something like this, Bobby must have thought I had testicles of titanium.

I opened my eyes and looked at him. He gestured out the windshield at a break in the greenery along the road. The woods were so tight and close, the driveway was black and depthless, like a bottomless pit to nowhere.

"We're here," he said.

Thirty-Four

The driveway, if it could be called such, was little more than a weedy strip that ran off narrowly into the woods. Bobby's patrol car crept along, undergrowth brushing along the door panels, as we looked for any sign that it had been recently traveled. We didn't want to be surprised by Kevin had he somehow survived and made his way up here to lick his wounds and plot his revenge. I noticed Bobby undid the strap on his holster and that made me wish I had brought my own gun along.

In a few hundred yards the driveway ended, and that was all it did, end. There was no structure, no clearing, not even sufficient space to turn a car around. If Bobby wanted to get back to the main road without risking his paint job attempting a three point turn in the narrow space, he'd have to drive in reverse.

We got out and stood beside the car quietly. All I could hear was normal forest sounds. That, and the thunderous pounding of my heart jackhammering in my chest. Even though Bobby was with me and carrying a gun, I didn't want to cross paths with Kevin again; I just wasn't up to it.

Sticking out of a nearby bush at my feet was the corner of a wooden pallet. I reached in and parted the vegetation, revealing three old bags of concrete stacked on top. They had been outside a long time, the paper wrapping weathered to pieces, the concrete inside the bags wetted and then dried into bag-shaped hardened blocks. I pushed through the bushes and stepped over the pallet, and found a stack of rotted pallets beyond, six, no seven, high.

"There's nothing here," Bobby said from his side of the car.

"I've got something," I called.

He came around the car and forced his way through the bushes to my side. He looked down at the concrete and pallets.

"So, it's a few old bags of concrete," he said.

I didn't reply; I was busy doing math. The three bags were forty pounders, which meant each made about two-thirds of a cubic foot of concrete. If the pallets held a ton, that would have been fifty bags, times eight pallets…

"If all of these pallets had held bags of concrete," I said, running through the numbers in my head, "he would have had over 250 cubic feet of concrete. And that doesn't count any pallets that he might have gotten rid of or stacked elsewhere."

Bobby's eyes widened, "You thinking a bunker?"

"Something," I nodded, "Something pretty big."

"You want to look around?" he asked.

What I wanted to do was call in a SWAT team and let them find whatever Kevin had built for himself, but it was just Bobby and me and help was far, far away. Plus Kevin, I reminded myself firmly, was dead.

"Sure," I said with all the enthusiasm of a guy hopping up onto an examination table for a colonoscopy.

It looked like we were on a path of sorts and so we stuck to it; maybe it was one that Kevin had used, or maybe it was just a deer path. Beyond the fear that at any moment Kevin might jump out and slash our throats, or a sniper round might take our heads off, the hike turned out to be pretty pleasant. It hadn't snowed this far north, and the going was easy. It was cold, but we were dressed for it, and the land was a natural wonder of trees and small creeks glassy with ice and there were interestingly-shaped chunks of rock, like someone had buried an ancient civilization and only the spires of their tallest buildings remained exposed. This is New Hampshire at its most wild and unspoiled.

We ambled in companionable silence, listening to the whisper of the breeze through the trees and various birdsong, and we literally stumbled over it, or at least I did. I caught a toe and lurched several steps before recovering. My first thought was that I had tripped on some random piece of stone, but Bobby stopped and dragged his heel through the leaves on the trail, exposing rusted metal. We knelt and used our hands – I used my one good hand – to clear away the debris, revealing a hatch about three feet across, mounted in a concrete lip, and secured with a padlock. I took the presence of the padlock as good news – if the padlock was on the outside that meant Kevin couldn't be on the inside.

Bobby grabbed and rattled the padlock; it was locked tight.

"You have any paperclips?" I asked.

He poked around in the various pockets and packets on his utility belt and seemed a little surprised that he managed to find a few. Better than Batman's utility belt as far as I'm concerned.

He handed them to me and asked, "You can pick locks?"

"Maybe," I answered.

I bent the paperclips into the best shape I could with my teeth and set to work. Right handed I can pick simple locks given enough time. Left handed, I didn't know. I honestly didn't think so, but it seemed worth a shot. The lock was not new. The internal mechanisms were worn and sloppy, and grit in the cylinder made the pins stick as I seated them in their place. Still, working left handed was challenging, and I was taking a long time. It looked like Bobby was going to tell me to give it up and call it a day – we could always come back with a pair of bolt cutters and a battalion of National Guard troops tomorrow – when the lock popped open.

He grasped the edge of the metal with the fingertips of one hand – the hatch had no handle – while drawing his gun with the other. He lifted it open quickly in a squeal of hinges and a shower of leaves and dirt, and pointed his gun into a empty concrete stairway that led down into the darkness, we couldn't tell how far. Bobby pulled a flashlight from his belt and turned it on, shined it into the hole. The beam was incredibly bright, almost like a wide laser beam that sharply illuminated every dust mote in the air, every granule of dirt that rained into the opening. The tunnel ended in a floor ten or twelve feet underground.

Bobby moved down the stairs, his gun pointed ahead of him. I followed.

The steps ended in a rough tunnel. Bobby found a switch mounted on the wall and flipped it. A line of bulbs stretching along the ceiling of the tunnel glowed with a pale light. I didn't hear a generator and didn't believe there was electrical service way out here in the middle of nowhere. I thought they were powered by batteries, and ones without a lot of charge left in them, judging from the way the lights dimmed.

The tunnel was concrete, poorly constructed using rough forms. The walls had not been properly sealed, and they wept water

203

which gathered in crude gutters in the floor, ran in gurgling rivulets into the distance. The place smelled unpleasant, of mold and mildew and something with a sharp tang underneath that I couldn't identify. Vinegar?

Bobby turned off his flashlight and tucked it away. He put both hands on his gun and gestured for us to move with a tilt of his head.

We advanced slowly, not out of caution because there was nowhere a surprise could come from in the straight tunnel, but because the tunnel was narrow and the ceiling was low. I had to stoop; Bobby had to hunch over and suck in his chest. He filled the hallway with his bulk, made a rasping noise as he brushed both walls with his shoulders, and I couldn't see a thing past him. I shuffled along in his wake, and when he stopped suddenly, I piled into him.

"Sorry," I said, "What's up?"

"A metal door," he replied. I heard him rattle a padlock. "Locked," he added needlessly.

"Let me try it," I said.

It took some doing, us passing each other in the space available and me all bulked up by my bandages.

"Was it good for you?" I asked when I had finally squeezed past.

Bobby barked a laugh and stood guard, his gun pointed back up the tunnel. Anyone trying to come at us from that direction was on a suicide mission. Bobby could have leisurely emptied his gun and reloaded it three times before someone could reach us.

The last bulb in the line was some distance down the hallway, so it was dark up against the door in Bobby's shadow. I borrowed his flashlight and took a crack at the lock. The first thing I noticed was that the flashlight was not good for close up work – it was way too bright, and I was forced to squint. The second thing I noticed was that this lock was neither old, nor worn, nor full of grit.

To work the lock I had to crouch down and clamp the flashlight in the crook of my neck, pinch one paperclip between the tips of the fingers exposed by the cast on my right hand, and hold the other in my spastic but otherwise good left hand. The lock pins were tight and springy, the chase well lubricated, and despite me putting a lot of torque on the cylinder, the pins had an annoying habit of snapping back as soon as I tried to set them and move on.

My neck and fingers cramped, my thighs burned. It was stuffy at the end of the tunnel, and my eyes were stinging from the bright flashlight and the odor of vinegar or ammonia or whatever it was that was much stronger here by the door, and I wasn't frigging getting anywhere.

I shut off the flashlight and put it down, slammed my cast against the door in frustration which made a flat, hollow sound and didn't budge a millimeter.

"Hello? Is someone there?" a woman's voice called from the other side.

"Hello?" I called back.

"Oh thank God!" the woman sobbed, "Help me! Let me out!"

"Are you injured?"

"No," she paused, "No, I'm OK. Listen carefully. My name is Cathy Oulette and I've been kidnapped. The man who did it is named Kevin Mercer, and he is very, very dangerous."

205

"Oulette?" Bobby said in a way that I wasn't sure if it was a question or not. He leaned over me. "This is the police," Bobby shouted, "We're here. We're going to get you out." More quietly to me he added, "I'm going to call this in. Stay with her."

"Who's Cathy Oulette?" I asked him, but he had already hustled a good distance up the hallway, no doubt fraying the shoulders of his coat on the rough concrete.

I heard the woman crying.

"Cathy? Cathy, listen to me. I'm with the fire department," I thought but didn't add that it was a fire department with a station about two hundred miles away, plus I was currently on medical leave. She didn't need all those details. "I'm going to stay right here until we get this door open. I'm not going to leave you."

"Be careful. Kevin could come back at any moment."

"No," I insisted, "he's not coming back. He's dead."

"Get the key from him," the woman pleaded. "Get the key and open the door. He always carries the key with him."

"He's not here, he's," I paused. How could I explain what had transpired to this woman? I couldn't, not quickly. "He's not here," I repeated.

"Get the key," the woman said as if she hadn't heard me. "He carries it on a ring in his pocket."

"He's not here," I said yet again, feeling like we were somehow talking past one another, that I was missing some vital element of this conversation. "He died several weeks ago, far away."

The woman gasped. "No," she said. "No, no, no, nononononononono," she moaned.

"What? What's wrong?"

"He's here," she whispered harshly, "He was here just a few minutes before you showed up."

My brain instinctively went into panic mode while I was still trying to understand exactly what she was telling me. Then I put it all together.

And then the lights went out.

Thirty-Five

Two quarts of adrenaline spilled into my bloodstream and my veins turned to ice. I could actually feel my eyes dilating, a not wholly pleasant sensation, but it did me no good. There was simply no light down there, none. Nothing coming through the cracks around the door behind me, and nothing I could see from the tunnel entrance far away.

I've met firefighters who have become claustrophobic, developed it after years of crawling around under houses and in low attics and in wall spaces. I've made light fun of them with some not-so-gentle ribbing and not-so-kind jokes. At that moment, I knew just how they felt. I couldn't seem to get enough air into my lungs, felt as though the walls were crushing down on me, the weight of all the earth above bearing down on them.

Kevin.

I strained to hear him. I heard the water gurgling in the gutters. I heard Cathy sobbing through the door behind me. Then I heard a faint scrape. A footstep? I waited. Another. And then another. This was followed by a lot of silence, and I found myself doubting that I heard anything at all. Maybe Kevin was not here. Maybe he hadn't turned off the lights. Maybe the batteries running them had finally run out of charge, and Bobby would be back in just a moment with the cavalry, and everything would be fine.

I was just starting to get my breathing under control, when Kevin, with an uncanny sense of the dramatic, whispered "Jaaaack."

I was still crouched, and I scrabbled around on the floor nearby in search of a weapon, any weapon, a chunk of concrete or a rock, but all I found was the flashlight, a tiny thing whose entire length fit completely in the palm of my hand, not a weapon at all. I grabbed it, thought about turning it on so I could at least see him coming, but didn't.

Kevin had turned off the lights, but I couldn't see him choosing to fight in total darkness. Sure, maybe he was trained in fighting blindfolded, and I wasn't, but the tunnel was narrow, and he had no way of knowing whether or not I was armed. If I had a gun, if I had thought to bring my gun, I could have shot blindly with a fair chance of hitting him. Kevin wouldn't take that risk, so he must have been able to see, must have been using some kind of night vision goggle.

Early night vision goggles had a serious flaw in their technology. With a little light, image intensifiers could project usable video to the wearer, but when looking at a bright light, the video became blinding. This was corrected in modern goggles, but the military keeps a pretty close lock on those. Could Kevin have gotten his hands on a modern pair? I was willing to bet that he couldn't. I was willing to bet everything.

But I had to wait until he was closer, use the element of surprise to the maximum advantage. I stood, keeping the flashlight tucked away in my palm. When I blinded him, he had to be

209

close so I could attack with, uh, my one good hand, or maybe I could club him with my cast. Once again I was working with a horribly incomplete plan.

He was giving me the silent treatment, and I needed him to talk so I could home in on him.

"Kevin," I said, "We won. Valerie and I beat you."

"You didn't beat me. You cheated," he hissed.

His words were smeared and clipped, so what I heard was 'You didn't meet me, you meeted.'

It took me awhile to translate that, and while I was working on it, he continued. "I'll give you crebit, yur harber to kill than I thought."

'...you're harder to kill...' Got it.

Distances were difficult to judge. He didn't sound close, but he didn't sound far away either. Keep him talking, I said to myself, I had to keep him talking.

"Many people have tried to kill me," I said, "few have succeeded."

He laughed at this. At least I thought it was a laugh, but it sounded like half-strangled choking, almost like a man drowning, wet and gasping.

"I'm gumma fish that."

'I'm going to fix that,' my brain supplied. In his excitement, his speech was getting worse.

"Once I'm dum wish you, I'm gumma go kill the mitch!"

"Mitch?" I asked.

"Mitch! Mitch! Mitch! MITCH!" he screamed so loud it echoed off the concrete all around me.

I didn't know who Mitch was, but it sounded like Kevin was very angry with him.

I was about to ask another question when I had the sudden premonition that he was close, very close. Maybe I felt a whisper of a breeze at his motion. I brought the flashlight up, angled it to where I thought his head was, and turned it on.

A beam of brilliant white stabbed into the darkness and struck Kevin in the face, and the image of him was burned into my vision like a photograph. He wore a pair of military green goggles over his eyes that made him seem somehow insectile, reminding me of low-budget Saturday morning horror movies on Chiller Theater with names like *The Wasp Woman* and *Mansquito*. He also looked terrible. I had gotten the best care that a government-run healthcare system could provide – insert your own joke here – but Kevin had been limited to strictly do-it-yourself remedies. He had lost a lot of blood, and he looked like a medical school textbook picture from the chapter on anemia. He appeared to have wired his own broken jaw shut, what I was pretty sure was bare copper electrical wire punching through the flesh of his cheek in a looping pattern like crude stitches. The cut on his neck was packed with gauze held in place with a worn, brown, leather belt. Bruising and swelling in his face made him appear almost alien, his skin tight and slick where it should be loose, slack and sagging where it should be tight.

His broken fingers were wound in filthy rags, his knife duct taped into his hand. I hate when people steal my ideas. The blade was dripping with fresh blood, what had to be Bobby's blood, and for a moment I felt panic racing around in my chest like a flock of startled birds before I managed to tamp it down into a roiling, hot ball in my stomach. I almost vomited on him then – how would that be for an opening salvo?

When the light struck him, Kevin screeched and reared back like a vampire exposed to the sunlight. He clawed the goggles off his face with one hand and struck out at me blindly with the knife. The blade was so sharp that I didn't even feel it slash the back of my hand, but my blood pattered to the concrete floor and the flashlight went spinning and ricocheting off down the hallway.

I moved in to do something, I wasn't sure what, perhaps pull the bandage off his neck and see if I could get that cut bleeding again, or punch him in the jaw and find out how much that would hurt, but Kevin proved far too fast for me. He stabbed at me with the knife, and I only barely managed to get my cast up between us. The blade skittered along the hard surface of the cast, sliced cleanly through the sleeve of my jacket, maybe cutting my forearm underneath, and then struck sparks against the wall. Before I could recover, he brought the knife up again and plunged it into my chest, the force of the blow driving me backwards. I hit the door which rattled in its frame. Cathy on the other side gave a cry of surprise or terror.

I lost my feet on the damp concrete and slid to the floor. Kevin stood over me, leaning onto the knife with his whole weight, pinning me like a butterfly to a collector's board. I grabbed his wrist, but couldn't pull the knife out, couldn't overcome his incredible strength.

He twisted the blade, seemingly surprised that I wasn't dying. I have to admit that I was surprised as well. I could feel the warm trickle of blood from the wound in my chest, but realized that between the heavy jacket and the bandage padding that the blade wasn't long enough to reach anything vital. The tip of the knife was pressing against a rib and the feeling as he twisted and grated it against the bone I'm at a loss to describe. Ouch certainly doesn't do it justice.

He changed tactics and clamped his free hand around my throat

212

and began squeezing with a force that made it feel like either he was going to crush my larynx or my head was going to pop. It was dark in the tunnel because the only source of light was the flashlight lying on the floor way down the hall, but my vision soon dimmed, and it became even darker.

I felt something stabbing me in the thigh, and thought in my confusion that he had somehow come up with a second knife, and a third hand, and was driving that weapon into me for good measure. I reached down and found that it was Bobby's pen in my pocket. It took some doing, but I managed to get the pen out, grasping it in my casted hand.

They say the way to a man's heart is through his stomach, but the way to a man's brain is through the orbit of his eye, or maybe through his ear, but the eye seemed a better target at that moment.

Faintly lit from behind, Kevin's head was only a vague shape above me. I drove the pen into the shadow of his face, I think hit him in the forehead, scrawled a bloody curve up into his hairline.

Both time and air were seriously running out.

I drew back and stabbed again. This time my aim was true and I hit him directly in the eye. I felt spongy resistance for a moment, and then a soft *pock!* as the eye burst.

Kevin shrieked and tried to pull away. I lost my hold on the pen which remained lodged in his eye, but I held onto his wrist, kept him close even though that kept his knife buried in my chest, grating against my rib. He released my neck and air rushed into my lungs, burning my throat. With a fumbling grab, he tried to pull the pen loose. I batted his hand aside and used the cast like a hammer to drive the pen deeper.

The first blow rocked his head back.

213

The second was accompanied by a loud sound, like the splitting of an old, rotten log with an axe, and his shriek was cut off abruptly.

The third drove the end of the pen flush against his face.

I'd like to think he was dead before he hit the floor.

Thirty-Six

It took me some time to gather myself, let the wooziness pass
even as Kevin's undoubtedly last breath came out as a thin
wheeze. I got up unsteadily and weaved my way down the hall
to retrieve the flashlight. It was slick with blood as I picked it
up, my blood. Under the beam of light I looked at the cut on my
hand and judged it superficial; at this point anything that
wouldn't kill me felt superficial. All the fingers worked. All the
nerves were intact.

I returned to Kevin, shined the light in his face. He was dead all
right; this time I was sure. Blood was welling up around the
little button at the top of the pen barrel, all that was visible above
the surface.

"Mightier than the sword, you son of a bitch," I said to him, and
then realized that he had been saying 'Bitch' not 'Mitch,' no
doubt referring to Valerie. Or maybe I was wrong and he really
hated some guy named Mitch. It didn't matter now.

Bobby.

As my adrenaline rush faded, as coherent thought returned, a wave of panic at what might have happened to him rose up, black and implacable, threatening to overwhelm me. After a grudging start, Bobby had come to support me in my mystery-solving. If I had led him up here and if Kevin had killed him, I wouldn't be able to live with it. A lot of people say that under a lot of circumstances, but I meant it literally. I didn't know if I would dine on the business end of the gun in my cookie jar or drink myself to death leisurely over the coming months, but somehow it would be the end of me. The very idea of losing Bobby and going on living was an impossibility, an equation with no solution.

I left Kevin and ran to the staircase. I looked back just once, sure that somehow his body would have disappeared, but it hadn't.

Almost as an afterthought, I yelled down the hallway to Cathy. "I got him! I'll come back for you." Maybe she heard me, but down the tunnel, through the doorway, probably not. She would keep; she wasn't hurt, and she wasn't going anywhere. Bobby was all that mattered at that moment.

I took the stairs two or maybe three at a time, barking both shins against the sharp concrete edges. At the top I stepped through the hatch and stopped, turned a full circle, certain I would see Bobby's feet sticking out from under a bush. Nothing. I looked for a splash of blood or a broken branch to indicate where Kevin might have dragged him. More nothing.

I ran down the trail, keeping an eye out for some indication of what might have happened to Bobby. It wasn't until I got all the way back to his car that I found him. The door was open, and he lay sprawled across the front seat, his feet hanging outside, blood down the backs of his pant legs, pooling on the seat and rubberized floor mats.

As a professional, I've trained for this moment for years and knew exactly what to do, so you would think I would have been able to hold it together, but seeing Bobby's blood blew that knowledge away in an instant. I ripped the radio mic from its hook on the dash and shouted "Officer down!" twenty or thirty times before managing to pry my fingers off the transmit button and giving the dispatcher an opportunity to get a word in edgewise. I gave our GPS coordinates; that was the best I had. I requested an ambulance, and then looked at my own bleeding hand and asked for two, perhaps three for good measure, and cops, lots of cops, and if they had one handy I wouldn't have turned down a bulldozer to widen the driveway. Then I dropped the mic and let the radio chatter build to a crescendo as emergency units vectored in on us from all directions

Memories of turning over Laura Hopewell and killing her fresh in my mind, I nonetheless eased Bobby onto his side. I had to see how badly he was cut.

All the blood made it difficult to see the thin, almost surgical slice across the base of his throat. I put two fingers against the side of his neck and felt something like a pulse going on in there, always a good sign.

The shell of my jacket was slick nylon, waterproof, not useful at all. I stripped it off and Kevin's knife, still piercing the jacket and stuck in the thick bandages around my chest, pulled loose. It fell to the ground just outside the car. The T-shirt underneath was sheeted with my blood – so much for Coed Naked Firefighting – but it was the best I had available. I removed it and rolled it into a wad.

"I think this makes us blood brothers," I said to Bobby as I pressed the cloth against the wound.

Bobby said nothing in return.

An ambulance responding out of Lincoln, Maine reported that they were leaving Route 16 and crossing the New Hampshire border. Was that really the closest ambulance? Where was the nearest hospital? I tried to assemble a map of the region in my head, and found it mostly empty space, but if that was because I didn't know what was up here or if there was nothing up here to know, I wasn't sure. I considered loading Bobby into the car and driving and then rejected the idea. With no firm idea where the hospital was, the ambulance was Bobby's best chance, and I didn't want to risk missing them if we took different routes.

Waiting, doing essentially nothing, was hard. Really, really hard. I muttered pointless phrases like, 'Hang in there, big guy,' and, 'Help's on the way.' Bobby gave no indication he heard me, but he kept on breathing which was job one as far as I was concerned.

I used one hand to work the radio, gave the dispatcher as much information as I had, talked about Kevin and Bobby and Valerie and I. My thoughts were a little scrambled and a lot of what I said was likely gibberish. I also gave updates of Bobby's condition in minute detail, every time his breathing hitched or his eyebrow twitched. Useless crap mostly. Thoughts of Cathy obliterated from my mind, I neglected to mention either her or the bunker.

I heard the first ambulance before I saw it, a squeal of metal louder than its siren as branches along the driveway scraped paint off the sides in long lines like the world's worst keying. It was followed minutes later by two State Police cruisers. The EMT's had a hell of a time getting gear out of their side compartments and a stretcher from the back of the ambulance around to the front, but they managed it and I let the pros take over. On my best day, all I am is emergency first aid trained, and this was far from my best day.

I was covered in my blood and Bobby's blood and some of Kevin's blood. I was a forensic scientist's wet dream. The cops, none too gently, forced me away from the side of the stretcher and peppered me with questions. From the information I had passed to the dispatcher, they knew me and my role in the events, but were jacked up and angry at the critical injury of another officer, and I was the closest target they could vent on. I let their anger roll over me like a wave without resisting and answered their questions when they paused to take a breath.

I had just started to tell them about the bunker when they were interrupted by the ambulance wanting to depart, which turned into something of a Keystone Cops show. The cops initially wanted one of them to stay and keep an eye on me while the other moved the vehicles, but then realized that simple math was against them – two cars, two cops. They admonished me not to move, then ran back to their cars and backed out rapidly, costing the state two paint jobs. The ambulance driver didn't even try to back out; he just bashed his way through a three point turn, crumpling both front fenders and smashing headlights and taillights galore. On the way out, a low branch sheared the light bar off the roof which fell to the ground with a crash of broken plastic. That left me standing alone in the sudden silence and swirl of exhaust smoke following all the activity.

Bobby on the way to the hospital, my thoughts turned to Cathy. I waited less than thirty seconds before scooping up my jacket because I was freezing cold. I shouldered it on as I ran back up the trail.

Down in the tunnel I envisioned that I would find Kevin's body had vanished, but he was as dead as dead can be, lying in the same spot I had left him, a few degrees cooler perhaps, but otherwise unchanged. I took the keys out of his pocket, found the right one, and unlocked the padlock. I let it drop to the ground and threw the door open.

Cathy knelt just inside on a piece of carpeting that was an incongruous, festive yellow. Her head was down, her eyes averted, her arms at her sides – a posture of complete submission. I was certain it was what Kevin demanded of her, this pose, how he expected her to be waiting for him when he came through the door. *Hi, Honey, I'm home.* I could taste bile at the back of my throat.

The room was an irregular concrete box, the floor layered in mismatched carpet remnants in circus colors: candy apple red, cerulean blue, fluorescent green. A sputtering Coleman lantern gave the room a garish light. There was a thin mattress lying on a metal frame, a military-style footlocker at one end. A bookshelf held boxes of cereal, cartons of crackers, cans of soup. A portable toilet, the source of the offending ammonia chemical odor, stood in one corner. Half the space was devoted to what was undoubtedly Kevin's idea of a playroom, where he had his fun – hooks and rings mounted on the wall, manacles and leather straps and all manner of madness. Envisioning Valerie chained up in this tomb, buried under I had no idea how much dirt and rock in one of the least-inhabited corners of New Hampshire, Kevin's plaything, filled me with a cold emptiness that the deepest voids of space couldn't hope to match.

Cathy hazarded a glance up at me, made a sound somewhere between a gasp and a whimper. She tried to jump to her feet, missed, stumbled to her knees, and used the wall to claw her way upright.

"I didn't think... I mean, I thought," she was unable to complete the sentence and the strength drained out of her. She fell back to her knees.

She had blonde hair and gray-green eyes and looked enough like Valerie to be mistaken for her sister. Kevin certainly had a type.

I took off my jacket and wrapped it around her. Even slimy with my blood, it was better than nothing, and that's what she had had on, nothing. Not a stitch. Of course she was naked. Yet more of Kevin's conditioning. There had to be clothing somewhere, perhaps in the footlocker; the temperature underground wouldn't have allowed her to survive perpetually naked. But she had my jacket and clearly wanted to get out of there, so rather than search for something else for her to wear, I helped her to her feet and led her through the door.

I ushered Cathy down the hallway, but she froze at Kevin's body. She moaned and shook her head frantically, unwilling to approach. I picked her up. She clenched her eyes shut and buried her face in my shoulder. Her paranoia put me on high alert, and I more than half expected Kevin to grab my ankle as I stepped over him, which of course he didn't.

My injured ribs didn't enjoy the activity, but I carried her up the stairs and down the trail. Another ambulance had arrived and the police, not having learned their lesson, had parked their two battered cruisers behind it.

I handed Cathy over to the EMTs. The cops started in on me again, covering much of the same ground we had already been over, and so my narrative was at the exact same point when the ambulance needed to leave. Keystone Cops, the sequel.

You might be surprised to learn that the next vehicle to arrive was a third ambulance, and again the cops parked it in. You might be surprised; nothing surprises me anymore.

Thirty-Seven

The next three hours of my life were spent at what became known later in popular media as 'The Dungeon.' More cops arrived, a lot more, so it seemed my request to the dispatcher had not been ignored. I heard second and third hand about Bobby's condition from them.

Bobby was going to be OK. There's no point in dragging that bit of suspense out, is there? It's not like I'm writing cheesy thriller novels.

It was his height that saved him.

Returning to the car to report our discovery, Bobby had opened the door and was leaning in to get the radio when Kevin had come out of the bushes and attacked from behind. Kevin's plan had most likely been to perforate both of Bobby's kidneys, but he had underestimated Bobby's height and couldn't identify his waist through the bulk of his coat, and therefore had stabbed Bobby twice, savagely, once in each butt cheek. That was something I planned to tease him about mercilessly when he got out of the hospital.

Bobby had straightened and Kevin had jumped onto his back, slashing the knife across Bobby's throat from behind. Again Kevin had underestimated his height, and so skipped the knife across both of Bobby's clavicles, avoiding the majority of the important stuff in his neck. Kevin had then leapt from Bobby's back and shoved what he thought was a dying man into the car, slamming Bobby's head against the doorframe and rendering him unconscious.

No joke – Bobby was seriously injured with a big concussion and a fair amount of blood loss, but he wasn't going to die, and that was all that mattered in my book.

Two detectives showed up and had me go through it all again while I sat on the rear step of the third ambulance and had my hand and chest tended to. The EMTs replaced the wrapping for my ribs with new padding twice as thick as the previous stuff. I ended up looking like the Michelin Man's fat cousin. I was pretty sure they were goofing on me, but didn't say anything.

These detectives were important, and someone moved their cars for them when it became necessary rather than interrupt their questions. Still, car jockeying became something of a spectator sport until a brush crew came with a bulldozer and chain saws to widen the driveway and clear a turnaround at the end. A ladies fire auxiliary showed up with food and drinks for the brush crew, and I managed to snag a hot cup of coffee and a pack of Twinkies. They were the first Twinkies I had eaten in thirty years, and I recalled someone had told me that they were not cooked; they were created as part of a chemical process that caused the cake to congeal, like blood. I had also been told that the cream filling was sweetened walrus semen. Bullshit I know, and yet I find the description somehow strangely compelling every time I eat one. Any hope of more substantial food departed with the brush crew and auxiliary, who left after the driveway was widened.

When the EMTs was done working on me, the detectives had me

lead them up the trail to the hatch, at which point they donned lint-free coveralls and little booties and left me standing outside shivering in the cold. Better out in the cold than down in the hole any day of the week as far as I was concerned. Had they asked me to give them a guided tour of the room, I would have refused. My excellent memory, which normally I see as a tremendous asset, was giving me a slide show with incredible and chilling detail from my one brief glance inside. The bare, stained mattress. The festive carpet remnants on the floor. The metallic glint of the Coleman lantern light reflecting off a manacle hanging from the ceiling. No, I didn't need to see any of that again. Thanks, I'm good.

Someone finally thought to bring me a blanket, though by that time my nipples were so hard they could have been used to cleave diamonds.

When the detectives emerged from the hatch, grim looks on their faces, they made arrangements to have me transported to the State Police substation in Littleton and from there on to the barracks in Concord. I had once spent several hours being questioned in the State Police barracks in Concord on a different mystery, so it was just like coming home.

It was there that I learned Cathy's story, how her husband and six year old son had been found beaten to death in their Berlin, Maine home two years ago. No one knew what had happened to Cathy, despite a police investigation that spanned both Maine and New Hampshire, until Bobby and I had found her. Two years in that hole. Unfathomable. How that particular case had lodged in Bobby's mind solidly enough for him to recall her name when he heard it, I planned to ask him when I had the chance.

In all the craziness I realized I had forgotten to check on Valerie, so I borrowed a cell phone from someone and called. She surprised me by answering. She had gone to her psychiatrist's appointment, and afterwards had felt like having dinner with friends. She had contacted some other firefighter wives who had come over bearing food. They were just cleaning up the kitchen and then planned to settle down and watch a rom-com. She didn't ask where I was or what I was doing, and I didn't offer. She would want to know that Kevin was dead, but I wasn't going to risk her good mood by telling her, not now. I told her instead that I loved her and would come home as soon as I could, and ended the call.

I felt buoyed. I knew this wasn't the last of it, not by a long shot, and that Valerie wasn't suddenly, magically back and whole. She would have days both good and bad ahead, but just this glimpse of the old her was more than I had allowed myself to hope for.

I returned the phone and spent some time being shuffled around various offices, handed off from detective to detective, and eventually I found myself alone in the same rectangular conference room as the last time, again drinking cups of the worst coffee in creation. Perhaps I would buy them a new percolator as a gift. The coffee was accompanied by a greasy box of tired-looking donuts. While I was hungry, I wasn't that hungry, and let them lie.

Someone had gotten me a shirt, which happened to be from a formal dress uniform, a colonel in the State Police if I was reading the rank insignia on the epaulets correctly. From the size of the shirt, the guy must have been a giant. My chest was festooned with medals. Didn't I feel special? I was joined by a stenographer and a guy with a video camera who could have also been the same ones as before, but I wasn't sure. They took seats and set up their equipment without so much as saying 'hi' to me. The cameraman braved one of the donuts from the box.

Shortly, in walked none other than my friend, state homicide investigator Doherty. He had replaced Brittany, his previous zaftig assistant, with an equally zaftig woman named Lauren. It seemed Doherty had a type as well.

When everyone had taken their places, I proceeded to go through it all for a third time.

The investigation was very much active, and our Q&A session was repeatedly halted whenever anyone came in to give Doherty an update. These were delivered in harsh and harried whispers, but the room was quiet, and I caught a lot of bits and pieces.

An entire investigative unit had been assigned to discover how and when Cathy had crossed paths with Kevin. Craig Lerner had himself gotten a lawyer and was refusing to answer questions about Kevin unless they were submitted in writing through his attorney. A lawyer lawyering up gave me a brief moment of lightness in what was otherwise a very dark day.

Cathy had told the doctors in the emergency room that up until about a month ago – time was difficult to judge down in the dungeon – there had been a second women held captive there with her named Molly Grimes. This news caused Doherty to storm out of the room and stand in the hallway barking orders for a solid ten minutes. A special forensic team with ground penetrating radar was dispatched to the scene, but a couple of cadaver dogs already up there were going nuts.

Doherty returned to the room looking like someone had let all the air out of his tires. He sat back down. It appeared like he was going to tell me to continue; the video guy restarted the camera recording. Instead, Doherty leaned back in his chair, made a slashing motion across his throat which reminded me of Bobby lying in a hospital bed somewhere. The video guy paused the camera.

I had thought the room was quiet before, but now it was positively hushed, like we had all collectively agreed to hold our breath.

"Molly Grimes?" I ventured cautiously.

Doherty took off his glasses and dropped them onto the table
with a clatter. He pressed his fingers against his eyes. Lauren
put a hand on his forearm, a warm and human gesture that made
me wish someone would put a reassuring hand on me.

"Out," Doherty said.

No one seemed to know what to do with that.

"Out!" he repeated loudly, which sent everyone scurrying for the
exit.

I didn't think he meant me, so I stayed put.

Once the last person had left and the door had clicked shut,
Doherty began with, "I was," and then decided to back up and
try a different route. "I used to run a special crimes division
down in Massachusetts before I came up here to New
Hampshire. We worked it all; whatever was highest on the
Governor's radar. Drugs, gangs, especially important murders."

He paused and looked at me to see if I was paying attention. I
was. I had no idea where he was going with this, but he held
every molecule in my body rapt.

"Five years ago, Molly Grimes was out with three friends for her
bachelorette party. They had rented a limo, hired a driver, ate
dinner on Boylston, went clubbing near the Common. The limo
was later found in Chinatown, some trash-strewn alley off
Kneeland, with the three friends and the driver cut to pieces
inside. Literally pieces. Jigsaw puzzles down at the coroner's
office. My division was instructed to work it, and work it we
did, for an entire year. Of Molly Grimes, we found not a trace."

He didn't continue the story from there; he didn't need to.
However it had happened, however she and Kevin had met, she
had been held captive for almost five years in the dungeon, alive,
waiting for a rescue which came too late. I also couldn't help

227

but realize that he had probably gotten rid of Molly to make room for Valerie. And with that, a dark day became a little bit darker still.

There was a knock on the door and a woman who looked like an accountant poked her head in. She gave a nervous little head bob and Doherty waved her in. She entered with an armload of fanfold computer paper pinned against her chest. As she leaned over to whisper in his ear, he told her tiredly, "Just say it."

She looked from him, to me, and back to him. She opened her mouth, and then closed it. She tried again. "I've been looking at the LLCs of the subject, Kevin Mercer. It's tough to follow, but there's evidence that an LLC in Virginia owns property."

"We've already found that property."

"No, no," she shook her head quickly, "a different property. One in Vermont."

I didn't know about Doherty, but I wanted to find a nearby bar and drink it dry.

I had to give him credit; he showed a level of control that I couldn't have faked at that moment. "Call the State Police in Vermont. Give them the address and send a liaison over to work with them."

The woman nodded efficiently and started to leave. He jumped to his feet and caught up with her before she cleared the doorway. "Tell them," he paused, "Warn them about what they're headed into."

She left and he stuck his head out into the hallway, called everyone back to their places.

And the interview continued. For hours and hours. By the time I got desperate enough to give one of the donuts a try, others had beaten me to them. No one offered to get me food, and I didn't ask. I wasn't sure if I was really hungry or just feeling like I should be hungry.

I did my absolute best to answer every question, tell them everything I knew, for Cathy, for Molly, for the bullet Valerie and I had so narrowly dodged. They had me sign my statement in triplicate, plus the label on the DVD the operator ejected from the camera, and as long as I was at it, they had me sign a picture of the knife collected at the scene, plus a statement identifying my jacket. You wouldn't believe the paperwork involved in taking down a multi-state serial killer.

Afterwards, the video and stenographic equipment was packed up and everyone else left. It was just Doherty and me again. He led me to the door, but stopped with his hand on the knob without opening it.

He turned to me and I thought he was going to offer me congratulations, a pat on the shoulder for camaraderie, maybe thank me for a job well done. Instead what he asked was, "How do you keep getting mixed up in this shit?"

"Hey, hey," I admonished him, "you're talking to a superior officer." I tapped the epaulets.

Doherty didn't smile, and as I ran it through my mind, I didn't find it very funny either.

"I think my wife wonders the exact same thing," I said quietly.

He stared at me with what I interpreted as pity, though that could have just been my state of mind.

"I'll get you a ride home," he said.

Thirty-Eight

Two words.

There's not a lot of great importance you can convey using only two words in the English language. I love you requires three. Eat shit and die is four. I'm from the government and I'm here to help takes nine, though it never fails to get a laugh, particularly in a roomful of government employees. Valerie, who in the aftermath spent much of her time cruising along on single word answers, and monosyllables for the most part at that, nonetheless managed to come up with two that completely tipped my world on edge.

She had been attending counseling sessions three or four times a week. I wasn't seeing anyone; I guess you could say I was self-treating. I've got plenty of Oxycontin for my hand and ribs, and taken with tequila it does my head some good as well. Maybe self-medicating would be a better description. Po-tay-to, po-tah-to.

I'll admit that I was curious what Valerie and her counselor talked about but didn't ask, partly because I didn't want to seem as though I was prying, mostly because I wasn't sure I really wanted to know. On her own, likely at the urging of her counselor, Valerie gave me little peeks into their conversations anyway.

These, I'm not even sure what to call them, revelations for lack of a better word, always blindsided me, hit me when I least expected them and was least prepared to deal with their content. I don't believe this was malicious on Valerie's part; she seemed to have little control over when they came out. They were horrors, infections, boils under her flesh bursting to be released, but the telling was hard, humiliating, caustic, an acid that ate away at her self-confidence and sense of security even as it brought relief.

One evening we were preparing dinner, pork chops with homemade apple sauce using late season local apples. I was trimming the pork chops, salting and peppering them before lining them up in the baking dish, while Valerie peeled and sliced the apples.

She turned to me, considered an apple that she held in her palm.

"He measured me," she said softly.

I immediately knew who she was talking about. The pronoun he always referred to Kevin now. He might refer to Kevin for the rest of our lives. He, him, his – Kevin had claimed them all. So although I knew who she meant, I still couldn't make any sense of her words.

"He, what? He measured you?" I ventured cautiously, uncertain that I had heard her correctly.

"He told me he measured me, for the gag. The ball had to be the right size. Too big and it would dislocate my jaw. Too small and it wouldn't," she swallowed, turned the apple in her palm, "it wouldn't keep me quiet."

She had said this last part so softly that I had to strain to hear it over the hum of the refrigerator.

I took the apple from her and set it on the cutting board, took her hand, cold as ice, and led her to the couch in the living room where the story came out slowly, painfully. She had been at NHPR, waiting in the green room for her interview which she told me was actually green, and not a particularly attractive shade. She hadn't had time to eat, and Kevin offered her an apple, the story of Adam and Eve in reverse, Adam offering the apple to Eve, leading her unto hell.

She had taken one big bite – it was all she had time for before she was ushered into the studio. I thought it likely that Kevin had timed it that way, held onto the apple until the last possible moment so all she could take was one bite, but I didn't interrupt her flow to bring up this point. It wasn't important anyway. Kevin told her that he had kept that apple, taking measurements of her bite mark to get the gag right, custom sized just for her. He told her this like she should be touched or perhaps flattered, that she should be impressed by his cleverness and thoughtfulness and all the trouble he had gone to for her benefit.

So Kevin ruined apples for us as well. We abandoned the pork chops and got Chinese takeout.

On another occasion we were lying in bed together. I had moved back into the master bedroom again after several months of sleeping in the guest room. We weren't doing anything, just sleeping in the same bed. For one, my hand and ribs didn't allow for anything else. For another, given what Valerie had been through, I thought sex, well, you know. When she was ready, I hoped I would see some signal, though I didn't know what I was looking for. Likely one of those support groups I wasn't attending could have helped me out there. While awesome for so many things, the Oxycontin didn't have an answer for this. So we were just sleeping in the same bed, and that in itself was wonderful, even though at her insistence we slept with every light in the bedroom and the adjoining bathroom and the upstairs hallway blazing.

Then one night just before lights out, metaphorically speaking of course, Valerie lay absolutely rigid, staring at the ceiling. I'm not sure she was breathing.

She said, "He made me watch."

He. Kevin again.

"Watch what?" I asked, feeling like I was playing the straight man, fulfilling my role in a particularly ghastly knock-knock joke.

"He made me watch while he beat that woman to death."

She went on to tell me the details of which I'll spare you. I could have interrupted, informed her that Kevin hadn't beaten Laura Hopewell to death, only mortally wounded her and that I had found her alive but dying. Again, it didn't seem like an important point.

Valerie filled our lives with these zingers, and over time I got a better picture of her time with Kevin, both from before, the little and at the time unnoticed things he had done to prepare and set his plan in motion, and when she was his prisoner.

My hand throbbed continually, and between that and Valerie's stories I upped my Oxycontin intake considerably. I prodded my doctor and got my prescription refilled. And tequila, you can buy that anywhere. I also convinced Tank, a friend and fellow Dunboro firefighter, to give me the remainder of the Vicodin that he hadn't used from a shoulder separation injury. Like taking candy from a baby. It was even easier convincing myself that I had it all under control, didn't have a problem, even as I went to the doctor and begged to get the prescription refilled a second time.

"You've got to be careful," he admonished me, "this stuff is really addictive." Then he shrugged, "Why am I telling you this? You're a firefighter; you've taken all the classes."

I laughed with him as I assured him, yes, I had taken all the classes, even as my mouth literally watered at the thought of fifty pristine Oxys – I supposed Oxy and I were good enough friends to be on a nickname basis – snug in their little childproof bottle, warm underneath a layer of cotton batting, waiting patiently for me at the pharmacy.

More time and more of Valerie's stories and more Oxy, with several Vicodin – I figured I'd call thm Vic – thrown in for variety's sake, passed.

The newspapers recounted Kevin's murder and kidnapping spree. The property in Vermont held a very similar dungeon to the one in New Hampshire, but it was empty. Cadaver dogs were brought in, and the results got ugly in a hurry. One day, the New Hampshire Union Leader put a line of photos across the front page, eight women that Kevin had kept in his two dungeons over a span of ten years, seven of which he had killed, Cathy the only survivor. Not to oversimplify Kevin's motivations, but all eight of them looked so much like my wife that it was eerie. Needless to say, I hid that paper deep in the recycling bin before Valerie could see it.

Two weeks later I came home to find Valerie sitting on the edge of the bed, looking at nothing but the wall in front of her. So much like my nightmares, I actually checked the wall behind me to see if someone had installed a closet door there. Finding no door, I nonetheless pinched myself as I came around the bed to face her to be certain I was awake. Does that even work?

"What?" I asked.

"I thought it was my fault," she replied, though perhaps replied is the wrong word, because I was pretty sure she wasn't talking to me. She continued, "I thought I was defective."

Her use of the word defective brought me back to our earlier conversation at the start of our hike, before Kevin, before everything, what felt like at least one lifetime ago. She was talking about her infertility, the knowledge that she would never be a mother to anything more than Tonk.

"We talked about adoption," she murmured, her gaze remaining fixed on the wall in front of her.

We had talked about adoption, about opening our home and giving our love to a child, but I couldn't understand what-

She spoke, interrupting my thoughts, "Could you love a child that was not your own?"

This last was definitely addressed to me, which she emphasized by turning her eyes in my direction. She looked up at me long enough to freeze my soul solid, and then dropped her eyes to her lap. I followed them, and noticed then that she held a pregnancy test stick in her hands. The indicator area showed a tiny blue plus sign. Without the instructions in front of me, I didn't know for certain what that meant, but I thought I had a pretty good guess.

When I looked back up, I found her staring at me. She gave the smallest nod humanly possible. Then she said two words. Two simple words that felt like plummeting into an abyss.

"It's his."

Afterword

If the ending of this story upset you, for that I am sorry. I figure there are enough mystery writers churning out sappy, happy Hollywood endings – the bad guy is caught, the hero gets the girl, all is right in the world – that I wanted to try and play with those expectations in my novels a little and see where it might take me. As an independent author unfettered by a publisher backed by a battalion of market researchers trying to force me into writing what they think will sell, I can tell the stories I want. This is that story. I have plans for the future of Jack, Valerie, and this child she now carries (you can turn the page and get a taste of that in the first chapter of the next Jack Fallon mystery, Night Calls), and I hope you'll come along for the ride, but I won't make any promises for a happy ending.

I also realize that I've taken a lot of liberties with the accuracy of GPS systems.

As for the firefighting stuff in this novel, The Brookline Fire Department rescued a Rhodesian Ridgeback that had been bitten by a beaver as described – that story is 100% true. It is also true that I took swift water training in the Merrimack River in freezing temperatures, in the snow, and it was cold and miserable and some of the best training I've ever done.

I'm always looking for more firefighter tales for future novels, so if you think you've got a good one, please send it along to psoletsky@gmail.com, and a signed paperback copy of the book I use it in will be yours. That email is good for anything else you might like to send along – comments, questions, criticism; I'm open to it all.

Thanks for reading!

One

My wife is pregnant.

After all that has happened, I really don't know how I should feel about that.

I ponder this a lot, especially at times like now, when I'm reclining in bed, a book open on my lap that I'm not reading. Valerie is in the bathroom performing her nighttime rituals which remain as much a mystery today as they were when we first married a little over ten years ago.

This baby is the product of rape. There, I said it, though the word *product* somehow seems too industrial, like she's manufacturing iPhones. *Outcome* for some reason feels no better. *Result?* At any rate, the man was someone who tried to kidnap her and kill me, and very nearly succeeded on both fronts, so you'd think this would be easy. Religious and moral issues aside, an abortion could solve this quandary. But as I've learned, nothing in life, or at least my life, is ever that simple.

My wife and I had been trying to conceive a child for a long time, over a year. We had consulted with a fertility specialist who discovered benign cysts in Valerie's womb. These are not life-threatening, but they make the odds of her getting pregnant quite low. The diagnosis meant essentially that she was infertile, or so we had believed at the time.

We bore this discovery with difficulty, its weight creating fresh stress cracks in our already-strained marriage. Valerie I think took it harder than I did, but that's only supposition on my part. We didn't talk about it or other alternatives such as adoption, not much, not directly, thus continuing the pattern of incommunicative behavior that had brought our marriage to its current sad state. We both had affairs, which probably didn't help things.

Then came the kidnapping, my fight for our survival, somewhere in there the rape, and now a pregnancy. This could be her only chance of having a child of her own.

Despite problems in our marriage, I love my wife deeply, and half of this baby would be hers. I try and focus on that, the half of the baby, Solomon-like, I would love. But you can't love half a baby. A baby is not like a carton of Neapolitan ice cream; you can't slice out the parts you like and leave the rest to get old and gummy in the back of the freezer, or at least the law frowns on that kind of thing. With babies, not Neapolitan ice cream. The law doesn't care a whit which flavors of Neapolitan you eat and which, after kidding yourself for months that you'll have company over one day and they'll finish the flavors you don't like, you ultimately throw away. Throwing away babies is obviously also frowned upon by the law. Now I'm sorry I brought the whole metaphor up.

I pass the book I'm holding from my right hand to my left. I flex the fingers on my right, and they move pretty well. The man who tried to kill me, the man who raped my wife, also broke most of the fingers on that hand. They have healed remarkably, and after eight weeks of medical leave from the Dunboro Fire

Department, where I'm a volunteer firefighter, I'm back in the saddle. Healed or not, moving the fingers was a mistake as it awakened a sharp, stabbing pain deep in my joints, something the doctors have been at a loss to explain. My bones they tell me are well-knit, my inflammation and swelling a thing of the distant past. I glance at my nightstand and the bottle of Oxycontin that resides there. I've already taken my before-bed pill, but consider taking another which I know will put the pain back to sleep. I pick up the bottle – just holding it relaxes me – but am dismayed at how light it is. I know there are nine pills left; I count out their dwindling number carefully each and every time I take one. I have this absurd fantasy that like rabbits kept in a small pen, they'll reproduce inside the bottle. They never do. This is my fourth refill, and I'm unlikely to successfully cajole the doctor into giving me another one.

I've had some doctors suggest to me that the pain in my hand is psychosomatic. That veers dangerously close to a dark territory I don't wish to explore.

With regret, I put the bottle back down unopened. I roll my neck, feeling the vertebrae pop and crack, and try and distract myself by returning to my previous train of thought.

Medically speaking, the child is just a collection of DNA. The father was a violent serial killer, but the child is innocent, a clean slate, in no way linked to the circumstances that created it, and with the father dead, the problems of shared custody will never come up. I'm a man of science. My PhD in physics proves that, even if the degree itself remains tightly rolled in the tube the university shipped it in because I never got around to getting it framed. I should be able to concentrate upon the science and love the whole child. Easy to think, hard to internalize. While I can be cool and logical about so many things, this understandably is not one of those things.

Perhaps the greatest irony of all is that I'm not sure she wants this baby. I'm sure she wants a baby, but this one? She exhibits

241

none of the glow of a typical pregnancy in my experience. Rather than smiling and rubbing her belly, maybe while humming Rock-a-Bye Baby, she drifts through her life like a depressed storm cloud, unable to muster the energy to even rain. She's been meeting with a counselor, and I keep hoping to see her mood improve as a result. While I never expected her to bounce back to her old self overnight – heck, I'm a long way from over it myself – time is passing, and though she has brief, very brief, flashes of the old her self, I'm beginning to doubt that she's on a path to recovery.

Valerie has been pregnant for ten weeks and she is going to be start showing soon, two weeks, perhaps four, maybe less. She's always been thin, and after the trauma of the kidnapping and rape has lost still more weight. Her baby bump could become evident any day now. Other members of the Dunboro Fire Department know that Valerie and I have been trying to become pregnant, so they're going to make comments when they notice. And what will we tell them? Or do we tell them nothing and let them assume the baby is ours?

This is a conversation we're going to have to have, Valerie and I, but if there's one thing I've learned over the last ten years of my marriage, and Valerie would be quick to tell you that I haven't, you can't make her talk about something until she is ready. Lying in bed, I wonder however if I should try and force the issue. As if in disagreement with this idea, a gust of wind slams against the house broadside, peppering flakes of ice-like snow against the windows. The gust tucks up into the soffit, gives a microscopic lift to the roof rafters in the attic space above me. They creak, and the air pressure in the house drops, a sensation I can feel in my inner ear and eyeballs. Our English bulldog, Tonk, must feel it as well, because in the corner of the room where he lies on his bed he lifts his head and looks around curiously. Then the wind subsides, and both Tonk and the rafters settle, the rafters with another creak, Tonk with a sigh.

"Did you feel that?" Valerie calls from the bathroom.

"Yeah," I call back.

"Windy."

"Yeah."

"Is it snowing?"

"Yeah." In truth I don't know if it's snowing or not and would have to get out of bed and lift the blinds to check, but the weather forecast predicted snow and I heard some rattle against the window, so it seems a safe guess. I consider that maybe she wasn't actually asking if it was snowing – there is after all a window in the bathroom and she could look outside for herself – but was instead trying to keep the dialog going.

I wait, curious if she will make another attempt at continuing it, but she doesn't. Maybe she decided that the conversation was too inane to persist, or perhaps I'm reading too much into the whole thing. Regardless, the abbreviated exchange convinces me that now is the time to try to talk to her, about us, about this child, about the future. If this marriage is to have any hope of survival, we must talk.

I hear the water shut off, the medicine cabinet squeak open and shut; these are sounds I associate with her nearing the end of her routine. I try and pick a good conversation starter, something gentle and compassionate. I discard "So, you're having some other guy's baby," as too confrontational, asking about her health as too circumspect, talking about the weather as too redundant.

A drawer in the bathroom opens, there is a clatter, and it closes. I've always thought the clatter is a hairbrush, or maybe a clip she might use to hold her hair up while she washes her face. I've never inquired. Whichever, it signifies the final step in her process.

243

My brain suggests starting with a joke, perhaps a reference to *Rosemary's Baby*. Stupid brain.

I don't have any idea how to begin this talk, but plan to fake it, figure it out as I go along. Adlibbing, that's what firefighters are supposed to be good at, and yet I find myself filled with dread as I enumerate in my mind the ways in which this discussion could go catastrophically wrong. I steel myself, gird my loins, take a deep breath, as I wait for the bathroom door to swing open.

And then my pager goes off. Saved by the bell.

64460458R00138

Made in the USA
Charleston, SC
26 November 2016